TAILS OF LOVE

LORI FOSTER
STELLA CAMERON
and
KATE ANGELL • DIANNE CASTELL • ANN CHRISTOPHER
MARCIA JAMES • DONNA MACMEANS • SARAH MCCARTY
PATRICIA SARGEANT • SUE-ELLEN WELFONDER

BERKLEY BOOKS, NEW YORK

THE BERKLEY PUBLISHING GROUP
Published by the Penguin Group
Penguin Group (USA) Inc.
375 Hudson Street, New York, New York 10014, USA
Penguin Group (Canada), 90 Eglinton Avenue East, Suite 700, Toronto, Ontario M4P 2Y3, Canada
(a division of Pearson Penguin Canada Inc.)
Penguin Books Ltd., 80 Strand, London WC2R 0RL, England
Penguin Group Ireland, 25 St. Stephen's Green, Dublin 2, Ireland (a division of Penguin Books Ltd.)
Penguin Group (Australia), 250 Camberwell Road, Camberwell, Victoria 3124, Australia
(a division of Pearson Australia Group Pty. Ltd.)
Penguin Books India Pvt. Ltd., 11 Community Centre, Panchsheel Park, New Delhi—110 017, India
Penguin Group (NZ), 67 Apollo Drive, Rosedale, Auckland 0632, New Zealand
(a division of Pearson New Zealand Ltd.)
Penguin Books (South Africa) (Pty.) Ltd., 24 Sturdee Avenue, Rosebank, Johannesburg 2196,
South Africa

Penguin Books Ltd., Registered Offices: 80 Strand, London WC2R 0RL, England

TAILS OF LOVE

A Berkley Book / published by arrangement with the authors

PRINTING HISTORY
Berkley Sensation trade paperback edition / June 2009
Berkley mass-market edition / December 2011

ISBN: 978-0-425-24506-4

BERKLEY®
Berkley Books are published by The Berkley Publishing Group,
a division of Penguin Group (USA) Inc.,
375 Hudson Street, New York, New York 10014.
BERKLEY® is a registered trademark of Penguin Group (USA) Inc.
The "B" design is a trademark of Penguin Group (USA) Inc.

PRINTED IN THE UNITED STATES OF AMERICA

10   9   8   7   6   5   4   3   2   1

CONTENTS

MAN'S BEST FRIEND   1
Lori Foster

A KNOTTY TAIL   33
Stella Cameron

NORAH'S ARC   59
Kate Angell

THE PURSUIT OF HAPPINESS   83
Dianne Castell

ATTICUS SAVES LISA   107
Ann Christopher

RESCUE ME   137
Marcia James

LORD HAIRY   167
Donna MacMeans

DANNY'S DOG   197
Sarah McCarty

SCAREDY CAT   231
Patricia Sargeant

A MAN, A WOMAN, AND HAGGIS   255
Sue-Ellen Welfonder

MAN'S BEST FRIEND

Lori Foster

CHAPTER ONE

It figured that on the most miserable night of the week, Erin Schuler would be the last one out. It was her own fault for staying so late, working well past closing just because . . . well, she really had nowhere else she needed to be. Her empty apartment wasn't all that appealing. Hanging out at the park was always preferable—when it wasn't so dark and stormy and cold.

The rain came in a torrent, soaking Erin as she locked the door to the park's storage shed and dashed for her car in the farthest lot. Tall, thick trees blocked what little moonlight might have penetrated the stormy sky.

At least she'd gotten the last of the mulch covered and all the tools put away before the skies opened up.

But now, with rain battering down on her, she could barely see two feet in front of her as she navigated over the gravel lot, mindful of shadows and night sounds. With her arms over her head, uselessly attempting to block some of the rain, she jogged fast—and tripped over something small and soft.

As she went down face-first, whatever she'd tripped over gave a surprised yelp, followed by a very heart-wrenching whimper.

She hit the ground hard and, hearing that sad little sound, jerked around and shielded her eyes with a hand. There, looking wounded, wet, and afraid, was an animal.

Her heart lurched as she stared at the small creature with large, glistening eyes. Shaking from cold and unease, she immediately went to her knees on the gravel and pulled a small flashlight from her bag. Shining it at the critter, she found herself face-to-face with a sodden puppy of indiscriminate breed.

"Oh, baby." Erin held out a hand. "There, there, it's okay. I'm sorry if I hurt you," she whispered. "I didn't see you hunkered down there."

The ball of wet, matted brown fur watched her from worried dark eyes. Whimpering, hopeful but afraid, it inched a little closer.

Very slowly, Erin got off her knees and went into a crouch. "It's all right, baby. You look as cold and miserable as I feel. Come here, now. We'll get warmed up together."

The dog's fur was filled with mud and probably unspeakable things, like ticks and fleas. But what the hell, she wasn't in much better shape herself now that the rain had soaked through to her skin and she'd fallen on the gravel lot. She pulled the little bundle up close and cradled it in her arms.

The puppy couldn't weigh more than three pounds and had the distinct look of neglect about it. In the three years she'd been working with the park, Erin had seen and rescued plenty of wild animals. But never before had she encountered a pup.

Not being a dummy, she wondered if someone had left the animal there, and if the creep was still around.

The little dog shivered in her arms and laid back its ears in a beseeching way. Holding it close to her chest, Erin unlocked her car and slid inside, then closed and locked the door. Relieved for that much security, she decided to take the dog to her apartment and see what she could do about making it comfortable.

She put the key in the ignition, turned, and . . .

Nothing.

"Crap." Her battery had died? Truly nervous now, she dug out her cell phone. "It's okay, sweetie. We'll be fine, I promise."

But when she opened her phone and the light came on, she said, "Crap times two." The battery was all but dead. Erin flopped her head back against the seat and groaned. *Stupid, stupid, stupid.* She had to hurry and call someone, or she'd be stranded here alone for the night.

The dog licked her chin in encouragement, and after a pat meant to reassure the pup, she tried calling her brother.

No answer. *Jerk.*

He was probably out having a great time somewhere. Not that he could have known she'd need him, but still . . .

Though it was summer, the freezing rain and cool night air sent shivers racing over her body. Who to call?

One look out the window and she knew she couldn't bother her folks. Not only would they have been in bed for hours, but she didn't particularly want either of them to be out driving in this horrible storm.

As to friends . . . well, she didn't have any super good friends who wouldn't mind venturing out late on a rainy night to save her socially dysfunctional butt.

That left her with only one choice: Gary Rutledge.

Never mind that Gary was probably asleep, or with a woman, or that she'd been avoiding him for a few months now. Erin thought of the last time he'd called, how frustrated he'd been that she claimed to be too busy to see him.

They both knew it was a lie. Only she knew *why* she lied.

But damn it, what she wanted and what he wanted were worlds apart. His life was already too full to add a serious romantic relationship, and she cared too much about him for anything less. She had enough problems in her life without fostering a deliberate heartache.

But even if he wanted what she wanted, he had big plans ahead and she didn't want to get in the way of them. And if she was totally honest, she had to admit that his newfound popularity and social standing intimidated the hell out of her.

Lightning crashed across the sky, followed by a deep belch of car-jarring thunder. The pup yelped pitifully. Erin jumped. "Wow," she said as she stroked the animal to calm it. It whined and tried to burrow under her arm. "Yeah, yeah," she told the dog. "I know. It's time to suck it up and make the call. I'll do it right now."

She'd ask Gary for help, but keep things cool and detached. Somehow.

Cooing to the dog, she dialed his number.

On the third ring, Gary gave a low, sleepy, "Hello?"

Well hell. She'd sort of hoped against hope that he wouldn't be in bed already, but it was obvious that she'd awakened him.

Erin cleared her throat and without meaning to, asked, "You alone, Rutledge?" If he was with another woman, she'd damn well crawl home in the storm before admitting she needed his help.

"Erin?" New awareness chased away the slumber in his tone. Voice now firm and demanding, he said, "What's wrong?"

Her phone gave a series of near-silent beeps, indicating an impending disconnect from a dead battery. Jostling the pup to keep it still in her lap, panicked at the idea that her phone would die any second, she rushed into speech. "I need you, Gary. I'm at the park, in the north lot, and everyone else is gone. Bring some towels. Maybe a blanket and—"

The phone blinked off.

Erin stared at it in horror, then let out a long breath. Had she said enough? Had he heard her location?

If so, surely he'd play white knight. Surely, he'd understand the seriousness of what she asked.

Surely he'd come alone, and not force her to ride back with whoever his current bed-warmer might be.

Rain lashed her window and lightning again lit the area, stretching ominous shadows and amplifying just how alone she was. If Gary didn't show up, she supposed she would have to start walking. It would take at least an hour just to get to the main thoroughfare, and the park roads were dark and narrow and . . . well, scary. But she'd do it if she had to.

Hugging the dog, Erin wondered how she always got herself into these fixes.

She needed to get a handle on her work schedule.

She needed a new car.

Hell, she needed a new *life*.

Cracking the window to hear any sounds that might be unfamiliar in the surrounding woods, Erin waited. The pup whined in confusion and discomfort. She felt like joining in.

After ten minutes that felt like an hour, headlights shot into the parking lot and a sleek, sporty car crept in. Hope mingled with nervousness, but she'd just have to trust that it was Gary. If not, she might have a bigger problem than she wanted to contemplate.

Silhouetted by his own headlights, the driver got out. Moving toward her in the darkness, he looked big and powerful. His car idled in the silent lot.

Erin swallowed.

He wore a long Windbreaker with the loose hood pulled up, hiding his features so it wasn't until he'd strode right up to her car and his gorgeous face was there against the window, frowning in concern, that she knew it was Gary.

Her knees turned to Jell-O.

He looked relieved to see her, but also a little pissed. Brown eyes narrowed, rain dripping off his nose, he said, "Open up, Erin, and start explaining."

* * *

Seeing Erin, sodden but safe and sound, helped a little, but Gary's heart still thumped in residual fear. Getting a "save me" late night phone call from her was not his idea of fun.

He'd called her right back, but she hadn't answered, and he'd thought the worst.

Now, knowing she was okay, he felt like yanking her petite ass out of the car and shaking her. She'd taken him from a sound sleep to panic in a nanosecond. For too long now she'd been dodging him, making him nuts, and then to hear her on the phone, so late at night, with not much more than an "I need you" demand . . . Well, she'd better have a good explanation.

He waited, getting more soaked by the second while she appeared to gather some things in the seat beside her. Without a word she put up her window, opened her door, and stepped out to shove a squirming, frightened pup into his arms.

Brows lifted, Gary asked, "What's this?"

"A dog."

He was in no mood for her unique brand of sarcasm. "I can see that, smart ass." Gary automatically opened his Windbreaker and held the dog to his warm chest. Muddy paws and a muddier belly scuttled in close, no doubt ruining his shirt. Poor little thing. "Where'd it come from?"

Erin kept her head down and closed her car door. "I found it when I got off work."

"Which was when?"

"Should've been hours ago, but . . ." She shrugged. "Since I lock up the place, I stayed longer to get some stuff done."

She still wasn't looking at him, and Gary didn't like that. "Why didn't you answer me when I called back?"

"Dead phone. I guess I forgot to charge it." Then, defensively, she said, "I'm lucky I got through to you before it went entirely kaput, or I'd have been walking home."

When lightning splintered the black sky, followed by several cracks of thunder, Gary took her arm and steered her toward his car. "Not real smart, Erin. You shouldn't be out here alone."

"Yeah, no kidding." Her short dark hair was plastered to her head, and rain water dripped over her face. As they walked back to his idling car, she hoisted a bag over her shoulder. "I'm sorry for the inconvenience, but—"

"Forget about it."

She started to say more when she saw the Audi and froze. "No, you didn't."

"Didn't what?" Gary hauled her the rest of the way to the car and opened the passenger door for her.

She didn't want to get in. "You drove your new Audi."

Now she hated his car, too? "So?"

She put her hands to her head and stood there in the pouring rain. "So it's a fifty-thousand-dollar car and I'm wetter and muddier than the dog."

He smiled. "I can see that."

Finally she looked at him—but it was with wide-eyed horror. "I can't ride in there!" She pointed at the front seat of his Audi TT interior. "I'll ruin your leather seats."

Icy rain made its way down the back of his neck. "The leather's treated. It'll be fine. Now get in."

"But . . . I'm muddy."

Impatience had him nudging her along. "The car can be cleaned." As she gingerly seated herself, Gary stared down at the top of her head and, feeling provoked, said, "You can help me with that on your next day off. Okay?"

Her gaze clashed with his, but only for an instant. "Uh, sure."

So much enthusiasm. He shook his head and put the pup in her lap. "The towels are there in the seat if you want to wrap him up."

"Him?"

Gary helped her to get settled. "He's definitely a boy dog. You didn't notice?"

She made an incredulous sound. "I was a little preoccupied imagining some whack-job who might have left the puppy there as a way to booby-trap me in the dark and deserted woods."

Smiling, Gary reached in and pushed wet bangs out of her face. She looked . . . adorable. Like a cute drowned rat. "Not too farfetched, really."

When she gave him a doe-caught-in-the-headlights look, he shut the door and ran around to the driver's side. Once inside, he stripped off the soaked jacket and stuffed it behind his seat. "You have to be more careful, you know."

"I know." She kept looking around the car with awe.

"It's just a car, Erin."

"A car that costs more than some houses."

"Hardly." He smoothed his hands over the wheel. "It was an indulgent buy. Don't make me regret it, okay?"

Carefully removing her soaked sneakers and putting them on a towel on the floor, she asked, "How could I make you regret it?"

"I'll explain later." She looked cold, so he adjusted the heater. "How's the pooch?"

"Sleepy, I think." As dry as Erin could get him, the pup curled up, rested his little furry chin on her thigh, and dozed off.

Gary propped his hands loosely on the steering wheel and watched her care for the dog. He liked the profile of her slender nose, her stubborn chin, the way her short dark hair curled when wet. He liked her gentleness as she comforted the dog. Hell, he more than liked everything about her, and had for some time now.

For him, Erin was reality in a world filled with facades.

Rather than spook her by saying what he really thought—about her—Gary commented on the dog. "He's cute."

"And small and too skinny." She pushed back her wet hair and groaned. "God, what a miserable night."

"Better spent in bed."

Wide eyes locked onto his face.

She was mute, prompting Gary to retrench a little. "I always sleep pretty sound when it rains. It's hypnotic."

Erin blinked and turned away. "I'm so sorry that I woke you."

"I'm not." He saw this as a great opportunity and planned to make as much headway as he could.

"I didn't know who else to call."

"I'm glad you called me."

She cleared her throat after that disclosure. "I tried my brother first—"

"And didn't reach him." Gary couldn't help his knowing grin. "Dave is out for the night, and maybe even the whole weekend."

The mention of her brother eased some of her tension. "He's too good-looking for his own good. He really needs to settle down."

"So do I." He and Dave had been friends forever and now, in their early thirties, they were both ready for home and hearth. Dave had held out because he was picky.

Gary had held out because he wanted Erin and no one else. She was worth waiting for.

She might not know it about her brother, but Dave was pretty serious about a new woman in his life and spent most of his nights with her. Because things were intense, Gary suspected Erin would soon be meeting the new woman. If she'd called Dave's cell instead of his home phone, she'd have reached him—in bed and no doubt busy.

Instead, he got handed a golden opportunity.

Thanks to Erin's faulty car and the unpredictable summer weather, she was temporarily stuck with him. If things worked out right, he could see to it that she was trapped with him all night. He'd finally have the chance to tell her, and maybe show her, how he felt about her.

CHAPTER TWO

Gary looked out the windshield as the plan formed in his mind. Ready to get things going, he pulled out of the parking lot. "Where do you think the dog came from?"

"I don't know. Maybe someone left him at the park, maybe he wandered in on his own." She smoothed shivering fingers over his crown, and tucked the towels in closer around him. "But I couldn't leave him."

"I would hope not."

She shot him a look. "You'd have taken him in, too?"

That annoyed Gary. From the moment he made it clear that he considered their relationship to be about more than friendship, she'd been seeing him in a different way. "Do you even have to ask?"

Her shoulder rolled. "I don't know. It's just that you have a busy career now. It's not like you have time for . . . a dog."

As a fighter whose popularity was fast growing in the SBC—Supreme Battle Challenge—mixed martial arts, he could only nod agreement. "And that means what? That I don't care about animals anymore? That I somehow became a heartless bastard who'd leave a puppy out all alone in this shit weather?"

Her anger sparked, too. Erin had a quiet temper, the kind that she conveyed with a really mean look. "You have an even busier social life."

"If you mean all the promotional crap, it comes in waves and doesn't have anything to do with who I am." Did his growing notoriety really put her off? Was that part of the problem? Damn it, he'd always counted on Erin knowing him. Not his fighting persona, or the guy in the magazine ads, but him, the man. "I'm the same person you've known since you were six."

"Yeah, right. When I was six, you despised me."

"I never despised you, Erin," he clarified. "But back then, to a couple of teenage boys, you have to admit you were a real pain in the ass." He could remember Erin in pigtails, dogging their heels wherever he and her brother went. Back then, she'd hated to be excluded for any reason. "Do you remember when you were eleven, and you hid in the bushes to catch me kissing Annie?"

Teasing right back, she said, "It was an education I'll never forget. I thought you were both so gross, but I couldn't stop watching."

"Until your mother busted you."

"Ha! She busted you and Dave, too. We all got lectured, and after that, Mom left the front porch light on all night so that you guys couldn't make out there anymore."

Gary laughed. "It was pretty embarrassing all the way around. You were such a pest."

She smiled, and that alone nearly did him in.

His hands flexed on the steering wheel. "You know, it wasn't until you were about seventeen that I stopped thinking of you as Dave's little sister, and instead realized how hot you are."

Her smile faded. "I am not."

"You most definitely are." In deference to the weather,

he drove slowly, taking twice as long to return to his place as he'd taken to reach her at the park.

"I don't know how you can say that, with the women who are always throwing themselves at you."

For the moment, Gary ignored her remark. "Back then, I had a hell of a time making myself remember that you were Dave's sister, and seven years younger than me."

She took a moment to pick a burr out of the puppy's ear, then said quietly, "That hasn't changed, you know."

"Plenty of other things have. We're now both grown adults with settled jobs."

"You've got to be kidding! You call being a fighter a settled job?"

Now he felt defensive. But Erin was the only woman he knew who had such a negative reaction to his choice of career. "It pays well, I'm good at it, and I love it."

After studying him a moment, she looked away. "I like it too, but . . ."

"You do?" He glanced at her in the shadowy interior of the car. She had her head down, petting the dog and doing her best to resist the chemistry between them.

"You're incredible when you fight." She glanced at him. "I've watched all your fights. You know that."

"I thought you hated it."

She shook her head. "But . . ."

"But what?"

"It's just that everything is so different now."

"I'm not different."

She rolled her eyes. "Look at what you're driving. And you've got that big, brand-new house. And face it, Gary, you're practically a sex symbol."

He took all that very seriously. "The car is just fancy transportation—"

"Now *muddy* transportation that smells like wet dog."

"Will you forget about that? It doesn't matter." How dare she think he was some fastidious jerk who fell apart over a little dog hair and mud? "As to my house, it's not that big, but it is comfortable and it has room for my gear."

"It has room for a shopping mall."

Gary locked his teeth and moved on to the most important part of her complaint. "And just so you know, I'm not interested in groupies. Anyone with a brain knows that hangers-on are phonies and not to be trusted. They're not the crowd you want around you. They sure as hell aren't people you want to tie yourself to."

Erin considered that for a long, quiet moment. "So you've never wallowed in the adulation, huh?"

"Hell, Erin, I'm thirty-two and I know what I really want, what I've wanted for a while now." If she'd just stop fighting him, they could both move ahead. "It has nothing to do with fancy cars, big houses, or one-night stands with women hoping to mark their bedposts."

The dog whined, saving them both from the awful silence that followed. Erin resettled the little ball of fur, and changed the subject. "I hope he doesn't have a lot of nasty ticks or fleas."

Seeing that as a perfect segue, Gary pulled the car into an all-night convenience store lot. "Stay put. I'll grab some dog shampoo and stuff and be right back."

She tried to protest, but he jumped out and dashed through the rain to the store's front door. Luckily they had a decent pet section. When he finished he had a dog dish, puppy food, flea and tick shampoo, a collar, and a leash.

He didn't mind the expense; if things worked out right, he'd name the little dog Cupid and call things even.

* * *

Erin stared at the haul Gary stored on the floor near her feet. Things were getting crowded, fast. "Good grief, did you buy out the store?"

He was even wetter now after facing the deluge to shop. "Just the necessities." He lifted the hem of his shirt to dry his face—which gave her a great peek at his impressive abs—and then settled into his seat. "It's likely he does have fleas, and you don't want those things to take up residence in your house."

"I suppose not." The thought of bugs crawling around didn't thrill her.

"To be safe, we'll bathe him on my back porch." Before she could complain, he explained, "It's covered."

She frowned at him. "How much do I owe you?"

"It's my treat."

"Oh, no." No matter how financially set he might be these days, she carried her own weight. From what she could tell, too many people were already trying to live out of his pocket, and she wasn't going to be one of them.

Besides, she'd already inconvenienced him enough. "I'll pay you back. I insist."

"Fine." He drove the car out of the lot. "We'll discuss it later."

Meaning he hoped she'd forget—but she wouldn't. "I want to see the receipt."

"Afraid I'll overcharge you?"

"No!" Gary was the most honest guy she knew. But he worked hard for his money.

He grinned to let her know he was teasing. "After his bath, we'll get him fed."

A lot of things had changed, but not that killer grin. It still had the power to make her goofy. But not so goofy that she wanted to be alone with him in his spectacular new home.

She'd seen it from the outside when she'd driven by without him knowing it, and that was enough to make her agog at the luxury of it. Her brother said the interior was incredible—and she just knew the high-end, designer furnishings would make her feel like a Podunk. But even if Gary wasn't so well-to-do these days, she didn't want to be alone with him long enough to bathe the dog.

Already her will had weakened. Give her half an hour of privacy with him, and she'd be the aggressor, asking him for things she knew she was better off not having.

Like his body.

The problem was that he'd been so caring about the dog, and so uncaring about the mess it caused, she didn't know how to refuse him. His shirt had to be ruined, but she prayed he was right about his leather seats. Heaven only knew what it'd cost to repair them.

But nice or not, just being with him in the quiet seclusion of his car had her thinking things she shouldn't. Erin cleared her throat. "I sort of figured I'd clean him up tomorrow at my place."

"And leave him dirty and tangled all night?" He shook his head, sending a wet lock of brown hair to fall over his brow.

Her heart gave an unsteady beat.

"No, it'll be better to take care of it now." Then, as if he thought better of things, he suddenly shot her a look. For that single instant of time, his brown eyes were direct and soul sucking. "You don't have other plans, do you, Erin? I mean, a date or something?"

The ridiculousness of that helped pull her from her daze. Her last date had been months ago and was a resounding flop that hadn't encouraged her to try again.

"Okay," he said slowly. "No plans." He looked pleased by that, but also put out by her reaction. "It was a legitimate question for an attractive twenty-five-year-old woman. You do know that you could date nonstop if you wanted to, right?"

In a fictional world maybe. But Gary was the very last person with whom she wanted to discuss her nonexistent romantic involvements. "I spend most of my weekends working."

He nodded. "You aren't high maintenance, so tell me why you take all that overtime?"

The truth would suffice. "I enjoy the work."

"More than dating?"

She couldn't think of anything but the truth. "There's no one I'm anxious to date."

Smiling, he said, "Want to tell me why?"

Letting out an exasperated breath, Erin stared at him. "You want me to say I have a thing for you, is that it?"

"Not just any old thing, no. The *real* thing. And you do, so why not admit it?"

The real thing? *Yeah, it was plenty real.* But regardless of his protests, he was now a celebrity of sorts, and win or lose, though he mostly won, he gained more popularity with every fight. Events took him to hotspots all over the country, and sometimes out of the country.

He wined and dined with celebrities.

He appeared in magazines and newspapers.

Gorgeous, sophisticated women vied for his attention.

Could he really be happy with a hometown girl he'd known since he was a kid?

Erin thought about it so long that Gary was pulling into his driveway without her even realizing they'd reached his home. Outdoor lighting made the grounds look magical. Even soaked and storm-whipped, the landscaping was beautiful. The long driveway led up to a four-car garage.

"You have a gorgeous house."

"It's comfortable—but a little too big for a single man." He put the car in park, looked at her for a long, heart-stopping moment, then he leaned over and kissed her.

No hands. No body parts touching.

But his mouth was warm on hers, and confident, and he tugged at her lips in a way that raised her temperature several degrees.

Wow.

For years, he'd played at being a pseudo big brother to her, but there was nothing fraternal about the way his mouth moved on hers.

Erin started to lean into him—and the puppy yapped, jumping up between them. Erin came to her senses just in time to realize that the little rascal had piddled on her leg.

"Oh, crap." She grabbed for her door handle to get the pup out of Gary's car. For a second there, her seat belt hindered her escape, but Gary released it for her, and he got out, too.

Luckily, the rain had slowed to a drizzle. Not that it mattered since she was soaked to the skin anyway.

Crouched on the muddy grass by the dog, she saw when Gary's big feet stopped near her. He said nothing, but Erin felt his watchful gaze.

Her blood still pumped too fast from that kiss, but she wasn't a complete coward, so she looked up at him—and got snared in his dark gaze.

Get a grip, Erin. She pasted on a false smile. "Now my jeans are wet with more than rain."

"Huh." His smile was genuine and full of promise. "Guess you'll need a bath, too, then, won't you?"

At that suggestive comment, her heart shot into her throat. She tried to think of something to say, but Gary scooped up the dog, took Erin's arm, and started them all toward a side door to his large ranch-style home.

He led her directly into the cavernous garage, where she saw a truck parked, and then into the attached laundry room.

An overhead light brightened everything and granted her a good look at the pup.

And Gary.

He set down the dog and let it go about sniffing everything. With both hands, he raked back his hair while kicking off his shoes. His clothes clung to him.

And then he grabbed the hem of his shirt and dragged it off over his head. One-handed, he tossed it over her head and into a laundry basket behind her.

Erin stared.

Gary had always had an athletic body, but since starting

the extreme sport of MMA competition, he'd gotten far too buff for her peace of mind.

Loose-limbed and casual, he stood there and let her look. Unlike some of the fighters, he'd kept his chest hair and she liked it. A lot.

His hips were super lean, muscular. The waistband of his wet jeans curled out away from his body. The material over the fly was . . .

She looked up at his face—and found him watching her far too intently.

Oops. Trying to be cavalier, Erin said, "You look great. In shape, I mean."

"Thanks."

Trying not to stare at him again, she kicked off her own shoes and stripped off her light jacket. "Do you have something we can use to bathe him in?"

When Gary didn't answer, she looked at him again, and found him standing very still, his jaw tight, his cheekbones slashed with color.

He stared at her chest.

She knew she wasn't overly endowed, and her physique in no way compared to his, so she crossed her arms under her breasts and asked, "What are you looking at?"

At her tone, his left brow shot up—and he continued staring. "This is in no way a complaint, believe me, but it seems a white T-shirt and bra go . . . completely transparent in that much rain."

CHAPTER THREE

Startled, Erin looked down—and squawked. The material appeared glued to her flesh, showing the outline of each breast. Even her ribs and her nipples were so visible, she might as well have been naked.

Horrified, embarrassed, and unsure what to do, she spun around, presenting Gary with her back.

He stepped up closer to her, and his voice softened. "Don't faint, okay."

Did he sound amused? If he did, she'd brain him.

Still in that light tone, he added, "I'll grab a dry shirt for you and be right back."

She stood staring blindly at a blank wall, her back to the door, when Gary flipped a navy blue shirt over her shoulder.

His finger went down her cheek, then fell away. "Take your time. I'll be on the back porch with the pooch when you're ready."

She'd never be ready.

It wasn't easy, but she managed to say, "Thanks," reasonably enough.

A few minutes later, dressed in his warm, dry shirt and with her courage shored up, she headed for the back porch. Along the way, she took the "gawking tour" of his house.

It really was fabulous, but it was still . . . Gary. Still cozy and comfortable, and not in the least ostentatious. She wasn't sure what she'd expected, maybe a designer's cold touch. Instead it looked like every other bachelor pad she'd ever seen, but bigger and with more furniture.

It looked like a house meant for a family, not one man. And that made her think.

Gary had left the patio door open for her, but pulled the screen. Through the doorway she saw a big covered back porch that housed a hot tub and wet bar. Beyond that was an in-ground pool, securely fenced. Tall hedges offered privacy.

Hearing a masculine laugh, Erin snuck up to the door and saw Gary on his knees beside a low dishpan filled with water. The dog frolicked and played, a true water baby, while Gary tried to suds him up. The dog shook several times, sending soap bubbles to Gary's head, left ear, and over his chest.

He said to the dog, "You're lucky I'm the one doing this, bud. Erin's not a wimp, but she wouldn't be too keen about those fat ticks hiding on your belly, or whatever that was you had stuck to your butt fur."

The dog yapped and jumped and splashed, and for some reason, tears stung Erin's eyes.

The scene brought about an old memory. She was eighteen and giving her parents' German shepherd a bath in the driveway of her family home. Gary and Dave, both twenty-five, were heading out of town on a fishing trip together, and had stopped by to see her parents first. While Dave went in to the house, Gary stayed outside and helped her with the dog.

Before long they were both soaked and laughing. It wasn't until Erin stripped off her shirt, showing her bikini top underneath, that Gary went all serious and started looking at her differently.

She'd dated boys, but at that point, Gary was a man and his attention had both flattered and frightened her.

Then suddenly, without a word, he'd stepped away from her and went to the front door to tell Dave to hurry up. They'd left minutes later.

For a long time after that, until she finished college, Gary was different with her. Still friendly but somehow more distant and, maybe, cautious.

After college . . . well, he outright flirted with her, but he'd already started fighting by then and in those early years, he spent as much time away as he did at home.

"Erin?"

She shook off the memories. "What?"

"You look like you're a million miles away." His smile held a question—and an invitation. "Stop daydreaming and come help me with this little spaz."

The dog bounced and splashed some more, making Erin grin. "He has gotten pretty energetic, huh?" She went out the door and sat down cross-legged beside Gary. Cupping her hands into the water, she helped rinse the dog.

He bounced out of the dishpan and jumped first on Erin, then Gary, before following his nose to a grassy spot off the porch.

She watched the dog with a grin. "You're good with him."

Gary studied her for a long moment, leaned forward. Erin held her breath but didn't move away.

Again he kissed her.

This time it was light and easy, as if he'd been doing so for a long time. She wanted more, but didn't dare say so.

He settled back to smile at her, and belatedly picked up on her comment. "He feels better clean, and you will, too."

With that said, he whistled for the dog, who came tumbling over to him.

Gary opened a towel and stood. "Hand him up to me."

Erin lifted the squirming dog and Gary wrapped him in a soft towel. Wiggling his whole body in happiness, the pup licked Gary's chin.

"I heard you mention ticks," Erin said for lack of anything better.

"I tossed them into the yard. Nasty things." He settled the dog against his chest. "You want to dump that tub and come inside? I think the little rat has to be hungry." He went in without waiting for her, but was still holding the dog when she entered.

"What's wrong?"

"I'm trying to figure out how to contain him in my kitchen, or do you think he'd be better off in my bathroom? It'll be closer to us."

Closer to *us?* Erin mentally floundered. Did she even want to resist? "Uh . . ."

"What?" He stepped past her to consider the doorway that led to his living room. "You don't expect me to drive you home tonight, do you? And even if I did, what would you do about your car? You'll need someone to take you over there to look at it, right? I'm good with cars. I can help with that."

He'd already done more than enough. She'd sooner pay a garage than impose on him further. "Gary . . ."

"I know that look, Erin. You're ready to go all independent and argumentative on me. And I can handle that. I like that side of your personality."

She would never understand him.

"But," he added with exaggeration, "I have a feeling I'll need my hands free to . . . *counter* your arguments. So hold those thoughts for just a minute, okay?" He set the dog down and went about opening a can of puppy food. The dog waited with bated breath, poised to leap, his ears up high.

The second Gary set the dish on the floor, the little dog attacked.

Erin's heart softened. Poor little guy. "He must've been half starved." She couldn't believe how fast he ate, which made her think of something else. She cast a sideways look at Gary. "I don't suppose you included potty training in all your plans?"

His bare shoulder lifted in a negligent shrug as he, too, watched the dog gobble down his food. "I think he's part pig." A half-smile kicked up the corner of his mouth and he looked at Erin. "Newspaper for tonight, more intense instruction tomorrow."

He really had thought about it. "So . . . is he your dog then?"

Lifting his hands, palms up, to remind her that they were now free, Gary grinned and came to her. He looped his arms around her waist and hauled her in close.

It felt right to be snuggled up against him like this, familiar but also new and exciting. Given their long history, the familiarity made sense; over the years, she'd had plenty of hugs from him. But that had been in friendship, and this was so much more.

"Actually," he whispered, "I'm thinking he'll be our dog. Mine and yours." His gaze drifted to her mouth and stayed there. "What do you think?"

Mine and yours? Did he mean as a couple?

Or was he just asking for help with the dog?

He did go out of town a lot, so he'd need someone to watch the dog when he was away. She'd be happy to do that. Her apartment wasn't big enough to accommodate a pet full-time, but she'd always loved animals and the little dog was so cute. . . .

"You're thinking about this way too much." This time when Gary kissed her, he took his time.

And he took liberties.

His tongue touched hers, teased, moved over her lips, and then sank in deep and hot. His hands stroked her back, and then her behind. He lifted her to her tiptoes and slanted his head and kissed her like a starving man.

Erin gave up.

It wasn't easy to focus, but in the farthest reaches of her mind, she was aware that he'd come after her without complaint. He'd been more than wonderful with the dog. And truthfully, she was tired of resisting him.

How could it hurt for her to stay the night?

He left her mouth by slow degrees. His hands remained on her bottom keeping her belly pressed close to his pelvis.

Still so near that she could see his eyelashes, he whispered, "Should I take that as a yes?"

She wasn't entirely sure about the question. "I guess so."

His smile went crooked. He relaxed a little more. "Way to boost my ego."

"Your ego doesn't need a boost."

"If you believe that, then you really don't know what you've put me through the last few months." He kissed her again, hard and fast. "Let's go before you change your mind. You can shower while I finish settling the pooch. After you've gotten more comfortable, we'll talk."

"About what?"

He winked. "Longevity. Commitment. Misguided intentions."

"Wow. Sounds . . ." *Intriguing.* ". . . heavy."

At the door to his bedroom, he stopped. "Towels are in the bathroom closet. Help yourself to my wardrobe if you see something you'll be comfortable wearing. I'll go take the puppy out again, then grab my own shower in the hall bath." He leaned into the room to take her mouth again. "Meet you in the bed in ten minutes."

With a pounding heart and fluttering nerves, Erin watched him go. Heaven help her, she could hear him whistling.

Unwilling to waste a single second of the ten minutes he'd allotted, she closed the door and hurried to the bathroom.

* * *

Anticipation had him rushing through his shower in record time. He thought of Erin showering, Erin naked.

Erin waiting in his bed. *Finally.*

Only half dry, he pulled on his boxers and peeked into the kitchen at the pup. After eating his fill and soiling the backyard, the little dog had plopped happily into the cozy bed he'd made for him.

Poor little guy.

He turned out the light and headed down the hall. Erin had left his bedroom door ajar, and when he looked in, he found her in the bed, the sheet pulled up to her chin. Except for the hall light shining into the room, it was dark as Hades.

Knowing he had to slow down, Gary stepped into the room, but left the door wide open. He'd waited so long for her that he didn't want to miss a thing.

"It's a good thing you worked late tonight."

Watching him, she asked, "Why do you say that?"

He walked around to her side of the bed and sat down on the edge. Resting one hand onto her sheet-covered thigh, he smiled. "If you hadn't, you wouldn't have found the dog, and he'd still be out there alone."

"Oh." She licked her lips. "Did you leave him in the kitchen then?"

"Yeah. I made him a bed out of an old flannel shirt. He's blocked in so he can't get out of the kitchen, and right now he's sleeping. But if he wakes up, we'll hear him."

"It breaks my heart to think what he's been through, how long he might have been hungry or afraid." She let go of the sheet and relaxed a little. "Now, here with you, he's a happy little guy. So thank you for . . . everything."

Gary took the edge of the sheet and eased it off her. She wore one of his T-shirts—and nothing else. "Thank you for calling me."

That made her smile. "I made you come out in the rain."

"No, you gave me a chance to convince you that . . ." He looked up at her, saw she was practically holding her breath, and figured, *What the hell.* "I love you, Erin. Have for a long damn time."

Her lips parted.

He stretched out over her and held her face. "I fell in lust with you when you were eighteen, and if it had been only that, I could have ignored it. But damn, Erin, you're smart and funny and I enjoy talking to you."

When she started to speak, he put a finger to her lips. "You have to understand that the more women I saw, the more women who came on to me, the more I realized that they might be okay for the short-term, but only you would work for the long haul."

"Longevity?" she asked.

"Yeah. Marriage. Kids."

Her mouth twitched into a smile. "A dog?"

He smiled, too. "It's a good start, right? I know I screwed up by giving you too much time, first to grow up, then to finish college."

"But then, you were away so often with the sport."

"I know, believe me. And when things finally seemed right, you started avoiding me."

She put her hands on his shoulders. "I think that's where misguided intentions come in. I didn't want to get in your way."

Gary touched her breast, her belly, and said, "There's nowhere I want to go without you."

Erin's expression softened with emotion, but as he continued to touch her, it heated with something very different.

"I've waited so long for you," he told her. Her body was sleek and warm and perfect for him, just as he knew it would be.

Making love to Erin was unlike any other experience. It was more, in every way. More emotional, more sexual, hotter and yet, sweeter. She wasn't reserved, not with him. They had such a solid background together, he knew in his gut that they'd never have secrets, in bed or out.

As he kissed his way down her throat to her chest, she gave a soft groan. "Once won't be enough, Gary." Her hands threaded into his hair. "Not for me."

Satisfaction added to his pleasure. "Not for me, either."

"I love you, you know. I always have. That's why I never date. No one could measure up to you."

His heart almost stopped. It felt like he'd waited a lifetime to hear her say that. "I love you, too. So damn much."

As he pressed one hand between her thighs, he took her nipple into his mouth and sucked gently. She was already wet, ready, and the sounds she made, the way she moved, pushed him over the edge.

He pressed a finger inside her, stroking, teasing, and when he knew she was as anxious as him, he levered away to don a condom, then moved over her.

He held her face. "This isn't just sex, Erin. It's a commitment."

"Yes."

Her heavy eyes and swollen lips pushed him, but he had to be sure. "Understand me, Erin. You worried about my car, my house, but material things don't mean shit, not without you."

Smiling, she hooked her legs around him and held him tight. "If you'll stop talking and get on with it, I promise to marry you. Tomorrow even, if that's what you want."

Gary's eyes flared. "I think I could wait until we tell the families."

"Fine by me. But for now, I need you." She pulled his mouth down to hers and kissed him, then kept on kissing him as he entered her, as they rocked together, breathing faster, deeper, until it became too much.

When he felt Erin coming, squeezing around him, he lifted up to watch her, so overwhelmed with love he wanted to shout. His own release hit him and he could do no more than put his head back and groan.

Afterward, he rested atop her, feeling her breath, the gentle beat of her heart against his. The minutes ticked by, but he didn't want to move, couldn't move. Her hands idly stroked his back, and every so often, she kissed his shoulder with lazy contentment.

Damn, he felt good. Better than good. He forced himself up to his elbows to see her, to tell her again how much he loved her.

A high-pitched howl split the quiet.

They both jumped, then Erin started giggling beneath him. "You woke up the dog."

"Me? It was you." Grinning, he sat up, did a quick survey of her relaxed body still sprawled on his bed. "Stay put. I'll go get Cupid and be right back."

She came up to one elbow. "Cupid?"

Gary winked as he grabbed up a pair of shorts and headed out the door. "Suits him, don't you think?" On the way, he detoured into the hall bathroom to get rid of the condom and put on the shorts. But by then the little pup had worked himself into a moaning, yelping fit of panic.

"Settle down," he crooned as he stepped over the barriers he'd erected to keep the dog in the kitchen. Cupid leaped in berserk joy at the sight of him, and Gary didn't have it in him to abandon the little guy. He held him and laughed as the dog tried to lick his face. "Let's hit the backyard first, then we'll see about getting some sleep."

Cupid took great pleasure in jaunting around the yard to do his business a half dozen times. When Gary figured he had to be done, he scooped the pup back up and carried him to his bedroom.

Erin had turned to her side and her head was resting on her arm. "Is he okay?" she asked as soon as Gary got into the room.

"Just lonely." He sat Cupid on the bed beside her and the

little dog spent a moment loving her before going to the foot of the bed, half crawling under the sheet near her feet, and slipping right back into a sound sleep.

Erin laughed. "He's too adorable." Holding the sheet in place, she sat up to pet the dog, and her smile faded.

Gary stood there watching her, basking in his newfound good fortune. She'd agreed to marry him. She'd said she loved him.

Life couldn't get any better than this.

"Poor little thing is exhausted, but I think he's scared and afraid of being left alone again. After all he's been through, it's no wonder he started crying." Erin peeked up at him. "Do you think it'd be okay if we just let him stay in here with us?"

With us. *Damn that sounded good.*

"Are you kidding?" Smiling, Gary got into bed beside her. "Cupid brought you back to me." He lay down and pulled her into his arms, and they both heard the little dog sigh in his sleep. "As far as I'm concerned, he can sleep anywhere he wants to."

A KNOTTY TAIL

Stella Cameron

"Listen up, Dickens," Madeleine said. "Looks like we're on our last chance. Blow this and we could be history."

Dickens lay on his back timing his next snap at a circling fly.

"Close your mouth," Madeleine told him, exasperated. "Flies are bad for you."

"Why?"

"Germs. Didn't Mother teach you anything?"

"I never met Mother," Dickens said.

"Oh, my." Madeleine sat with a thump on a wad of tartan fleece and scratched her ears, one at a time. "Of course you met her."

"How's that?"

"You were *born*, Dickens. That's when you met Mother. So did I."

"Only in passing," Dickens said. He snapped at the fly again. "I don't remember a thing about her."

"Don't feel bad," Madeleine said. "She probably doesn't remember us either."

She looked Dickens over. Like her, he was in good shape for a five-year-old dog, but that was probably because of the Jack Russell bits of them. They did a lot of jumping around to stay fit.

When she and Dickens got adopted this time, Madeleine had heard the man at the adoption place say, "These terrier mixes are hardy. And they're loyal, too. Never any trouble. They don't bark or bite or get fleas . . ." Well, maybe he hadn't said the part about the fleas, but he had gone on and on about how perfect they were. Madeleine and Dickens were afraid the woman deciding if she could take a *brother and sister go together* would figure there must be something *really* wrong with them and look at another dog. But the woman visited with them in the petting area and said, "Yes."

Madeleine still trembled just thinking about how relieved she had felt.

"You think she's gonna keep us?" Dickens said.

Madeleine sighed. He talked a good story, but inside he was as scared as she was that this second adoption wouldn't work out, just like the first one. Where they'd been before their people moved and had decided, "It's too expensive to ship a couple of mutts." Madeleine had heard that. She was always hearing stuff because, unlike Dickens, she listened and faced up to things.

"Do you?" Dickens pressed, sounding worried now.

"She'll keep us if we're what she wants," Madeleine told him. "We gotta be good. We only gotta bark at strangers and then we gotta look terrifying if she needs us to. No whining, begging, scratching, chewing, or peeing and pooping where we're not supposed to pee and poop. Got that?"

"*Sheesh,*" Dickens said. "Life's hardly worth living."

"*Dickens.*"

"Yeah, yeah, keep your hair on. We've been here a week and I haven't messed up yet, have I?"

"Nope."

"Do you think we'll get to go in the house in winter?" Dickens asked.

Their new person, name of Rose Gibb, kept them in a big run at the side of her house. It got pretty warm since it was summer and even though the lot was on a hill, this part of Georgia was having a long, humid spell. Fortunately Rose had made sure there was a roof over part of the pen so it was easy to get out of the sun.

"If you don't forget to go where you're supposed to," Madeleine said, looking at a corner of the pen where Rose Gibb scattered fresh shavings each night. "She's got to trust us not to do what she doesn't want us to do where we're not supposed to do it. Then I think she might let us in."

Dickens settled his mouth together in a wavy line all the way around. It was his grumpy look.

"What?" Madeleine said.

"I want her to like us. That's dumb, but I do. She looks like she does sometimes but . . . it would be okay if she scratched my head."

Madeleine blinked. "Me, too." Bright sun could make her eyes sting. She perked up her ears. "Hush. Someone's coming."

* * *

Those two canines didn't know it yet, but they were going to help Clawdia accomplish something important. She stood behind a big clump of orange flowers, put all four of her feet together and sat down.

With her beautiful, sleek tail curled around just so, she knew what a stunning picture of feline perfection she made.

From there she could see the ugly dogs through the flower stems. Dogs were not known for intelligence, so they wouldn't notice her if she didn't want them to.

At first she had been furious about the arrival of the two white, black, brown, whiskery, and who-knew-what-else creatures. This was her hill. Hers and Simon's. Simon was her person and it was one thing to have Rose Gibb living up here—after all, she had been there first—but *dogs*?

Clawdia's skin quivered over her well-toned muscles. Never mind, she was a pragmatist. Opportunity took many forms, even the form of dogs and she would use them.

She and Simon lived in a large, luxurious house trailer in the middle of a fine stand of trees across from Rose's little house. Simon ought to be blissful and completely satisfied up here drawing his cartoons and looking after Clawdia, but humans could be contrary. Simon was pining. Imagine it. Pining after Rose Gibb.

Fiddlededee, she would have to suck it up and approach the beastly dogs.

Slowly, with exquisite grace, Clawdia stepped her way across grass that needed a good mowing. She undulated her spectacularly supple spine back and forth so that her rear and her head took a look at each other with every pace. And her tail stood tall like a ship's mast, the very end tipping forward . . . like a tiny, fluffy flag.

The question was, could she dumb herself down enough to be understood by these lowlife creatures?

Look at that. They're staring, the rude things. "Good afternoon," she said. She would not turn her face away, she would not, would not. She needed their help.

All they did was wiggle their stubby whiskers and sniff.

"I said, good afternoon. You're looking, *mmm*, somewhat better today."

"What d'you want?" the bigger one said, although neither of them were an impressive size. "You didn't have anything to say yesterday, or the day before, or on any day that I remember."

She stretched. "One must have standards. Talking to you at once would have been forward."

"I'm Dickens. This is my sister, Madeleine. What d'you want?"

Typical lack of grace. "My name is Clawdia. I live over

there." She indicated the lot on the other side of Rose Gibb's fence. "I'm with Simon Falzone, a superior sort of person."

"Good for you," the other one, Madeleine, said. "We're with Rose Gibb and we think she's nice."

"You haven't been here long enough to know," Clawdia said. "But, as a matter of fact, I think she's nice, too, and so does Simon. Unfortunately, she's a bit graceless and shy, and he, being a male, is naturally obtuse."

"Ob—"

"Obtuse," Clawdia repeated, curling her lip. "I expect you'd understand better if I said he's *thick* sometimes. She's shy and bumbles about, so he thinks she doesn't like him. But of course she does. What woman wouldn't?"

"We haven't met him," Madeleine said. "So we don't know about that, do we?"

Clawdia sashayed closer, raised her nose and did her best to look down on Dickens and Madeleine. "Do you think you'll be staying long?" She had almost said "long enough for my purposes," but thought better of it.

The smaller dog, who had rather nice dark eyes if one made oneself look, said, "This is our home now," sounding, Clawdia thought, a bit defensive for some reason.

"It's my opinion, and I'm never wrong, that Simon and Rose want to be friends." She flipped her tail. "You're going to help me arrange for that to happen."

The bigger dog muttered what sounded like, "Uppity alley cat," but Clawdia must have misheard.

"How would we do that?" Madeleine asked.

"Don't bother your heads with all the details. I'll let you know when you're needed."

She could have sworn Dickens said, "Tabby menace," under his breath. She stared at him really hard and curled her lips when he looked away.

"I hear Rose's car," Clawdia said, twitching her ears back. "Do as I tell you. I'm going to sacrifice myself and you will, too. We're going to pretend we like each other."

* * *

Rose drove from the dead-end lane into her driveway and parked.

Today she didn't feel as nervous about coming home to the dogs she had impulsively adopted. A doctor at the hospital where she worked as a pediatric nurse had suggested that since she lived up here on her own she ought to get a guard dog. She hadn't liked to suggest that she wasn't really alone since Simon Falzone was across the lane.

The moment she opened her door, heat hit her face. She gathered her purse and a bag of groceries from the back seat and took them inside.

Dickens and Madeleine were the first pets she had ever had. She shouldn't have allowed herself to be talked into taking two dogs, but once she saw the way they sat there, side-by-side, looking at her with such hope, she hadn't had the heart to walk away from them.

If she could look after sick children, she could certainly take care of two little dogs who needed her. *Be honest, Rose, you need them, too.*

She needed something or someone. Self-sufficient she might be, but she could get lonely.

Come on, buck up, girl. Get on with it.

Nothing she had bought needed to be put away at once. She must keep on track and do exactly what she had promised herself. Exercise was what she needed, and so did the dogs.

When she had changed from her uniform into a new black cotton jogging suit and sneakers, she went through the kitchen door to the side of the house. Her responsibility for making sure Dickens and Madeleine got long walks would help change her own life. She couldn't turn herself into a raving beauty, but she could work on the "pleasantly plump" bit.

Her neighbor, Simon Falzone, popped into her mind as he did far too often. With her arms crossed, she stared across to where his trailer, if you could call something that big a trailer, was parked. He would be over there drawing, and brooding. Simon brooded a lot. She sighed. Brooding suited him, added to his mystery, and she was certain he was hiding a sense of humor and a heart of gold.

Tall, slim in a muscular way and with the bluest eyes she'd ever seen, she did wonder why he didn't have a wife, or at least a woman in his life. Oh, he probably did. The idea that he didn't was wishful thinking on her part.

Fanciful thing that she was!

Rose snapped to and clapped her hands when she approached the dog run. "Hello, there," she said, opening the heavy wire door. The run had already been there when she moved in two years earlier. "Walkies time. We're going for real walkies today, not just down the lane and back. I'm dressed for the part now."

The dogs got up. They looked at each other, then back at her before wagging their tails, which Rose found odd.

"Do you like my new suit and shoes?" She pirouetted for them, then held up one foot at a time. "Snazzy, huh?"

Furtively, she checked around to make sure she was completely alone before she laughed at her own expense.

When she led the dogs from the pen, Simon Falzone's big tabby cat walked straight up to her. Rose stood still, amazed. Clawdia—Rose had heard Simon call her that— was one of those aloof cats that ignored you, but here she was actually *rubbing* herself around Rose's legs.

The cat moved on and went right up to Dickens and Madeleine.

Rose clutched the dogs' leashes tight and felt shaky. How horrible it would be if they got into a fight. Simon would be furious if his cat was hurt.

"Clawdia," she said. "Kitty, kitty, good kitty. Dickens and Madeleine, don't you be mean to Clawdia. She's our neighbor."

All three animals looked at her for the longest time. If cats could sneer, Rose thought the expression on Clawdia's elegant face would be a sneer.

"Oh, my," Rose said and felt herself sag with relief. The cat nuzzled Dickens and Madeleine who just stood there and . . . Madeleine licked Clawdia!

"You are so good," Rose told them. "Sweet, dear things. You could teach the world a lot about different people getting along."

Awkwardly, she patted each animal's head. The cat flashed her tail. Dickens and Madeleine wriggled a little.

The dogs walked around Clawdia, who purred loudly and curled up in a puddle of sun by the run door, as if waiting for her friends to get back.

* * *

Simon liked loblolly pines. He liked their long, spiky needles and the sound of their name. He also really got into their sharp scent. This was a good place, up here on this hill. He wanted to stay. Or he thought he did most of the time.

Then there were the encounters with Rose.

Darn, he'd lost all his social graces when it came to women, unless he wasn't interested in them. That meant he did just fine with every woman he encountered—except Rose Gibb.

He had bought a place up here to get out of the city. The lot was perfect, remote and with just the right sized clearing for his double-wide house trailer. Everyone who knew him wondered why a successful, syndicated cartoonist lived where and how he did. Let them wonder. This was where he wanted to be.

His life would be bliss if it weren't for Rose. "That's not what you mean, Falzone," he muttered. "It would be perfect if you *had* Rose."

He got hot all over, then cold. What was the matter with him? He was thirty-five and sophisticated, so why did one sweetly beautiful woman with a quiet, charming manner, reduce him to quivering incoherence?

"Forget it. You've got work to do. Clawdia!"

He left his drafting table and shoved open the door to his screened-in porch. Clawdia liked to curl up out there on the seat of his bentwood chair.

The chair was empty.

"Clawdia!" He raised his voice a notch. She was one of the inspirations for his cartoons, which had always featured cats.

First he toured the whole trailer but when he didn't find his buddy, he went outside and called her name repeatedly.

He did worry about her being outside on her own in case something large, alive, and predatory took a fancy to her, but she didn't usually venture more than a few yards from home.

The light had started to fade.

Concerned, Simon strode rapidly along the cut that led through the trees to the lane beyond. "Clawdia," he shouted.

Rose came into view, climbing the hill. Two white dogs with black and brown splotches came with her. Simon could hear Rose breathing hard and he frowned. With all the running around she must do at the hospital he was certain she was fit, so why was she out of breath?

He considered turning back before she saw him. *Oh, hell*... "Hey, there, Rose," he said. What kind of man ran away from a woman he wanted to see?

"Hello, Simon."

She *was* panting. He looked at the dogs. They weren't leaping around much either.

"Been for a walk?" he said and felt ridiculous.

"Yes."

Rose never said much.

"Whose dogs are you babysitting?"

"Mine," she said.

He nodded, and squinted. "You got two, huh?"

"Two, yes."

"You decided against starting out with one?"

Rose stopped a few feet from him and the dogs promptly sat, then flopped all the way down. "They're together," Rose said.

"A pair?" Simon asked.

"Brother and sister."

"Ah." They looked as if they had terrier in them, maybe Jack Russell, but there was Sheltie in the full tails and pointed noses, and the ears weren't right for Russells. "They're cute."

"Yes."

"You went for a long walk?"

"Yes."

This was getting hard. "You'll put us all to shame," he said. "You'll be so fit."

Rose gave a short laugh. "If I get rid of some fat it will be worth it." She flushed scarlet to the roots of her curly blond hair.

"What fat?" he said. He shouldn't say anything at all, he guessed, but he hated to see her embarrassed like that. "You don't have any fat to lose. You're just right."

Well, she didn't . . . and she was just right. She had the kind of figure a woman ought to have as far as he was concerned.

"Take care," she said and scurried off so fast the dogs had to scramble to their feet and run.

"I was looking for my cat," he called after Rose. "Clawdia. She's a tabby with long legs and pretty markings. Her tail—"

"Oh, yes." Rose turned around at once. "Clawdia was visiting at my place. I'm sorry. I should have made sure she went home but I didn't think. I'm not practical about things like that. Um, she could still be here."

"Great."

"No, what am I thinking?" Rose said. "She wouldn't be here now. That was a couple of hours ago when I . . . well, you don't care if I was leaving for a walk two hours ago."

He did. Yes, he cared a great deal what Rose did. "I see," he said. "If you do see her, could you give me a call?"

She fluttered a hand. "Yes."

"Here." He fished his wallet from his back jeans pocket and took out one of his cards. "My number's on here. We should know each other's numbers anyway, just in case there's ever a reason . . . If you need help or just need something or someone, call me. Please call me."

Once more she blushed. "Thank you."

She hurried through the opening in the wooden fence around her property and quickly left his view.

For a while Simon stared in the direction she had taken. He noted the roof of her house, tiled blue, and trees: ash, oak, pine. He hadn't actually been into her yard but he imagined it would be filled with flowers.

"Simon!"

He heard Rose call his name and took off after her. His feet pounded on tamped-down bark and pine needles in her driveway. The little yellow Astra she drove stood in front of the one-story house.

"Rose, where are you?" He couldn't see her. "Rose, what's happened?"

She came from the far side of the house. "Clawdia's still here. I don't think she wants me to pick her up or I'd bring her to you."

Simon slowed down. He took a narrow path that led past flower beds encircling the house. Just as he'd imagined, there were tons of flowers and standing where she was, the setting sun turning her blond curls into a bright nimbus around her face, Rose looked just right. Her eyes were dark brown and bright with intelligence and, he had to admit, uncertainty.

"I'll get her," he said. He was unsettling Rose. That made him angry with himself. "Don't trouble yourself. You go about your business and I'll deal with the cat."

"Well—"

"Really," he said grimly. "She's making a nuisance of herself. I'll make sure it doesn't happen again."

* * *

"It's scary out here in the dark," Madeleine said, later that same evening. She and Dickens huddled together inside the roomy wooden shelter Rose had provided for them. "Do you think anything could get in here? Like a bear, I mean?"

Dickens snorted. "A *bear*. I should think not. If a bear came anywhere near I'd scare it off." He squeezed closer to her.

"Would that be before or after he ate you?" Madeleine said and immediately felt mean. "Sorry. You're trying to make me feel better. I wish Rose would take us in with her. We'd be ever so good."

Now Dickens was shivering although it was a warm night. "I like her," he said. "I like the way she talks to us, too, like we've got minds."

"We do have minds, silly," Madeleine said.

"Didn't she look nice in that outfit she was wearing?"

"Very nice," Medeleine agreed. She thought about their walk. "I love getting out but once Rose starts, she doesn't quit."

"Nope," Dickens said. "She goes like a machine. And she doesn't know about letting us sniff and stuff. I'm worn out."

"Did you get a whiff of that big, black rock with the moss on it? Wow, I want to check that out again."

"Don't rub it in," Dickens said. "I was on the wrong side of Rose. Missed the whole thing."

Madeleine yawned. "If I wasn't nervous, I'd be sleeping like a dog."

"You are—"

"Yeah," Madeleine snapped. "I know, I *am* a dog. And I'm dog-tired." She sniggered.

They fell silent. Lightning bugs zigzagged in the gloom.

"Do you believe what the alley cat said?" Dickens said.

"Try to be kinder," Madeleine said. "She's a snob without a cause and you should feel sorry for her."

"She's got a big head and a bigger mouth," Dickens said and made a grumbly sound. "What's in it for us if Simon and Rose start liking each other a lot?"

"Clawdia's person turns all happy," Madeleine said.

"He does scowl a lot," Dickens remarked. "But I still don't see why it should make any difference to us."

"You know cats," Madeleine told him. "Selfish bunch. She'll probably get better food or something. We won't get anything."

"You sure of that?" Dickens said.

Madeleine thought about it. "Nope. Rose could get happier, too, if Simon's happier and does nice things for her."

"What would he do?"

"How would I know?" Madeleine said. She was tired but too nervous to sleep. "Scratch her ears? Pat her back?"

"*Mmm*," Dickens said with a longing sigh. "What about scratch her belly? I bet that would make her so happy she'd definitely let us inside at night."

* * *

She only had nine lives and the way things were going, or not going, she'd use them all up before Simon and Rose got together. That being the case, Clawdia thought she would end her days still putting up with Simon's unpredictable moods. Unpredictable moods meant divided attention for a deserving cat, and that would not do. It just would not.

He'd locked the door to the outside before he went to bed. She knew how to get out easily enough—through a window in the bathroom—but from the noises Simon was making, he could erupt from his bedroom again at any moment.

Sounds of the bed groaning and the sheets tugging while Simon tossed around came from the bedroom. He would get more crotchety by the second.

Oh, grow up and calm down, Simon. Why couldn't people be more like cats; too sensibly concerned for themselves to need anyone too much.

Actually, she did need Simon. She even liked him, which could be inconvenient.

He was making so much noise he'd never hear her leave.

She shot through the trailer, imagining the picture of lithe speed she must make, and vaulted through the window over the bath.

Clawdia kept running and didn't stop until she reached the pen where those two dogs were.

"Wake up," she said, careful to keep her voice down. "Tonight's the night. We've got to act."

From the painted wooden box with a hole cut out in the front for a door, came Madeleine first, then Dickens. They snuffled and Clawdia was reminded of a former life when she had lived, very briefly, on a farm. Pigs snuffled. *Yuck!*

"It's nighttime," Dickens said.

"I wouldn't have known that if you hadn't told me," Clawdia said. "I don't know how long it would take to get my person over here if I left it up to him. We have to do something drastic to make him come."

Dickens yawned so hugely his teeth glittered in a big, white oval with a dark hole in the middle. Clawdia didn't like the way it looked.

"We've had a hard day," Madeleine said. "We're worn out."

"We don't have time for your problems," Dickens added. "I'm going back to bed."

"Bark," Clawdia commanded, ignoring his rudeness. "Bark really loudly."

Madeleine was horrified. "Why would we do that?"

"Just do it."

"We will not," Dickens said. "You want to get rid of us, that's it. That's it, isn't it, Madeleine?"

"Is it?" Madeleine said. "Has all this talk of yours been a plot to make us bark at night and wake up Rose? So she'll decide to get rid of us and you'll have this lovely hill all to yourself again?"

Clawdia was speechless.

"Well, was it?" Dickens asked.

"Ungrateful wretches," Clawdia said. "If I wanted to get rid of you, you'd already be gone. I want you to help me for the good of everyone concerned. Now, bark."

"Won't," Dickens said.

"Bark because there's a fearsome beast hanging around waiting to eat you."

"There isn't," Madeleine said, but her teeth chattered a bit.

"No," Clawdia said. "There isn't. But we want *them* to think so."

"They won't though," Madeleine said. "They'll just think we're a nuisance. And when they come to tell us off, and Rose says how she's taking us back to the adoption place, you'll be off in your cozy bed again, laughing at us."

Clawdia had a good think. "I see your point. But you're suspicious creatures and you're wrong. I've seen the way Rose looks at you and she likes you. That means you're good for her. That means she's nicer, which will make Simon want to be with her even more—enough to *finally do something about it and get it over with before he drives me mad*!" She took a huge breath and tried to calm down.

"Barking won't do it," Madeleine said quietly. "But I've got an idea."

Clawdia didn't recall asking for ideas but she kept quiet.

"We'll dig a hole under the fence and you'll come in. In the morning they'll find us asleep together in our doghouse and then they'll know we want to be together. So they'll get together. How's that?"

"Stupid," Clawdia said without preamble. *Asleep together in their doghouse? Holy horrors, what an alarming thought.* "It won't work."

"You come in," Dickens announced. "We'll get ourselves all wet from the water dish, rough up our fur, then set up a ruckus. Once they come running, we go in the doghouse like we're hiding out together. Protecting each other because we got attacked. We'll make the hole under the fence *huge*, big enough for a tiger to come through."

"You're not normal," Clawdia said. "There aren't any tigers up here."

"A nasty great racoon could hurt us." Madeleine spoke in a breathy rush. "Or a mongoose, or . . . a snapping turtle.

What does it matter? They won't know what it was but they'll see us together and take us inside to keep us safe right away."

"And since I belong to Simon," Clawdia said, "and you belong to Rose, they'll have to stay together to look after us."

"Will they?" Dickens asked, sounding doubtful.

"Of course they will," Clawdia told them and started scratching up dirt at the bottom of the wire fencing.

"Cats are useless," Dickens said and went nose-to-wire with the fence, spread his back legs, and set to work excavating a large hole the way it ought to be done.

*   *   *

Two in the morning.

Simon stared at the readout on his clock and surfaced from the fog between sleep and consciousness. He hadn't actually slept at all yet.

Rose was gorgeous. Everything about her was all-woman. If he held her she would be warm and soft—feminine.

He growled under his breath, threw off his twisted covers, and sat on the edge of the bed. "Ask her over for a cup of coffee, or a glass of wine. On the porch where she'll know she's not threatened."

On the porch of his isolated trailer, surrounded by big, dark trees and with no other living soul for miles around. Sure, she definitely wouldn't feel threatened in those circumstances.

It was hopeless.

"You love me anyway, Clawdia," he said and winced. Who said anything about love? "I did. I must be mad."

"Come on, girl. Off the bed so I can make it habitable again." He patted around near the bottom of the mattress where Clawdia settled each night once she decided she wasn't going to be allowed to go hunting small critters.

She didn't meow, like usual.

He felt emptiness, the sense of being completely alone,

and flipped on a light. No Clawdia anywhere that he could see.

Fifteen minutes later Simon knew his cat wasn't in the trailer. After a further half an hour, he was certain she couldn't be anywhere in the immediate vicinity. If she was, she'd come when he called her. She was good about that.

A tromp to the lane with the aid of a flashlight still didn't produce his cat. He wished he didn't care, but he did. A lot.

Across the lane moonlight silvered oak leaves and settled a subtle gleam on the roof of Rose's house. She would be sleeping. No way could he either wake her up or try to sneak around her yard looking for a cat. Or could he?

* * *

"Intruder," Dickens said and clamped his mouth shut to stop himself from barking. He ran back and forth, glaring into the darkness.

"Shhhh," Madeleine said.

The hole wasn't finished but Clawdia slithered beneath the fence and popped out on the inside of the pen. "What is it?" she said. "Why are you fussing? We're not ready yet."

"Intruder," Dickens said through clenched teeth. He pulled his lips back from his gums and growled deep in his throat. He couldn't keep still. "Intruder," he yelled.

"Intruder!" Madeleine echoed, and let out a howl.

Dickens leaped about, all of his feet shooting into the air at the same time. He hurled himself against the wire with a rattling crash.

* * *

"Good heavens," Clawdia said. "You're both mad. Where's the water bowl?"

"No time," Madeleine shouted. "There's someone in the yard. Bark. Hurry up and bark."

Bark? Clawdia narrowed her eyes and listened. This intruder issue wasn't her thing, but she was in *their* territory

so she would go along. She raised her head and yowled as
hard as she could.

*   *   *

Rose flung herself from the bed and stood up, her heart
pounding.

The dogs were barking.

They'd been quiet every night until now.

Don't put on a light. Whoever was out there would see
exactly where she was in the house if a light went on.

Whoever?

She fumbled about for the phone and tried to hit the right
buttons. At least she managed to illuminate the panel.

The noise got louder, the barking, and the shrieking.

Rose pulled on her robe, then she held still and listened.

Dickens and Madeleine barked and howled, but there
was another sound. Wailing and, she thought, snarling.
Another animal was out there.

She tore open the bedroom door.

What could it be?

If there was a coyote out there it could probably climb the
fence and get the dogs—her dogs—those poor little things.

There wasn't time to get help.

Running, her long nightie winding around her ankles and
slowing her down, Rose rushed through the house to the
kitchen. The only weapon she could think of was the garden
rake she'd left leaning against the wall just outside. That and
as much noise as she could make were all she had to fight with.

She wouldn't do anything stupid, just try to frighten the
attacker away.

Sobbing now, she wrenched the door open.

*   *   *

Damn it!

He'd forgotten about the dogs. They were going mad.

Shoot!

Kicking away the flip-flops he'd shoved on, Simon sprinted for the dog pen, murmuring what he hoped were friendly sounds as he went. "It's okay, boys," he said. Why hadn't he found out their names? "Okay, okay. Good dogs. Quiet down. It's okay. You want treats? Shut up, you little punks! Shut up, damn you!"

He burst around the corner of the house and something hard smashed onto his naked left shoulder.

Rose screamed. A motion sensor flooded the area with light and he saw her, arms raised, hands clutched around the handle of an evil-looking rake—and her eyes shut tight. She screamed again.

And the rake, this time while he flinched at its sharp tines, slashed toward him again.

"Rose," he said, grabbing the rake and colliding with her. "It's me, Simon."

The dogs howled madly and he heard a shrill caterwaul.

The woman in his arms clung to him as desperately as he held her.

* * *

Rose had never expected to have Simon Falzone, shirtless, shoeless, his jeans riding low on his lean belly, sitting in her kitchen.

She had never expected such a thing, or visualized such a thing—but she would never forget it now.

"Are you sure it's okay with you for me to be here?" he said.

Did he have any idea how she felt having him with her? He wanted to be there; she could feel it in his smile and the open, interested way he looked at her.

"I'm glad you're here," she told him.

His smile widened. "You make good coffee," he said. "I admit I'm addicted."

"Me, too."

They had decided on coffee once the adrenaline stopped pumping and their combined energy hit around zero.

"I think you should think about having Madeleine and Dickens in the house when you're at home," Simon said. "Not that it's my business."

"No, no, I agree with you. I never had pets before and the run was there so I used it. Look at them—they're so cute."

The two dogs lay, side-by-side, on the mat inside the kitchen door, with their heads resting on crossed paws. Their brows had shot up as if they knew they were the topic of discussion.

"Nice dogs," Simon agreed. He had returned all of his attention to Rose, who felt warm under his gaze.

"Clawdia's amazing," she said. The cat sat at a distance with an expression of serene disdain on her haughty face. "Really beautiful."

"Really beautiful," Simon murmured.

Rose got up and piled oatmeal cookies on a plate. "These were only made last night," she said, setting them on the table in front of him.

"I've lived up here for six months," he said. He took a cookie and ate it in three bites. "That means we've known each other for six months."

She didn't know where he was heading with that remark but she thought she liked it. "I guess so."

"Would you let me take you out to dinner tomorrow night?" He looked at his watch and grinned. "Make that tonight?"

Flustered, Rose turned her coffee mug around and around. "You don't need to do that. You're feeling bad about what happened out there."

"Yes, I am. But that's not why I need to have dinner with you. I just need to—and want to. Will you?"

Both dogs got up, walked to sit at her feet, and stared up into her face. They almost looked as if they were trying to tell her something.

"Look at them," she said and scratched each one between the ears. She got licks from rough tongues.

"You're not answering me."

"I'll cook for you," Rose said in a rush. She didn't want him to go out of his way. "You don't seem to like going out much."

"You've noticed," he said. "I like knowing that."

Rose rubbed her forehead. "Sorry, I shouldn't tell you how you feel about things."

"Why not? I don't go anywhere, or not often. But that's because I haven't had a reason to. I'd like to take you into town if you'll let me."

She looked back into his blue eyes. "Thank you, then. Yes."

"Great!"

He looked too happy to be putting on an act.

Impulsively, Rose touched the back of his hand and said, "I read your cartoons. Your drawings are wonderful."

Simon stared at her. "I know when you get home each day."

"What?" She leaned closer. "What do you mean?"

"I listen for your car. I like to know you're back safely."

She swallowed.

"Does that feel threatening to you?" he asked.

"No," she whispered. "Look at this." She got up and pulled a scrapbook from the top of the refrigerator.

Simon took it from her and set it on the table. Slowly, he turned pages, although she could tell he wasn't really seeing the cartoon strips she continued to clip and paste each day.

"I scared you badly tonight, didn't I?" he said, resting a hand on top of the book.

"I could have killed you." She laughed and heard a touch of hysteria in the sound.

"We could call it a weird beginning, only we'd already begun, hadn't we?"

She thought about him listening for her car, and her daily sessions with the scrapbook. "Looks like it."

"I'll come over for you around six, if that's okay."

"Perfect. I was going to go walking again but I'd rather go to dinner with you."

"We could walk together tomorrow," Simon told her. "I do a lot of climbing around out there on my own."

* * *

Dickens spoke from the side of his mouth, "I think I'm going to be sick."

"Not in here," Madeleine said sharply. "Go to the door and whine. Now."

"Not really, silly," Dickens said. "It's these two. They're soppy over each other."

"*Mmm.*" Madeleine sighed. "It's lovely."

"Sometimes we have to suffer irritation for the good of all," Clawdia said from her spot not far away. "The end justifies the means."

* * *

Simon wanted to touch Rose. Just touch her, feel the softness of her skin, her warmth, but he figured he'd better take it slowly.

"It's kind of nice to have some routine," he told her. "If you're serious about the exercise we could make it a standing date. Not that you need it for anything but keeping fit. You're perfect."

He closed his fool mouth. What was he thinking, going on like this?

Rose smiled. "Thank you." She turned pink again. "I've got to be a responsible pet owner and get these guys out regularly."

Simon had to work at not trying to take her in his arms. "They don't always have to come," he told her quietly.

* * *

Madeleine looked at Dickens who promptly rolled on his back with all four feet stuck in the air and said, "No, we don't always have to come." He muttered, "Save the dogs. Walk the woman."

* * *

When Simon got up to leave, Rose didn't want him to go. She also couldn't tell him that.

He scooped up Clawdia and draped her around his neck. The cat looked smug and comfortable there. She would feel much the same in the cat's position, Rose thought.

Simon opened the kitchen door to the side yard and stood, silhouetted against the darkness outside.

Rose held the door handle. "That was really nice," she said. "Think of the lengths I went to, getting you over here." She laughed softly.

"That's what you think," Simon told her. "How do you know I didn't carry Clawdia over here to make the dogs bark, just to get close to you?"

"You didn't, but it's a nice thought."

He kissed the corner of her mouth, softly, gently. "Every thought I have about you is really nice, Rose. See you at six."

Rising to her toes, she slipped a hand between his neck and Clawdia and quickly pressed her mouth to his. She stepped away and said, "See you at six."

NORAH'S ARC

Kate Angell

CHAPTER ONE

"Get your goat off the hood of my Corvette!"

Mike Kraft's voice carried into Norah Archer's office on a gust of wind. His arrival fluttered and shuffled the papers on her desk. So much for her orderly paying of bills.

Norah pushed to her feet, faced off with the six-foot contractor with the dark hair and eyes and steam shooting out of his ears. "Don't blame Houdini for escaping." She shifted the blame. "Your bulldozer operator keeps clipping my fence posts and loosening the chain link."

"There's no room for a petting zoo in an industrial park," Kraft shot back. "You should have moved your animals when Tampa Feed and Seed went out of business."

Norah rounded her desk, met him sneaker to steel-toed boot. The man was tall, and she hated talking to his chest. A very thick and solid chest covered in a white button-down, the sleeves shoved to his elbows. His forearms were tan and dusted with dark hair. A TAG Heuer wrapped his wrist. No wedding band.

She angled her head just as he dipped his chin, and their lips nearly brushed. His aftershave hinted of sunshine and sandalwood. He had a masculine mouth and a morning's worth of stubble. She'd never seen him smile.

Confrontation was not her style, yet when it came to her animals, she'd go down fighting. "Norah's Arc was on the outskirts of town long before you spread your cement and asphalt. So back off, Kraft."

A tendon in his jaw jumped and a snarl broke as he jabbed a finger toward the door. "One hoof dent in my fiberglass and your ass is mine."

Her ass would never be his, thought Norah. She didn't, however, want Houdini in the parking lot, jumping from car to car. The pygmy goat would cause a ruckus.

Norah pushed past the contractor, cleared the office door, and took the wooden steps two at a time. The summer day proved overcast, the roll of thunder deep in the distance. Hurricane season was upon them. It rained every single day.

She walked briskly along the brick path toward the side lot. Mike Kraft kept pace, his stride long and purposeful. His scowl was as dark as the gathering storm.

The goat's bleat drew her to Kraft's Corvette. Houdini stood two feet tall and weighed twenty pounds. He had a mischievous streak a mile long.

The little buck pranced on the hood as if he owned the sleek black sports car. Dust and dirt collected on the fiberglass, but Norah didn't see any dents from his hooves.

Relief sank bone-deep. She didn't need a lawsuit.

Nor a call to Animal Control.

She prided herself on the upkeep and security at Norah's Arc. Twelve years and she'd never had an escapee. Not until Kraft Construction tore up the land around her petting zoo, damaging the fences and scaring the animals.

"Houdini, down," she ordered.

The goat's return bleat proved an outright refusal as he shot from the hood onto the sunroof.

"He's climbing." Mike ground the words out.

"Goats are cliff-dwellers," she quickly explained. "The boulders for his pen have yet to arrive. His pen mate Hermes doesn't mind the grass and dirt, but Houdini is going through puberty and wanting to show his muscle. He likes to climb and be king of his mountain."

She turned a wistful look in his direction, asked, "Got boulders?"

Mike actually nodded. "We set water lines this morning. My bulldozer operator hit a lot of rock. Get his goat butt down and I'll deliver the granite and gravel."

Norah patted her thigh. "Houdini, want to play?"

Mike Kraft watched as the crazy zookeeper trotted *away* from the goat.

Houdini gave a bellowing bleat, then stomped his hooves. Hooves that were still on the roof of Mike's Corvette.

Bleat, prance, leap. The goat jumped from the roof to the hood and onto the asphalt parking lot. A playful bleat and Houdini chased after Norah Archer.

Mike couldn't believe his eyes. Norah's laughter rent the air as Houdini ran up behind her and butted her with his tiny horns. She grabbed the goat by one horn and used it as a handle to gently control him, then slowly walked Houdini back toward Mike.

They made a picture, the woman with the wild auburn hair, light blue eyes, and slight build walking her caramel-colored, coarse-haired goat. Norah was a small woman for the big job of zookeeper. Maybe not so big, Mike recanted. From what he'd seen, every animal at the petting zoo was miniature. From the horse, donkey, zebu cow, potbelly pig to the zebra, all came pint-sized.

Two by two, they came in pairs. Each had a mate.

Mike caught Houdini nipping the back pocket on Norah's jeans. Distressed jeans with more tears than denim. He noted the long rip at her knee, as well as the shorter one at the top of her thigh. Lady had nice legs.

"Any dents?" Norah interrupted him checking her out. Together they crossed to his Corvette.

Mike ran a practiced eye over the fiberglass. Outside of the dirty hoof prints there were no dents or scrapes. "Goat is cleared to go back to his pen," he stated.

He noted her relief, the deep sigh as she blew out a breath that fluttered her bangs. She dug into the front pocket of her jeans, pulled out a twenty-dollar bill. The sparkle returned to her eyes and her smile broke. "A deluxe wash and wax on Houdini." She offered him the money.

Which Mike refused. "Keep the twenty. No damage done."

Houdini sniffed and bit at the bill between Norah's fingers. She jerked her hand back before the buck ate Andrew Jackson.

Mike watched them walk away. His daily confrontations with Norah had become routine. From the first shovel of dirt at the ground-breaking ceremony, he and the zookeeper had faced off over property lines, parking spaces, and where she dumped manure.

She was feisty and argued with him as no other woman had dared. Her high color and determined fight for her animals both frustrated him and held his respect. He was under contract to build Cambridge Square and didn't have time to pacify a pygmy goat.

Houdini's interference had cost him an hour. An hour better spent pulling permits at the courthouse. He scratched his jaw, shook his head. The government center would have to wait. All because he'd gone soft and offered to haul boulders so Houdini could be king of his mountain.

Mike crossed the parking lot and circled the freshly cemented foundation for the industrial center. Sidewalks would be formed tomorrow. He located the bulldozer operator, pushing dirt over the water pipes. He instructed the man to load and haul the boulders to the back gate of Norah's Arc.

He then took the return path to the main office. Ancient

banyan trees shadowed the brick walkway and yellow hibiscus bordered the sides. The scent of rain hung heavy on the air. A storm cell brewed over the Gulf, now edging the shore. Most of the petting zoo's visitors had headed for their vehicles.

He knocked on the office door, only to find it locked. After several inquiries of the employees, he located Norah inside a pen with two babydoll sheep. The zookeeper was on her knees, bottle-feeding the smallest of the two.

He opened the gate and entered without her permission. Her lips parted in surprise. "Boulders are at your back gate," he told her as the chug and rumble of the bulldozer broke the calm before the storm.

Norah pushed to her feet, pressed her walkie-talkie, and called for assistance. She then left the tiny sheep and headed toward the goat pen. She trapped Houdini and Hermes in their little red barn while Mike, the bulldozer operator, and six staff members hauled and arranged a granite mountain. They built the base wide, stacking to a ten-foot plateau.

Mike then went on to straighten the corner post and secure the fencing that contributed to Houdini's earlier escape. He made a mental note to remind his heavy equipment operators not to cut so close to the property line.

Standing back, Mike watched as Norah released the pygmy goats. Hermes circled the boulders, the tiny doe curious but cautious. Houdini scaled the granite, bleating his superiority on the top rock. The goat ruled his world.

There was a round of applause and everyone dispersed. Norah came to stand by Mike. She thanked him with a light touch to his forearm and a few soft words. "You've made Houdini one very happy boy."

"If your goat's happy, then you're happy?"

"My animals are my life."

He crossed his arms over his chest, looked down on her. "Lady, you need to get out more."

"I date." Norah met Mike's gaze. "When I have time."

"Time isn't always on your side, is it?"

"The petting zoo keeps me busy."

"Which means no man in your life?"

"No man at the moment," she confessed. Her animals held top priority. Second place didn't settle well with most men.

Overhead, thunder rolled and storm clouds skidded across the sky. The wind broke like hot breath against Norah's skin, creating an intimacy born of heat, lightning, dark shadows, and Mike Kraft's proximity.

The man stood close, very, very close.

She studied his face, deeply tanned, angular, and cut with character. His body was honed from physical labor. He was a good-looking man, even if he wasn't fond of goats.

Lightning jagged off to the east. Thunder soon popped, and Houdini bleated. A steady drizzle forewarned the wrath the storm was about to unleash.

Hermes trotted toward the red barn in the corner of the pen. Houdini was less bothered by the rain. He came down from his granite mountain, circled behind Norah, and butted the back of her right knee.

He butted her hard enough that her leg bent. She tipped forward, right into Mike Kraft's chest. A thickly corded chest that flexed and felt hot against her palms.

Mike's broad hands secured her hips, steadying her. His touch was as warm as the shower of rain.

There was a faint but visible loosening to the set of his shoulders as Mike widened his stance and Norah eased between his thighs. The wet denim of her jeans outlined her hip bones and flat stomach. His erection strained behind his zipper.

The wind blew in her ear, and the rain sluiced between them like slippery hands. Water pooled at their feet. Yet neither sought shelter.

"This is crazy," she breathed, embraced by both man and the sexual hum of their bodies. His scent was rich and sexual.

"Beyond crazy," he agreed as he looked at her through narrowed eyes inked by dark lashes. There was a curious hunger and heat in his gaze. He appeared about to kiss her.

His kiss came on an inland clap of thunder. Driving his hands into her hair, he drew her up on tiptoe for a kiss that turned as wild as the elements. He tasted of desire and promised satisfaction.

They kissed until the storm passed. Until the Florida sun broke through the clouds and the hiss of steam drying on the brick sidewalks turned the petting zoo into a sauna.

It was Houdini's bleat that reset reality.

Slipping his hands past her wet and wildly curling hair, Mike Kraft stroked the vulnerable length of her neck, the fine line of her jaw. He was acutely aware of how small she seemed against his big body. Lady was tiny.

Her white "Norah's Arc" T-shirt clung to her teacup breasts, the cotton transparent and telling as her nipples poked against the satin cups and into his ribs. The dip at her navel was visible as well.

Soaking wet, her jeans stretched and slipped, riding low on her hips. Narrow, fragile hips, a hand-span wide.

Ever so slowly he released her, this woman who both aggravated and aroused him. Her face glistened, and her blue eyes were wide, her expression dazed. A blush heated her cheeks, as much from embarrassment as from his whisker burn.

She backed away from him, only to land ankle-deep in a puddle. Her sneakers got a second soaking as water crested the shoe laces. She looked down at her feet. "Some storm."

Mike glanced to Houdini. "You've got one wet goat."

A goat now shaking off like a dog.

Norah collected herself. "I need to towel him down." She moved toward the small barn where Hermes now stuck her head out into the sunshine.

Mike watched as Norah retrieved two brown towels. She tossed him one, then moved to pat down the little buck.

Houdini allowed her several swipes before he grabbed one
end and started chewing on the border. Norah lightly tapped
him on the nose, but he ignored her.

Within seconds it became a tug-of-war between the zookeeper and her goat. "Give me the towel." Norah's gentle
order fell on deaf goat ears.

Houdini held fast. His ears flickered and his tail twitched.
He bared more teeth as Norah dropped to her knees. The
towel went taut and ripping rent the air.

"Need help?" Mike asked as he slung the towel around
his neck. "Maybe if you let go, Houdini would, too."

Norah rolled her eyes at him. The second her gaze left
the goat, Houdini released the towel. Caught off guard, she
tumbled backward and straight into the mud.

The imprint of her bottom remained long after Mike
offered his hand and tugged Norah to her feet. She felt soggy
and squishy and in need of a shower.

"Houdini won," Mike said as the pygmy goat snatched
the mud-caked towel and took off for the barn with his prize.

"I'm a good loser where he's concerned," she said, a smile
in her voice. "I purchased Houdini after two petting zoos
had returned him to a local goat farm. He'd been called
incorrigible and a menace. He bores easily, and is always
on the lookout for a new adventure. He's an escape artist.
Here at the Arc he gets testy, but he's also quite sweet."

Mike had yet to see the sweet side of the goat.

Norah, on the other hand, had left him curious. They'd
argued for weeks, neither giving ground. Yet amid the wind
and rain, they'd come together and kissed until their lips
went numb. She tasted of fresh rain and willing woman.

The lady could kiss.

She'd twisted him tight.

He took her in. Her hair was electric and her eyelashes
spiked. Goose bumps rose on her arms. Her T-shirt and
jeans stuck to her skin. Mud caked her ankles.

"You're soaked to the bone," he told her. "You need to

change clothes." And so did he. Yet he dragged his feet in leaving.

He had the unsettling urge to follow Norah Archer home, to strip her down, then work her up until they lay sated and smiling at the ceiling.

He shook his head. He didn't do spontaneous.

His life was organized to the second most days.

Yet Norah proved a distraction. She played hell with his self-control. He'd put his life on hold to build a boulder mountain for Houdini and then stood in the middle of a goat pen exploring the zookeeper's mouth.

Mike's body buzzed.

His blood hummed.

He had Norah on the brain.

Yet dedication to his job had him hitting the road, when he'd rather spend an afternoon getting to know both her and her body better.

"Work calls," he finally said.

"For me, too," she reluctantly agreed. "Thanks for the boulders."

"The mountain should keep Houdini occupied and off my job site."

"We can only hope so."

CHAPTER TWO

"Boss, you need to see this." Mike Kraft's foreman motioned him to the sidewalk. The man pointed to the front entrance to the main building. "Vandalism."

Destruction on a job site wasn't new nor was it pleasant. It did, however, prove damn costly. Over the years, Mike had faced graffiti, broken glass, and torn up shrubbery. What surprised him most was the vandals had struck at midday.

His gut clenched and the cheeseburger he'd eaten for lunch settled heavily on his stomach as he crossed to his foreman. What he saw set his teeth on edge.

"Guess we know the culprit," the foreman said.

Every muscle in Mike's body went tight. Allotted an hour for lunch, his crew had formed the walkway, poured the concrete, then dispersed while it set. Sixty minutes was just enough time for a deviant goat to do damage.

Houdini bores easily. Norah's words hit him hard.

The goat was at it again. The little buck had broken from his pen and crossed the parking lot. Instead of a child's handprints marking a special occasion, Houdini had set his front hooves in the cement and turned in circles. He'd then trotted down the full stretch of the sidewalk. The goat's trail was warm and easy to track.

Mike stormed Norah's Arc.

He found the zookeeper in Houdini's pen, hosing off the buck's hooves. Norah was on her knees, her wild auburn curls caught in a ponytail. His gaze swept the smooth curve of her shoulders, then lingered on her slim waist and sweet round bottom. Twenty-four hours, and the memory of her kiss seduced him. His jeans grew uncomfortably snug. He shifted his stance. Twice.

The pygmy goat's bleat drew his thoughts off Norah and back to the sidewalk. There were no tourists in sight, so he swung open the gate and entered the pen. "Washing away the evidence?" he growled.

She looked up, her expression as guilty as Houdini's.

"Your goat owes me forty feet of 'crete," he told her. "He's damn lucky the cement was still wet, otherwise the industrial park would have a permanent statue of a goat at its entrance."

Nora set the hose aside and pushed to her feet. "Houdini heard the cement truck arrive. Sounds interest him," she defended her goat. "The loud whirl of the mixer left him curious."

"There was a lot of heavy machinery in the parking lot this morning," he returned, a hard edge to his voice. "Not everyone's on the lookout for your pygmy goat."

He caught Norah's shiver, knew her heart would break if anything happened to Houdini. "Why weren't you watching him? How'd he escape?" he demanded.

"I have staff checking on Houdini throughout the day. He slipped past the last person on duty." Her sigh was heavy. "I was with the potbelly pigs, recycling water for Pudding and Pie's mud hole, when one of the workers notified me that he'd disappeared. By the time I got to Houdini's pen and found where he'd dug under the fence, he'd returned. His hooves were caked in fresh cement. I grabbed the hose and washed him down."

While Houdini'd had a grand old time, Mike Kraft was visibly ticked. The man was all dark eyes, tightened jaw, and gunning for goat.

Norah's heart had quickened when he'd entered the pen. Their attraction held strong.

She didn't, however, have the words to pacify him.

"Houdini's cost my company time and money," Mike stated. "This can't continue."

"I'll reimburse you," she quickly offered.

"You'll go broke paying off Houdini's debt."

She licked her lips. "We're sorry."

"How sorry?" His gaze held on her mouth. He looked mad as hell, in an aroused, might-kiss-her sort of way.

Her throat worked.

And her tummy went tight.

She locked her knees to keep standing.

He leaned in, as if drawn to her.

His breath brushed one corner of her mouth.

Anticipation sparked, hot as the afternoon sun.

Her eyelids lowered.

Her lips parted.

And Mike pulled back.

A curse broke as he gained control. Jamming his hands in the pockets of his jeans, he cut her one last look. "Keep your goat penned."

Norah watched him walk away, all straight spine, stiff legs, and significant erection. He had a great body. Big, strong, impressive. Too bad he was so anti-goat.

Moments later, a young girl came to stand by the fence. She held out her hand, offering Houdini a small oatmeal and molasses baked biscuit, sold for a quarter at the Food Arc.

A delighted bleat and Houdini trotted to the fence. With the greatest care, the little buck took the all-natural treat.

The girl's father took a dozen pictures of his daughter feeding Houdini. The buck nuzzled the girl's hand, his coarse hair tickling her palm and making her laugh. Norah's chest swelled. Albeit a scamp, Houdini could be sweet.

Too bad Mike Kraft believed him delinquent.

* * *

Houdini was twenty pounds of trouble.

The goat needed a full-time keeper.

Two days had passed, and the buck was at it again, causing Mike Kraft yet another headache and delay in construction.

The paper trail told Mike all he needed to know. Houdini had once again escaped his pen and made mischief. A set of architectural plans had gone missing.

It had all gone down within fifteen minutes. Mike had left his temporary office to speak with his foreman. He'd left the drawings with all his notations spread across his desk. The door had been wedged for ventilation.

On his return, the door stood fully ajar. Six architectural sheets had disappeared. The tiled floor was littered with tiny bits of paper, all chewed up and spit out.

To fuel the fire, the buds on a bouquet of flowers he'd bought Norah as a peace offering following their last argument had been chomped off. Petals from the small sunflowers and deep blue iris lay strewn on the floor. Only the green stems remained in the crystal vase. Nibbling had untied the azure gauze bow.

A coarse caramel-colored hairball closed the case on Houdini. How could such a small goat make such a big mess?

Norah Archer had promised to keep Houdini penned. She hadn't kept her word. The pygmy goat had escaped a third time.

Mike followed the paper trail, across the parking lot and along the brick sidewalk of the petting zoo. He came upon Houdini and Norah at the exact moment the zookeeper discovered the buck's thievery. Her eyes were wide and one hand covered her heart. She appeared horrified Houdini had shredded page after page of diagrams.

The goat's ability to drag six rolled sheets of plans to his pen mystified Mike. The pages were big and bulky. He'd been one determined little buck, but perseverance was not to be admired in this case. Houdini had scrapped Mike's notations.

Mike was damn mad.

"What have you done?" He heard the catch in Norah's voice as she approached the goat. She dropped to her knees and stared at the mess. "Mike's going to—"

"Hang him by his horns?" he finished for her. He passed through the gate, came to stand before Houdini.

The buck didn't fear him. If anything, he chewed faster before spitting a paper wad.

Mike went down on one knee and salvaged a half sheet yet to be devoured. The remaining bits of the plan were the size of peas.

"Houdini loves paper," Nora rushed to say. "He's fascinated by the crinkling sound. He doesn't actually eat the paper. He rolls it around in his mouth and chews."

"Then spits." Mike ducked a spit ball.

"Here's a piece you can save." She smoothed out a damp corner edge. Her hand shook as she passed it to him.

He studied the drawing. "Goat spit smeared the lines."

She hesitated, asked, "Do you have another set of plans?"

"*This* set contained my notes and designated changes."

Norah Archer leaned back on her heels, leveled her gaze on him. "How did Houdini get your plans? Weren't they in your office? Wasn't the door locked?" Houdini had yet to pick locks.

"I'd left the door cracked so air could circulate," he explained. "Your goat hit and ran like a master thief."

"An open door is an invitation for Houdini to visit," she told him. "He's very social."

"Your goat came uninvited and destroyed a costly set of drawings."

Nora pursed her lips. "Of all the papers in your office, Houdini stole these particular plans?"

Mike nodded. "He had his choice of magazines, today's newspaper, the phone book or the plans."

She scooped up the remainder of the paper, pushed to her feet, and defended her goat. "Guess Houdini finds Cambridge Square as distasteful as I do."

Mike rose up before her, tall and agitated. "Three strikes, Norah." He tapped off his words on three fingers. "Houdini's climbed on my Corvette, ruined my sidewalk, and chewed and spit out my architectural plans. His escapades are getting old."

Her chest rose and fell, her heart heavy. "We'll do better," she promised.

His expression indicated he didn't believe her for a second.

High above, the sky clouded. A breeze slid between them, the air cool against the heat of his temper. Loose strands from her ponytail fanned her cheek, catching at one corner of her mouth.

It was Mike who tucked her hair back. The full press of his thumb against her lips held her silent as the callused pads of his fingers swept her cheek and secured the strands behind her ear.

His hand splayed along her jawline as the tip of his thumb made a slow pass across her mouth, teasing her lips apart. He stroked the inside of her moist lower lip, his touch slow and intimate. And a total turn-on.

Withdrawing his thumb, he dipped his head until their noses touched. "Tie a bell around Houdini's neck or install an electric fence. Just keep him off my construction site, understood?"

"Got it." Her voice was too husky to be her own.

A glance at Houdini, and Mike left the pen.

Norah blew out a breath. Her goat was a scamp. They didn't, however, need another strike against them.

She wouldn't let Houdini out of her sight.

CHAPTER THREE

"Houdini's disappeared." Norah Archer's shoulders slumped as she faced Mike Kraft in the side parking lot. She looked shaken and scared, her eyes all red and puffy. She clutched several Kleenex tissues in her hand.

He squinted against the late afternoon sun. He'd called it quits for the day and was about to climb in his Corvette. Instead he closed the car door. "Your goat's gone missing?"

She nodded, her voice watery. "I've kept a sharp eye on Houdini all week. He was with me in the miniature horses' pen while I was rubbing cream on Angel's and Astro's hooves to enhance hardness. It took me six minutes. When I looked up, Houdini was gone. I've searched for him for hours."

A cold trail for a lost goat would be tough to track. "You need my help?" Mike asked.

"If you have time."

He'd make time for this woman who looked as if she'd lost her child, not a petting zoo goat. "Do we walk or drive?"

"We'll walk," she told him. "I'll put Hermes in her harness. Houdini adores her. He'll hear her bleat and come to us. I'll bring Houdini's Red Flyer. He likes to ride."

Mike rolled his eyes. A goat and his wagon. Unbelievable.

Dusk purpled the sky. It would soon be dark. "I'll grab a couple of flashlights from my office," he said. "We'd better get started."

They separated, met again at the main gate. "Which way?" he asked.

"North," she said, glancing at her watch. "It's feeding time and Houdini will be hungry. There's an empty field close by. Goats are Weed-wackers."

They walked at a clipped pace, Hermes on a leash between them. Mike pulled the Red Flyer. Time and again Norah called Houdini's name, until her voice grew hoarse.

Passersby cut them strange looks, which they both ignored. There was a pygmy goat on the loose. Houdini needed to be in his pen by bedtime.

Norah's heart stopped when they arrived at the field and there was no sign of her goat. Vegetation grew wild; there were knee-high flowers, weeds, and an overturned palm tree.

Mike left the wagon on the sidewalk and tromped across the acre. He swung his flashlight through the darkening shadows as he covered every inch of land. Lines of concern soon scored his features. "No sign of hooves. No pulled up weeds," he said grimly.

Panic hit, and her stomach squeezed.

Her knees went weak. She sat down in the wagon.

Absolute stillness settled around them, thick and defeating. Mike came to stand beside her. He curved one hand over her shoulder, gently squeezed. "Don't give up. Let's keep looking. We'll find your goat."

Norah nearly jumped out of her skin when Hermes bleated, shrill as a whistle. Her little nose sniffed the air.

Soon her ears twitched and her tail wagged. She began tugging on her leash.

"Hermes has picked up Houdini's scent." Norah was on her feet and moving fast.

Darkness hit fully, and the timer-set streetlights illuminated the sidewalk and street corners. Norah kept pace with Hermes; Mike followed with the wagon.

Another block and Hermes stopped at a public park. She pawed the ground. Then head-butted Norah's leg. Norah bent and scratched the little doe's ears. "Where's Houdini?"

Again Hermes bleated.

A return bleat broke the night air. A frustrated, forlorn bleat that sent Norah running toward the sound.

Mike was on her heels. He held both flashlights and shed brightness across the darkened park. "There's your goat." He pointed toward a playground where several old tires sat upright at varying depths off the grass. The tires provided jumping challenges for children. Apparently Houdini had tried to play, too, only to get his horns stuck in several connecting metal links on a low chain that secured the tires to the ground.

His next bleat asked forgiveness. Houdini sounded sorry he'd run away. Sorrier still he'd caused Norah so much worry.

Norah fell to her knees. Her hands shook as she tried to pry his small horns free. Blood trickled from a gash in his head, a result of his struggle to free himself. He was in need of doctoring.

Anxious for his freedom, Houdini stomped his hooves and jerked wildly. His bleat was now belligerent.

Norah struggled against Houdini. She needed him still.

Mike hunkered down beside her. "You hold the flashlights and I'll free him."

Norah watched as his big hands turned gentle. Even after Houdini sidekicked him, Mike soothed with soft words and a stroke down the buck's back.

Hermes chose that moment to nuzzle noses with Houdini through the metal rings, which calmed the goat long enough for Mike to disengage his horns.

Freed, Houdini tossed his head and bleated his lungs out. The pygmy goat was as loud as any wolf baying at the moon. Norah opened her arms and Houdini came to her. She hugged the goat so hard she nearly choked him. Hermes wanted her fair share of affection. The doe butted her way between Norah and Houdini.

They were a family, Mike realized. As crazy at it seemed. Norah loved her animals, even the escape artist who sent her into the night to find him.

Mike swept one flashlight over the playground equipment. "Houdini came here to play?"

Norah nodded. "Pygmy goats are as inquisitive and active as children. Houdini can jump through tires, walk the low teeter-totter, climb the wide steps onto the platform of the wooden fort."

She pushed to her feet. "It's time to go home. Ride, Houdini?" She patted the bed of the red wagon.

The goat hopped in.

Mike led the group, pulling the Red Flyer.

Norah and Hermes trailed behind.

They returned to the petting zoo, tired and ready to call it a night. Once in his pen, Houdini jumped from the wagon and trotted to the barn. Out of her harness, Hermes soon followed.

Norah exhaled, tired and relieved. She would doctor Houdini shortly. At the moment, she was indebted and grateful to this man for finding her goat. She wasn't certain she could have gone it alone.

She cleared her throat. "I owe you—big."

His smile was slow and very male. "Big works for me. I'll collect tomorrow." He brushed a soft kiss against her brow, then departed, leaving Norah as high on anticipation as she was on Mike Kraft.

* * *

Morning rose to overcast skies.

And the sounds of sawing, hammering, and drilling.

Once dressed, Norah stepped from her resident office, called to one of her staff. "What's going on?" She raised her voice over the noise.

"Construction in the goat pen," her employee shouted back. "Mike Kraft and a dozen workers showed up at dawn."

On a Sunday? With Houdini safe, she'd slept like the dead. She hadn't heard them arrive.

All around her the air resounded with deep male voices and a whole lot of banging. Norah jogged down the path to her goat pen. She dodged a small forklift, then circled a trailer from McCumber Lumber. She moved to the fence, and stopped short.

What Norah saw, she would never forget.

Her throat thickened and her heart warmed as she watched Mike Kraft in action.

Throughout the pen, construction workers built a playground. Cemented in the ground, huge electrical spools stood up like tabletops, great for climbing. A twenty-foot commercial water pipe allowed Houdini and Hermes an opportunity for hide-and-seek. The goats could trot the full inside length and surprise each other at the opposite end. Their bleats would echo inside the pipe.

A low narrow beam would show off Houdini's gymnastics skills. Set in the far corner of the pen, a wide staircase curved around the base of an ancient Banyan tree, climbing to a tree fort. The structure was intriguing. Houdini would be highly entertained. He'd never be bored again.

Amid the commotion, the little buck stood beside the contractor. Houdini's horn had been wrapped in gauze. Mike gently scratched the buck's ears.

Wide-eyed and twitching, Houdini was alert to Mike's

every order and movement. Hermes peered from the barn, taking shelter against the shouting and whirring buzz saws.

Through it all, Norah focused on Mike in his gray T-shirt and jeans. He wore a black baseball cap backwards, dark sunglasses, and a tool belt on his hip.

With his back to her, she took in the tempting bunch of his muscles along his shoulders, the flex of his biceps, his amazingly tight butt as he hunkered down and helped anchor the last of the three tractor tires.

Houdini bleated, looked to Mike as if asking permission to play. "It's all yours, buddy," Mike said, as he and the other workers stepped back.

Houdini ran wild. Bleating, trotting, prancing, the little goat tried every piece of playground equipment once, then started over again. Hermes joined him, all sniffing and twitching, and slower in her exuberance.

It didn't take long for both goats to play tag.

Houdini won the game by climbing the boulder mountain and bleating his superiority. Hermes pawed the base, waiting for him to come down and go a second round.

To the west, clouds thickened and the sky bore a purple haze. Humidity weighed heavily, the air in need of a cleansing rain.

"Hey, boss, we're going to take off," one of Mike's workers called to him. "It's going to storm."

Mike had hoped for rain. He'd noticed Norah's arrival. The harder it rained the better. He wanted her wet and willing and needing him bad.

Mike dismissed the last of his men, then turned to the zookeeper. She leaned against the fence, a small woman wearing a white tank top, black jeans, and a big smile. In that instant he realized she meant something to him. Beyond their attraction, he liked her as a person. She cared for her animals as strongly as a mother for any child.

Mike hoped she'd care for him, too.

Even Houdini had gotten under his skin. Mike wished the little buck would butt Norah in his direction now, but it didn't take the goat to draw Norah to him. She came on her own. She entered the pen, amid a clap of thunder and the first fat drops of rain.

Hermes bleated Houdini off his mountain and coaxed him to the barn. Mike swore the buck winked at him in his retreat.

"Two by two," he said as the pygmy goats took shelter.

Norah looked up at him. "Life's better with a mate."

He nodded his agreement.

Tucking her into his body, he kissed her long and slow. She tasted of cleansing droplets, deep need, and shared happiness.

As he held her tightly, Mike thanked the heavens for rain and romance. He was also grateful to Houdini, a pygmy goat with a whole lot of attitude and a mischief for matchmaking.

He faced a future with the zookeeper.

Along with all her incredible animals.

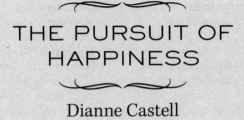

THE PURSUIT OF HAPPINESS

Dianne Castell

He loved this woman with all his heart and that was the problem.

Rex Barkley held on to a last bit of control as he kissed the soft inside of Jane's delicious thighs. He wanted to make this good for her, prove his love for her, not that making love did that all by itself.

"Rex! I need you now! You're driving me crazy."

Thank God, he thought, his lips devouring hers and he slid into her soft wet heat. He loved her and she loved him . . . probably. Damn! Did that word have to pop up now?

In one last stroke she climaxed, taking him with her. The whole city of Savannah tilted, least it felt that way every time he made love to beautiful, intriguing Jane Louise Garrison.

"What you do to me, Rex." Jane sighed as he rolled them over, her on top, her pearl necklace swaying gently as her long auburn curls tumbled down around their faces. She smiled, her brown eyes clouding with dreamy euphoria that turned his insides to fire. He stroked his hand down her spine, the sweet scent of their lovemaking filling his head and his small apartment over the clinic. His love for her filling every part of him.

But did Jane Louise feel that way about him or was he just . . . convenient? A love of the head more than the heart.

"You're perfect, you know that, sugar." Her pink inviting lips formed the words an inch from his. "You're strong, steadfast, loyal—"

"Honest, trustworthy, faithful, low-maintenance." He pointed to the little black and white dog of questionable parentage perched on the dresser. "Just like Maxwell. Your dog and I are two of a kind." Did he really just say that?

She giggled. "And don't you go selling my pup short, now. He's the best, just like you." She buried her face against Rex's neck, her lips kissing and sucking and doing magical things to his earlobe. His insides clenched, and his limp dick lost its fatigue. See, that was more of the problem. He was consumed by her, but was he just good old Rex to her? Always there when she needed him? Well, he'd find out soon enough . . . like today. Before he and Jane Louise got any more involved, he had to tell her what was going on in his life and the only way they'd get through it was if she loved him way beyond *probably*.

"We need to talk," he said in his most even voice as he tried to ignore his clenching gut. What if she ditched him? Turned him down flat? What if she thought he was out of his freaking mind! He'd had that thought once or twice himself.

"You'd better not be telling me you're married and have a wife and kids tucked away over in Beaufort. If you do, I swear on Mama's blueberry cobbler I'll cut your heart out with her silver serving spoon." She glared but there was a twinkle in her eyes. He hoped it was there ten minutes from now. "So, do I go get out the spoon and desert china?"

"No tableware needed. A sense of humor might help or a love of adventure depending on how you look at it."

"You know my family, humor and adventure are constant

companions. That's why I adore you, Rex." She grabbed his shoulders and brought her mouth to his, her nipples hard and firm and delicious. When it came to sex, he and Jane Louise were perfect together, but what about the rest of the time? He kissed her. The real-life times when they weren't in the sack.

Maybe there didn't have to be a rest of the time. Screw life. Maybe they could just stay in bed and handle the screwing that way. But . . . "I need you to help me fix a problem." He hated adding more to her already crazy life.

"Well now, I don't know diddly about veterinarian stuff but I'd be tickled to give you a decent biscuit recipe. Yours are like . . . dog biscuits. Last time I tried one I think I chipped a tooth. But Maxwell loves them. Can't get enough and they do seem to make his coat nice and shiny." She wound her fingers into Rex's hair, giving him a loving look until her cell phone rang.

Not now, dammit, he thought. Not when he'd finally gotten up enough nerve to risk it all and tell her. With Jane Louise reaching across him to the nightstand he had just enough time to plant another kiss on the sweetest skin that belonged to the sweetest girl in all of Georgia.

"It's Mamma," Jane said, studying the little phone screen. Her jaw clenched, then unclenched, then tightened again. She eyed the clock on the nightstand. "And it's not going to be a good thing if she's calling me in the middle of *General Hospital.* What has Mamma gone and done now? When God was handing out common sense, Fanny Lou was last in that particular line right behind Aunt Sadie, Uncle Will, Cousin Hilly, and the rest of the Garrison clan."

"Maybe she thought you were working over at the Foxy Snoot today and when you weren't there, she wondered where you and Maxwell were? Maybe she just wants you to pick out a new purse or something."

Jane gave him a slit-eyed look.

"Right. *General Hospital.* What was I thinking?"

"It's not that I don't love Mamma and all my kin to pieces, but I plucked out three more gray hairs this morning and at this rate of family agitation I'll be bald before thirty and that's only six months away."

Letting out a deep breath, Jane answered the phone, paused, rolled her eyes, cracked her knuckles, then downed the two Tums that Rex handed her before she disconnected. "Okay, here it is in a nutshell. Mamma says it's a surprise for me, which means it's for her and one that is truly outlandish because she wouldn't tell me one clue over the phone. Something's up." Jane Louise nibbled her bottom lip. "I'd better go right now before things get worse."

Jane slid from the bed and snagged her dress off the lamp. It had been one of those can't-wait-to-get-you-in-bed moments. Her hips twitched and he knew it was for his benefit. *Thoughtful girl.*

"Now what was it you wanted me to help you with? Oh, yes, the biscuit recipe." Jane hopped on one foot then the other while pulling on her heels and combing her hair with her other hand. How did she do things like that? *Amazing creature.* "You stop by the house a little later on after you have office hours and I'll give you Aunt Sadie's prize concoction." She blew Rex a kiss off the tips of her fingers and he could almost feel it land on his cheek. "You stay just the way you are, you hear. Rock-bottom normal."

"Boring."

"I like boring." She opened the door, snagged her purse in one hand and Maxwell in the other, then let herself out.

So much for spilling his guts. He could have interrupted her but when a Mamma situation surfaced, Jane had enough hassle. And now he was going to add to it. He wanted to marry Jane Louise, make her life easier, help her deal with her family. Even have babies with her despite the questionable gene pool that scared the bejeebers out of him. Of course, Jane's love of family more than made up for that glitch.

But he didn't want a wife who saw him as a security blanket, a woman who loved him because he was the logical choice, because he was the easy choice. He didn't want a wife who only needed him. Rex glanced at the western sky. Tonight he'd find out if she really loved him in spite of . . . everything. In seven hours they'd be together forever or they'd be history. And that possibility pained him to the depths of his soul.

* * *

Jane parked in front of the white Victorian that needed a paint job, roof job, gutter job, and had been the Garrison family home with random additions here and there for six generations. It was one of those places where the doorknobs stuck a little, the lights shorted out for no good reason and every stick of antique furniture, every bit of cut crystal carried over from Ireland, and every piece of sterling silver hidden in the cellar away from those damn Yankees during that unfortunate Northern occupation had a story all their own. Jane undid Maxwell's puppy seat belt. She slid him into the navy stripe purse she rented from the Foxy Snoot, then headed for the front door painted half red and half green because Mamma couldn't make up her mind which. A car horn tooted, drawing Jane's attention to a . . .

"Oh, please." She groaned to Maxwell. "Don't let that be Mamma sitting behind the wheel of that pink Mustang convertible. Please let it be another fifty-five-year-old woman with Hollywood sunglasses, bouffant hair and a polka dot scarf sitting there."

"Yoo hoo, Jane Louise, honey. Over here. Looky what I have." Mamma gave Maxwell a pat, then took off her glasses, her big blue eyes flashing. Jane found a Tums in her skirt pocket. That it was lint-coated and a little mushy didn't matter.

"Mamma where did you get . . . why did you get . . . how are we going to pay . . . take it back!" Jane ate the Tums.

"Now before you go getting yourself all out of kilter, hear me through. I got this deal from Jeremiah over in Garden City . . . which is nothing at all like a garden I might add and I'm never going to get used to that. It's just a jumble of concrete and weeds and I don't know why on Earth they don't fix the place up. Anyway, someone over there turned in this little beauty with only a few teensy weensy thousand miles on it so I got Henrietta here for a steal. Isn't she precious!"

"Steal is the only way we can afford Henrietta."

"And don't the two of us appear right smart together?" Mamma fluffed her hair and looked sublime. "Like you and Maxwell, we're a team."

"Maxwell's from the shelter, eats a thimble full of food and doesn't get ten miles to a gallon of gas."

"Well, your Aunt Sadie and Uncle Will will think Henrietta is a fine idea."

"They think their chicken taxidermy business is a fine idea."

"Roosters are a prize possession in these parts, you know that."

Jane wanted to add *so are horses* but thought it best to keep that piece of information to herself. Mamma tossed her long scarf over her shoulder, the silk polka dots floating off in the autumn breeze just like Jane's protests. "I need to be off now and show the garden club ladies my new ride. That's what the young man at the car dealership said. *Lady, that is some sweet ride you have there.*"

"I thought T-Bone and the guys were fixing up the Suburban for you. The Suburban's a fine car and it's paid for."

"T-Bone's a good mechanic and a fine man, and I'm sure that there car is just peachy for someone. But for me to pick a blue '88 Chevy over a new pink car! Mercy!" Mamma giggled, looked more thirty than fifty-something, and purred off down Julian Street pretty as you please without a care in the world. She could do that because she and the whole rest of the Garrison clan left all the caring up to Jane Louise. It was her duty to take care of them all and that was fine. *Aren't we lucky as a bouquet of shamrocks to have Jane Lousie in the family to get us through.* How many times had she heard that? A bazillion. To the point where she often wondered if she was adopted. 'Course she wasn't. She was the spitting image of Big Daddy . . . minus manly hair patches, a hundred and fifty pounds, catastrophic cholesterol, and the ability to drink anyone under the table . . . God rest his soul.

"Jane," came Rex's voice behind her. "Did I just see Mamma in a pink convertible? Sweet ride."

"No ride. She should walk. Take the bus. Skip. A unicycle would work, though Mamma on a uni is a bit over the top. But *that* we could afford." Jane snagged Rex's arm, dragged him behind the row of blooming magnolia trees in the front yard, put Maxwell down and threw her arms around Rex and kissed him. She added a good deal of tongue to help forget the Mustang and get her brain infused with more pleasant thoughts. Rex was a very pleasant thought indeed with his black hair, gray eyes, fine build, incredible lovemaking skills, and abundant sanity. His strong protective arms slid easily around her, making her feel warm and secure just like he always did. His hands cradled her bottom, bringing her close to his glorious arousal. "I can always count on you to be here and make things right."

She felt him stiffen all over and when they were in this type of situation there was usually only one stiff part of Rex's anatomy. "Are you okay, sugar?"

"Fine as can be." He grinned but it didn't quite reach his eyes. *Now what?* "This is a nice welcome," he added before she could ask him what was going on. "Mamma needs to buy cars more often."

"Don't you dare even think such things, Rex Barkley. My family's loopier than ever today. Mamma and the car. My aunt and uncle out recording rooster crows for a CD they're putting together to go with their business. It must be a full moon tonight or the stars are lining up in the heavens or something." Her lips drew his bottom one slowly into her mouth, her insides doing a slow Savannah meltdown over him.

"Now that you mention heavenly bodies . . ."

"Are you talking about little ol' me?" She administered little love bites to his chin and did a suggestive wiggle in his arms.

"Yes." He panted. "Definitely you, and that planet thing doesn't come along as often as you think. Some combinations just happen every five years, in fact. Transits of Venus is one. It's where the Earth and Venus line up with the sun and did you know that Venus is the goddess of love and that's a very powerful goddess and—"

"And what about the goddess you have right in your arms, Rex Barkley?" She stopped biting and thumped his chest with the flat of her hand. "I'm kissing you like crazy here in case you didn't get the point. This is called making out and if you're lucky, mister, maybe I'll even let you get to second base." She winked. "I so do like you getting to second base, Rex."

But instead of taking her up on her offer, he held her hand and led her over to the front steps. "You'd better sit down, Jane Louise."

"What on Earth is wrong with you?" He set her on the top step and pulled the bottle of Tums from his pocket. "You forgot these at my place and you're going to need them."

Jane jumped up, the *something's wrong* feeling back in full force. "Are you breaking up with me? That must be why you're acting like . . . like you're from my family." She threw her hands in the air and walked in little circles around Maxwell to try and get calm. "How could you do this and on such a pitifully rotten day when—"

"I'm not breaking up with you, Jane." He followed behind her. "I just have this problem. I'm not exactly what I appear to be."

She stopped and faced him. "You're going to go and tell me you're gay? That's what Jimmy Harris told Ida Jones when he wanted to break up with her. 'Course it was a big fat lie and she went after him with that derringer her daddy keeps in his desk drawer and—"

"We just made incredible love an hour ago. I think the gay issue is off the table."

"Right. Off the table." Jane pulled in a deep breath, feeling a bit better. "Well, you're acting all weird and no one knows weird better than me."

"I'm . . . Oh, boy."

"You've already established that, give me something else to go on."

"I mean I'm . . . I'm . . . I'm a werewolf. There, I said it, it's out in the open and it's true and I'm going to try and fix it . . . with your help so we don't have to worry about this any longer and we can get on with our lives."

She stared at the most handsome man God saw fit to put in the great state of Georgia and tried to imagine him as a . . . "How dare you, Rex Barkley. You think I'm a blooming idiot because I'm a Garrison. If you want to break up with me just say so, you don't have to fabricate some idiotic—"

"You think I'd make this up? Good God! Would anyone make this up? And why would I?"

"A werewolf? Even if this is Savannah and for sure some mighty strange things happen around here all the time, a werewolf is completely . . . nutty. And here I thought the gay excuse was pitiful and I have no idea where Big Daddy's derringer is these days and what do I say to everyone who wonders what happened to us being together? That I broke up with Rex because he's a . . . wolf?" She stomped up the stairs. "I doubt if any man ever wanted to break up with a woman as much as you do to dream up a story like this."

He took the steps two at a time and pulled her into his strong arms that weren't very pawlike at all. "I love you."

"Are you going to howl at the moon for me? And how does someone get to be a werewolf? Eat those dog biscuits of yours?"

"See, that's the very point. Think about it. Why would I like those unless I was what I said I was? Why do you think I have the biggest vet practice in Savannah; why I wrote that book on how to train your dog that everyone swears by; why I opened the shelter where you got Maxwell; why I know where to find the strays all over Savannah? I have unusual communication skills and I get around. We all do."

"We?" Jane felt her eyes bulge to cover her face. "All?" Her voice shrank to a squeak and her head started to spin. "There are . . ." She couldn't get the word out.

"Five."

"Holy mother in heaven." She blessed herself and plopped down in the wicker settee. "Five werewolves in Savannah. You must think I'm the most gullible female east of the Mississippi."

"Not exactly werewolves so much as . . . dogs. Minerva's powers aren't as strong as they used to be, thank heavens for that much. Ever see that 'Dogs Playing Poker' picture." Rex shrugged. "That's us. We took a picture during one of our poker games and a friend of T-Bone did the painting. The dog that found the missing girl in Forsythe Park last week, that was T-Bone. We all sort of crossed Minerva in one way or another over the years. Never *ever* tell Minerva that her scones aren't as good as the ones at the Pink House, or refuse to accompany Minerva's bitchy niece to the spring cotillion or take Minerva's parking space at the Piggly Wiggly. If you do any of those things, the next time there's a full moon you are in for one hell of a surprise and it just keeps happening every full moon from there on out."

"Let me guess, you're going to live forever."

"It's just a dog and moon thing and damn inconvenient to say the least and I'm tired of giving myself rabies shots and if you'd ever had a case of fleas you'd remember it."

"Well, thank God you weren't neutered."

He crossed his legs and looked pained. She stood and felt his head. "You're sick, that must be it. You have one of those raging fevers where you go delusional and your brain turns to Jell-O. I had that happen once when I ate some of Cousin Hilly's barbecue sauce. Fried my brain for a week, couldn't remember my own phone number. You have a fried brain."

"You can break the spell for me. For us. We were cursed by the same spell, we get uncursed by the same spell. Least that's what it says in the curse book."

"There's a book?"

"Lots of books. Old, dusty, smelly books. You can get them on eBay."

She buried her face in her hands. "You are so full of crap, Rex Barkley."

"And let me tell you that can be a real problem when there's a full moon. Do you know how many fireplugs there are in Savannah?" He winked. "A little werewolf humor."

"Damn you, Rex. I've known T-Bone and his cronies for years and Mamma is right fond of him and I have hopes they'll get together one day."

"With this curse he'll fit right into the Garrison clan when he and Fanny Lou do get together."

"It's all a lie because you want to break up with me."

"Once a month, sometimes twice I stay at home, right? When the moon is full."

"Can't remember about the moon part but you stay home to catch up on paperwork, write your book, on call at the clinic." Rex arched his brow as if to ask, *Are you sure?* She gasped. "I do not believe—"

"Yes, you do and the only way for me to break this spell is with your help. Tonight, one hour before midnight because that's the hour for doing good." He pressed a paper into her palm. "This is how to do it, Jane. Explicit directions on what you need to do to help me, to help the others. It has to be done with one true love and that's you." He kissed her hard. "Totally and completely you. With a full moon the Transits of Venus and you and me together."

"But—"

"Rescue me, Jane." His eyes were dark as midnight and sincere. How could this be sincere? He held her tight as if he might never hold her again. She felt sad, desperate, and confused. "I love you, Jane. Love me, too."

"I can't do this." She took a step back, straightened her spine and organized the brain that had served her well all her life. "My entire family is eccentric—I think that's the understatement of the century—and I'm the sane one, the logical one, the one who doesn't need a shrink and this is shrink territory big time. You just want to dump me and know this will do the trick because I hate this kind of behavior. It's the easy way out. I won't say anything because everyone knows my family's reputation is loopy enough already and I don't want to add to it by putting myself in that category, too."

She crumpled the paper in her palm and threw it across the porch, the white ball bouncing over the edge and into the bushes. "Well, it worked. You and I are officially done, Rex Barkley. You got what you came for, now you can leave."

His eyes met hers for a second, making her want to jump into his arms and say she'd put on a witch hat and dance naked on the rooftop if that's what it took to keep Rex with her. But she couldn't. She was the reasonable one and she intended to stay that way. Someone in the family had to!

"Remember I love you, Jane. Always will, till the end of time. I'm sorry you don't feel the same." Rex walked down the steps and headed for the sidewalk. Maxwell hopped out of her purse and trotted after Rex, his bouncy fur and curled tail fluffing in the breeze till Jane scooped him up and tucked him under her arm. "Traitor."

He barked at Rex's retreating figure and suddenly looked . . . sad. Yes, that was it all right. One sad little dog. Droopy puppy eyes, no tail wagging, and pathetic whiney sounds Jane had never heard before. "Now I have a psycho dog to go with my psycho family and boyfriend."

But that was just it. Rex wasn't her boyfriend anymore and it was all his fault. Werewolf? This was a breakup, pure and simple . . . though a werewolf story sort of took it out of the simple category.

She sniffed and wiped her nose on the back of her hand. Mamma would have a hissy at such behavior, except right now Jane didn't care about Mamma and Southern manners that one followed to the grave no matter what the circumstances. All Jane cared about was Rex and that he was gone; and as much as she wanted to say good riddance, she didn't feel one bit good about anything.

* * *

"Well, what happened now?" T-Bone Boon glanced up from the raised hood of a Suburban as Rex entered the deserted garage. A red neon sign that read CAR ER flickered in the window, illuminating the evening dusk outside. "You look like something the cat dragged in, Bubba, meaning it's gotta be woman troubles and with you that's Ms. Jane Louise. Not a nicer girl in all Savannah if you're asking me. You're lucky to have her. So, what did you go and do to mess things up?"

Lingering exhaust and gas fumes hung in the air, engine belts, hoses, and vintage Georgia license plates decorated the walls along with an autographed picture of Dale Earnhardt Jr. and "Dogs Playing Poker." Rex sat down on a case of Valvoline feeling tired clear through.

"Did you ask her to marry you and she turned you down flat? I can't imagine such a thing. The girl's crazy about you. And I use that word in a good way, considering her family roots and all."

"Or is she just crazy about my lifestyle, my normal lifestyle that is a far cry from her family's? I feel like she's attracted to me because . . ."

"You're normal as blueberry pie."

"Until I told her I was a werewolf. Weredog to be more accurate."

T-Bone dropped a wrench back into the tool chest, the clank echoing through the garage. He stared at Rex. "Are you out of your flea-bitten brain?"

"And I told her you were one, too, and that I needed her to get us out of this cursed situation by helping me out tonight. I even gave her the directions." Rex handed T-Bone a screwdriver. "Then she threw me out."

"And you're surprised? Her family's crazy as a bunch of waltzing pigs. She's had her fill. Maybe it's for the best. If you two get together for real, do you want to be dragged into that loony bin?"

Rex nodded at the Suburban. "And who exactly does that piece of crap belong to? You sure aren't working on it after hours for your health. You've got the hots for Fanny Lou and everyone in town knows it."

"Except Fanny Lou," groused T-Bone. "All I am to her is the local grease monkey. You're giving up too easy on Jane Louise. You need to talk to her. Find out how she really feels about you now that she's had time to sit on what you went and told her."

"Does the idea of your boyfriend being a werewolf improve over time?"

"Tonight's a full moon and all the stars a man could want are out there to work all sorts of magic. A good evening to make things happen, least that was your plan. So go for it. Find Jane Louise. Be a pity to let this night pass without even trying to get her to come around. How long have you been looking for the right girl? Someone who excites you, makes life worth living?"

"About as long as you have. But I have to know I excite her, too."

"Then don't just sit there like a bump on a log. Find out how the girl feels. Before tonight you were common as an old sweater to Jane. But hell, every man needs to embrace his wolf side now and then." T-Bone faced the open door and the rising moon and let out a long low howl that came from the very depths of his soul.

* * *

"What in holy blazes was that?" Mamma asked, her evening cup of tea poised halfway to her mouth. "Sounds like a . . . wolf. And right here in Savannah." She made the sign of the cross. "Saints preserve us, what is this town coming to?"

Jane stopped spooning honey into her Earl Grey and stared out the window into the darkness, the silvery beams of the full moon weaving in and out of the live oaks. She shivered. "Impossible. Absolutely impossible," she said to herself more than to Mamma.

"You look as if you've seen a ghost."

"Rex broke up with me today," she said matter-of-factly. "The big jerk," she added because it was definitely a fact. "And of all the excuses in the world he said he was a—you're going to love this—a werewolf."

Mamma's eyes rounded. Not exactly the head-for-the-hill response Jane thought she'd get. Maybe the next news would get to Mamma. "And that T-Bone and his cronies are werewolves, too. Something about crossing Minerva. Now I ask you, Mamma, if that isn't the most pitiful excuse for breaking up with a girl you ever heard? He knows I'd never buy such a story and that was an excuse to get rid of me and end the relationship. He succeeded. I thought Rex was more of a man than that. If he wanted to end things then he should just do it."

"Minerva you say. And T-Bone? How . . . interesting." Mamma's eyes twinkled with some faraway look. What the heck was that? Where was the cry of unbelievable nonsense? The accusation of *the man's out of his brain?* Instead Jane got, "I never would have expected such a thing of T-Bone, but now that you mention it . . ." She smiled.

"Uh, we're talking werewolf, as in fiction and over the

top even for the Garrisons. You know and I know there are no such things as werewolves, right, Mamma? Fiction."

Mamma sipped her tea. "Sweet pea, this *is* Savannah. Stranger things have happened. Around here fiction and fact get mixed up all the time." She absently ran her finger around the rim of the tea cup. "Did you know werewolves are supposed to be magnificent lovers?"

Jane remembered Rex making love to her that afternoon and she dropped the Haviland china cup onto its saucer, cracking it smack down the middle. Her blood ran hot as the water in the kettle on the stove and her insides ached for . . . Rex.

Mamma stared straight ahead, not so much as an eyebrow flinching at the dropped china. "Well, now, I'm guessing you do know all about that lover part firsthand." She stood and took her cup to the sink and rinsed it. "I wonder how T-Bone is getting on with my Suburban? I suppose the least I can do is pay him a little visit tonight."

Mamma straightened her shoulders, her eyes wistful as she glided out of the kitchen more than walked. "Don't wait up now, you hear."

"Mamma! What are you thinking? What are you going to do?" Jane fanned herself with the linen napkin but not because of what Mamma said or what was on her mind about T-Bone but what was on Jane Louise Garrison's mind about Rex. He was an incredible lover, not that she had all that much experience but she knew enough to tell the difference between *wow* and *ugh* and Rex was all *wow*!

She could feel him fondling her breasts, his mouth on the inside of her thighs, his erection pressing into her, slowly, deliberately, hard as steel, and unyielding. Her legs quivered and her heart nearly beat right through her blouse. No man was that good in bed unless . . . unless . . . and suddenly there he was beside her, taking her hand and leading her out onto the porch. "I didn't hear you come in."

Incredible moonbeams fell over them, a million stars

dotted the sky. "Because you were thinking of me, of us together," he said in a low husky voice. *Dear Lord, husky? Least it wasn't Chihuahua or poodle.* "I want you to believe in me, to believe in us with all your heart."

His gray eyes were liquid fire, his hands at her waist, warm and possessive. If he howled, she'd pass out cold. "You want me to believe—"

"Yes." His lips took hers in a hot kiss that was not canine and all man and seared her soul and stole her heart. "I love you." His hot breath mixed with hers. "If you don't believe another thing, believe that. We belong together, and only you can make it happen. Feel with this." He put his warm hand to her heart. "And not this." He kissed her forehead.

"Why are you doing this?"

"For love."

She pushed herself out of his arms. "I can't, Rex. I can't live this way. Maybe you do love me, maybe you don't want to break up, but for sure you aren't the guy I thought you were either. What happened? Where's my Mr. Mellow, the good old Rex? The Rex I fell in love with?"

"I'm right here, sweetheart. Take this leap of faith for us."

Stepping back she shook her head. "Do you know I never believed in Santa because it made no sense? A big fat guy coming down a skinny little chimney, no way. The tooth fairy? Who would give up good money for old teeth? Fantasy is not me, Rex, and I didn't think it was you either. You were so . . ."

"Logical. Predictable."

"I've got to get out of here. I'm so confused. I'm losing my mind. Maxwell! Maxwell, where are you, baby?"

When the little dog came to the screen door, she opened it, scooped him up, snagged her purse and the leash from the counter, and ran back past Rex to the sidewalk. No stopping, no looking back or she'd believe white was black and black was white or anything else just to have Rex in her life. But she looked back anyway and he was gone and she never felt more rotten than right this minute.

Snapping the leash onto Maxwell's collar, she set him on the sidewalk, adjusted her purse on her arm and together she and her dog headed down St. Julian. She crossed Reynolds Square, then Warren, then Washington, one little park more beautiful than the other. See, these were normal thoughts, like everyone else's in Savannah out walking this time of night. She was in control of her life, of her thoughts, just the way it should be. Street light dappled the grass and bushes. Live oaks joined their branches forming a canopy overhead. Horse-drawn carriages clattered over the cobblestone streets. Children ate ice cream from a vendor. And a dog with a fine black and white coat stopped at the crosswalk waiting for traffic to pass as if he were . . . human?

Jane watched the dog. Self-assured, proud, part of the city. "Get a grip, Garrison," she muttered to herself, not getting a grip at all. "It's just a dog, right? Someone's pet. Yet . . ." She shuddered at her own question. Scooping up Maxwell, she dropped him in her purse and ran, not having any idea what she was running from. She crossed Houston, turned down York, not quite sure where she was.

Stopping to catch her breath, she leaned against the side of a boarded-up brick building ready for renovation. Quiet, calm, peaceful. All was well here. She could get herself together.

"Give me the dog."

"Huh?" Jane looked up to a scruffy man holding a knife. "Do you believe in werewolves?"

"What?"

"Werewolves? You know, mythological creatures. Do you believe in them?"

"What the hell have you been smoking, lady? Just hand over the damn dog." Jane squeezed her purse handle, holding it tight to her side. "I can get a lot of money for that flea hound. Women go ape-shit for those purse dogs."

"And you can go straight to hell."

Not a good answer because the man came at Jane with the knife. *Oh, crap!* She ran because she left her pepper spray in her non-dog purse. She tripped and went sprawling and the bastard snagged the purse right off her arm. "Give me back my dog!" she screamed, Maxwell's retreating yelps tearing at her heart. "I'm coming, baby. Mamma's coming."

She took off but she wasn't quite fast enough. Where was that adrenaline rush people had in an emergency? Maxwell's little fuzzy black head disappeared around the next corner. *Crap! Crap! Crap!* She ran faster but so did the bastard till a big dog lunged out between the bushes and landed smack on the bastard's back. Maxwell jumped out of the purse and attacked his hand, making him drop the knife.

"Ouch! Damn it all! Help!" His words were mixed with growling and snarling. "Get 'em off! They're killing me."

"One can only hope."

The man squirmed and thrashed around on the sidewalk like a landed fish. It was hard to get up with two dogs having him for dinner and a really pissed off woman tying his feet together with a leash. Jane retrieved her cell from her purse, took a picture for Maxwell's Facebook page, then punched in 911. The big dog stopped and gazed up at her, gray eyes dark and mysterious. He gave a little yip, then trotted off down the alley. "Rex?"

"My name's Joey," the guy said. "Who'd have a stupid name like Rex. That's a dog's name."

Or a werewolf's. She needed a martini. After handing Joey over to the cops she decided two martinis were in order. And as she got closer to home she decided on three martinis, because Mamma and T-Bone were in the pink Mustang parked in the driveway behind the magnolia bushes. And they were necking like teenagers!

Without breaking a kiss, Mamma gave Jane a little finger wave as she walked by. Her mother had a better sex life than she did. Not fair. None of this was fair except for Mamma,

who seemed to embrace the werewolf idea with much enthusiasm. Why couldn't Jane have some of that enthusiasm?
She sat down on the porch steps.

"Are you okay, Sweet pea?" Mamma asked as she came
up the walk a moment later. She sat down next to Jane. "You
look a bit frazzled and that is not a usual look on you."

"It's been a frazzled kind of night."

"I think it's been an *I miss Rex* kind of night." She gave
Jane a hug. "You think too much, Sweet pea. You got to let
your heart have its way once in a while. Granted, the Garrisons let that happen on a regular basis and you get to pick
up the pieces, but just this once don't think, just go do whatever you have to do to be happy and don't ask questions.
You won't be sorry, Jane Louise. You deserve to be in love.
Rex is a great guy. He loves you beyond words. Listen to
your mamma just this once." She kissed Jane on the cheek
then strolled back to the magnolia bushes.

*   *   *

Bonaventure Cemetery was a really creepy place Rex realized as he hunkered down in the bushes and waited for Jane.
Would she come or not? Did she love him enough to do this
for him, for them? It was asking one hell of a lot, especially
for logical, rational Jane Louise Garrison. Damn it, his ears
were cold, his nose was cold, even his damn balls were cold.
He liked summer so much better, except for flea season.
There was rustling, then footsteps and Jane Louise walked
into the little grassy clearing to the headstone marked Mr.
Bentley. He was the Schnauzer who kept Lilly Bentley company for twenty-two years in this life and now into the next.
A dog ritual needed to be on a dog grave.

"This is crazy," he heard Jane say as she turned away,
his heart sinking in despair. He wanted more than anything
to yell back, "Don't go." But he couldn't. He'd said all that
he could and now it had to be her choice. Did she love him
or love who she thought he was?

Jane turned back. *Yes!*

Grumbling, she laid out the paper he'd given her earlier, the one she'd crumpled up and tossed across the porch but now had. Taking a stick she drew a circle around the grave, then added seven white candles with five dog biscuits and one raw steak in the middle, just as his instructions directed.

Moonbeams cascaded down on Jane, her soft curls swayed as she lit one taper, then the next. She knelt down in the circle, her lovely body silhouetted against the golden light. "I cannot believe I'm doing this," she muttered. "I am completely crackers and belong in the loony bin . . . or I'm in love." She sighed. "Definitely love." She held out her arms to the sky.

> Hail, hail, hail, great wolf spirit, hail
> A boon I ask thee mighty shade
> Within this circle I have made
> Release Rex a werewolf strong and bold
> Release him to me to love and hold

Rex's heart beat wildly. She did it! She did it for him. She loved Rex Barkley. The dog strolled out of the bushes and into the clearing. He wagged his tail.

Jane gasped. "Rex? Oh, my God, Rex? Is that really you? You were the one in the park. You saved me and Maxwell. Come here so I can kiss you on the nose. Least that's what you have written here on the paper. If this winds up on YouTube I'm having you neutered." She licked her lips. "Here we go. Are you ready? I'm not sure I am." She closed her eyes and kissed him.

Her eyes fluttered open. "All right. I did everything that you said. So switch into a man. Abracadabra. Alakazam. Hocus-pocus. Poof. Come on, do the poof! Hey, come back here. Don't you dare walk off into those woods, Rex Barkley." She stood. "Rex, damn it! Get back here. Where are you going? Rex?"

"I'm right here, sweetheart," Rex said as he brushed leaves from his jacket and walked out of the woods to Jane Louise, his Jane Louise. He slid his arms around her sweet body and kissed her incredible lips that he feared he would never kiss again. "God, I love you. You rescued me, Jane."

She squeezed his arms and shoulders and gazed into his eyes. "It is you. It really is." Her eyes got a little squinty. "But was the dog who was just here you or a dog you trained? Are you . . . were you . . . really a werewolf, Rex?"

He laughed. "I'm just a guy in love with a girl. A magnificent girl. I'm yours, all yours. Did you know, werewolves are wonderful lovers." He winked. "Want to go home and see if that part's changed?"

"But . . . but . . ." She gazed around at the candles and woods and moonlight. "I have no idea what just happened here."

"All that matters is you love me completely with all your heart. That you love me as much as I love you."

She shook her head, then nodded and shrugged. "You're right, I do love you. You may not have been the guy I always thought you were and that's okay. I love you now no matter who you are or what you are. But one of these days, you'll have to tell me what really happened. Were you . . . weren't you?"

"A werewolf brought us together, Jane. Now we have the rest of our lives to love each other. Nothing is more normal or logical than that."

ATTICUS SAVES LISA

Ann Christopher

CHAPTER ONE

"I'm in love with you, Lisa," said Cruz Shaw.

Oh, my God.

Stunned paralysis set in, rooting Lisa Evans's butt to the sofa and her jaw to the floor. Her fingers tightened reflexively around her glass of zinfandel, threatening to snap the stem, and she worked hard to loosen them, to breathe and gather her thoughts.

She'd been staring with deliberate focus across the living room at her brother Keenan and his therapy pet, a capuchin monkey (she always thought of them as organ grinder monkeys) named Atticus, trying to pretend she was only peripherally aware of Cruz sitting next to her, but so much for that.

The possibility of Cruz loving her had all sorts of unwanted emotions jamming her throat, clogging it. Surprise and dismay were there and, hidden deeper but no less powerful, tiny flickers of . . . joy?

Joy? No way. Not her.

Ruthlessly self-protective, as always, she stomped out the good feelings and focused on the rest. Years of practice had

made it easy to suppress any desires she might have; she
knew where her duties lay. Once, long ago, she'd had a girl-
ish dream or two, but now she was all about responsibility.
She was a caregiver for whom a love affair was not an option
and never would be again—period, end of story, turn out
the lights, and lock up as you leave the building.

The smartest thing she could do, and she was a *very*
smart woman, was to focus on a few key things: her career
as a radiologist, her brother, and her charity work. Sexy men
like Cruz didn't make the list and never would. And that
meant she would have to protect herself from the simmering
want in his dark eyes, the fresh scent of sandalwood and
spices on his light caramel skin, and her own weak body's
reaction to him.

It wouldn't be easy, of course—nothing ever was with
Cruz—but she could do it. She had to do it. *But . . . how
could she do it?*

She hesitated, stalling for time and trying to think.

Think, *Lisa. Think, think*, THINK.

*Cruz Shaw, software engineer, her younger brother's
best friend and a man she'd known for most of her thirty-five
years, thought he was in love with her.*

This was exactly the announcement she'd dreaded and
feared. There'd been something new in the way Cruz looked
at her lately, something smoldering, intense, and scary. That
was why she'd been avoiding him and ignoring his phone
calls. She'd known in her gut that this conversation was
roaring straight at her, a freight train of trouble racing along
at full speed, but that didn't mean she was ready for it right
now, tonight, in the middle of her little dinner party to celebrate her brother's return to work.

Tonight was meant to be about Keenan and his accom-
plishments. She and Cruz were supposed to be celebrating
three things—first: Keenan's recovery to the point that he
could return to his job as an architect; second: his firm's
eagerness to accommodate his wheelchair and permanently

curled fingers; and third: his new dexterity now that he had the help of Atticus's tiny hands.

Hadn't she made Keenan's favorite meal: roast beef with garlic-smashed potatoes? Hadn't she peeled apples for the pie, opened bottles of wine, and lit candles on every flat surface to create a festive atmosphere here in her cozy living room with its comfy sofas, pillows, and animal sculptures? Wasn't Earth, Wind & Fire's music being piped through the built-in speakers? *Earth, Wind & Fire.* The *upbeat* stuff, not the ballads.

How had this turned into a scene of seduction and longing?

They ought to be discussing *Keenan*, not love. But Keenan was far away across the room, near the fireplace, playing with Atticus and oblivious to the unfolding drama between his sister and his best friend, and Lisa was trapped on the sofa with the sexiest man in the world.

"Are you even going to look at me?" Cruz murmured in that dark, silky-sexy voice that promised endless nights of pleasure for the woman lucky and brave enough to share his bed.

Cornered, Lisa took her time glancing away from Keenan and into Cruz's face, but she could only turn her head so slowly, avoid the inevitable for so long. At last her gaze connected with Cruz's, and electricity flowed between them, shocking and bright.

Man, was she in trouble.

If only Mama had told her that trouble didn't have to be a dark alley with a strange man in a trench coat. Trouble could be an invited guest to her home. Trouble could be a tall man she'd known for years, one with flashing eyes and gleaming black hair that curled around his ears.

Trouble could be sitting right next to her.

Impatient now, Cruz watched her with those intent brown eyes. The harsh line of his jaw tightened with the kind of determination that made her want to abandon all pride and just run as far away as she could get. His sensual mouth was thin now, the full lips grim and hard. There would be no escape from dealing with him tonight, Lisa knew, no reprieve and, worst of all, no mercy.

"What are you doing?" she whispered, surprised her dry throat could generate words. "What's gotten into you?"

One corner of his mouth turned down in reproach. "Don't play dumb, Lisa. It's a waste of time."

Yeah, she'd figured as much, but she'd try a stall tactic or two anyway. "I don't know where this is coming from. This is not the time or place—"

"If you hadn't been avoiding me like a coward for the last two weeks," he said implacably, "we wouldn't have to do this here."

Stung and desperate—it was just like Cruz to tell the truth in all its brutality—she switched to a new gambit: negotiation. "Let's talk tomorrow then. We can have lunch . . ."

"I don't want lunch from you." His gaze slipped to the curve of her cleavage in her strappy black dress, highlighting what he *did* want. "And you blew your chance to do this your way. So now we're doing it mine."

Shooting a quick glance at her brother—Keenan was feeding Atticus mini-marshmallows from a small cup now, a rare treat, and the monkey was chittering with rapture— she leaned closer to Cruz and lowered her voice.

"I know you've always had a . . . a . . . slight crush on me, yeah, but you shouldn't confuse that with *love*."

This was sugarcoating it, of course. Cruz had been wild about her since that long-ago first day of school when she was fifteen and ten-year-old Keenan had brought home his new friend from the fourth grade, a recent transplant from Miami. She'd seen the spark in Cruz's eyes even then; she wasn't blind. But there was a world of difference between the puppy-dog looks of a pre-pubescent boy and the hot, naked want radiating from Cruz now.

"Go ahead and tell yourself I'm not in love with you." Despite his calm voice, she could see his growing frustration in the flush that crept across his cheeks. "It's probably less scary than having to deal with what's between us."

"There's *nothing* between us." The lie was automatic and easy as long as she didn't look him directly in the eye. "Why are you doing this? For sex?"

"Lisa," Cruz chided.

It was a real talent he had, saying her name in a way that made her edgy and ashamed, scared and aroused, and all at the same time. The question had insulted his honor, she knew, and he didn't like it. As Keenan's best friend, he understood very well that Lisa was off limits as a sex buddy—*it was a Player's Club rule, wasn't it, to never seduce your friend's sister?*—and Cruz would never in a million ice ages suggest such a thing.

This knowledge, perversely, terrified her. The thing between them was about far more than sex; she knew it even if she wasn't ready for it. Just like Cruz had to know that whatever desperate untruths came out of her mouth—she'd claimed there was 'nothing' between them, and even managed to say it with a straight face—were a smokescreen for her to hide behind.

"What are you two whispering about over there?" Keenan looked around at last, a bemused frown marring his smooth forehead.

"Nothing," said Lisa.

Atticus the monkey, fussing now that he'd devoured the last of the marshmallows, turned the empty cup upside down, shook it, and tossed it to the floor in obvious disgust. Then he began a systematic and frenetic search of the tricked-out wheelchair's many pockets, looking for more treats. The bright blue leash attached to his collar jangled with each jittery movement.

Keenan ignored the monkey and narrowed his suspicious eyes at Lisa and Cruz. "You look like you're plotting something."

"Please," Lisa said quickly, rolling her eyes for emphasis.

Cruz made a low, rumbling sound of dissent but didn't contradict her.

"So . . ." Shooting a sidelong warning look at Cruz, Lisa forced some cheer into her voice and prayed that her face wasn't as fluorescently red as it felt. God only knew how Keenan would react if he knew his best friend wanted his sister and she just didn't have the energy for *that*. "When're you giving Atticus his little thank-you present?"

"Right now. I'll go get it. It's in my room." Keenan used his stiff hands to turn his chair around, but one of the wheels hit the empty marshmallow cup. "Atticus," Keenan said, indicating the cup. "Pick up."

"Eeee-eeee-eeee," Atticus complained, looking into Keenan's face with wizened brown eyes. Lisa had no problems understanding the monkey-speak. The little guy couldn't have been clearer if he'd opened his mouth and said, *May I please have more marshmallows? "Eeee-eeee-eeee?"*

Keenan frowned down at Atticus. "Don't you back-sass me, boy."

There followed a quick but intense staring contest, which Keenan seemed to win. Whining and muttering darkly with disappointment, the battle for additional marshmallows lost, Atticus hopped down to the floor, flashed a bright red image of Elmo and pals on his diapered bottom as he picked up the cup, and jumped back into Keenan's lap.

The two rolled off down the hall leaving Lisa alone with Cruz.

Silent and defenseless, she waited for divine inspiration to help her deal with this man, this mess, but none came. Cruz let her fidget and watched as she ran a hand through her hair, shifted in her seat, and avoided his gaze. That was another talent of his: letting her stew in her own juices. Along with making her laugh, making her think, and tying her belly into delicious, quivering knots.

With no rescue in sight and no available options, she

asked Cruz the scariest question she could think of: "What do you want?"

For several beats he didn't answer, but the dark emotions leached away from his expression and left something worse: open adoration. Not the glimmers of admiration she'd seen here and there over the years when she'd caught him watching her in an unguarded moment. This was worship, the kind of fierce love that men killed and died for. This was the searing brand of a man beholding his dream woman, the answer to his prayers, and the future mother of his children.

And Cruz didn't even try to hide it.

In a gesture so unspeakably tender it nearly killed her, he raised one gentle hand and cupped her cheek. Lisa melted into nothingness, lost forever to the sensation of his hand on her body.

"I want you to forgive yourself for the accident."

This, of all things, was not what she'd expected. She stiffened with shock and the overwhelming need to escape, but he tightened his fingers in her nape, forcing her to listen.

"I want you to let go of your brother because he's got Atticus now and he's got his job back. He's ready to start living his life again and he doesn't need you as much as he did before, but *I need you.*"

The ringing vehemence in Cruz's last three words startled her. So did the turbulence in his eyes, the urgency. As though he *did* need her. As though nothing in his life could ever be right without her.

And she . . . God help her, but that flicker of joy was rising again, stronger this time. The fear was still there, of course, dominant and unchallenged, but the joy wasn't quite so easy to beat back.

Nor was the desire that surged hot and thick through her blood, or the insistent ache between her thighs. She wanted Cruz's hands and his mouth, the slick hard slide of his sweaty chest against her breasts, the relentless thrust of his body into hers.

The want was too big to hide; she shuddered with it and he *knew*.

"Lisa." His glittering gaze latched onto her lips as though he could already taste her. "You need me too, don't you? I can feel it."

Much as she wanted to surrender, on this point if nothing else, Lisa wasn't fool enough to think he was only asking about her sexual need for him. "I can't—"

"I want you to stop being afraid, Lisa," he said, cutting off her *can'ts* and *won'ts* and *no's*, as though he could stamp them out of existence if he caught them early enough. "I want you to think about how happy we could be together."

He paused. The weight of his silence told her that his biggest want, the most important one, was about to hit her hard—a TKO right between the eyes, and she was right.

"I want you to marry me," Cruz told her.

CHAPTER TWO

Lisa gasped and jerked away.

Cruz knew he'd made a serious tactical error, the kind that would've gotten him sent straight to the brig followed by a nice court martial if he'd been in the military. *Shit*. He should've jammed his fist in his big mouth rather than tell her how serious he was.

On second thought . . . no, he shouldn't have.

Stronger than the fear that he'd ruined his relationship with Lisa before it even got off the ground was the feeling of euphoria. Relief. Triumph. Because he loved this woman. Deeply, desperately, passionately loved her. Had always and would always. And it was past time she knew it.

Yeah, and it was past time for a few other things, too. She needed to stop working herself to the bone at the hospital and then coming home to care for Keenan to the point of exhaustion. And she needed to lose the haunted shadows under her sweet brown eyes, gain a little weight and, most of all, forgive herself.

Looking at her now, though, none of that seemed possible. She was skittish and just needed an excuse to run and hide.

Little did she know there was nowhere on Earth he wouldn't pursue her and no stone he'd leave unturned to get her in bed and keep her there. *Poor thing.* Her hiding days were over starting right now. He—*they*—had waited long enough, and tonight was about new beginnings for all three of them: Lisa, Keenan, and Cruz.

And he prayed that soon—*please, Lord, soon*—she would let him make love to her. The thought made him so hot, so excited, that he had to back away a little and creep up on it. Take it nice and slow.

What would he do if he could touch Lisa like he wanted to?

Well, first he'd filter his fingers up through those black curls . . . sift them . . . inhale them. And her neck. He'd slide his nose down that smooth brown column, find her pulse, and press his tongue to it. Wallow in the taste of her, the smell of her, the feel of her. There was a perfectly round black mole on the right-hand corner of her mouth that'd always drawn his gaze—as if *that* berry red mouth and *those* plump lips needed any highlighting—and he'd kiss it. Then he'd work his way to her mouth. . . .

God, he wanted her. He was hard with it, sweaty with it, desperate.

But she . . . yeah, she looked like she'd been smashed with a mallet.

"You can't be serious," she said, her breath ragged.

"Yeah," he told her. "I can."

"We've never even kissed."

"I've noticed," he said sourly. "But we'll make up for that real soon."

"I'm never getting married. I couldn't even make my engagement work, remember?" There was a definite note of panic in her voice now. "And you're divorced, so you shouldn't take this so lightly either."

He knew what she was doing: throwing out excuse after

excuse, whatever she could think of, as if she could talk him out of loving her. Like he'd say, *Yeah, good point—I don't want to marry you after all.*

She was wasting her time.

"Here's the thing, Lisa," he said, unable to keep the fervency out of his voice even though, judging by her platter-sized eyes, he was scaring her more by the second. "That guy wasn't right for you and I'd never've gotten married if you were available. You should've waited for me. You *know* that in your gut, don't you?"

"I don't know anything—"

She broke off and looked wildly over her shoulder down the hall, where the rubberized sound of approaching wheels on the hardwood floors was growing.

"Oh, God, here comes Keenan again. Please, please, Cruz, I'm begging you—can we talk about this tomorrow?"

For one beat—two, maybe—Cruz felt guilty for pressing her like this, but he kept his eyes on the prize and the momentary weakness passed. "It's not going to be easier tomorrow, *Lisita.*"

Lisa went absolutely still. "Don't call me that—"

"*Shhh.*" Temptation got the better of him, or maybe it was just that he was tired of fighting it after so many years. Aware of Keenan's imminent arrival and knowing, but not caring, that this wasn't the right time, Cruz leaned in, irresistibly drawn to those lips.

Just a taste, he told himself. *What could it hurt?*

She made a small peep of surprise but didn't pull back, so he took that as permission. No, more than that—it was an invitation, especially when he saw the smoldering heat in her eyes as they slipped to half-mast.

"*Querida,*" he murmured.

By now he was almost shaking with the force of his desire and excitement. Keeping his eyes open so he didn't miss one detail of her reaction, he licked her. Ran his tongue slowly . . . slowly . . . across her mouth and savored the faint traces of wine and the sweetness that was purely Lisa. And then he pressed one gentle, lingering kiss on her dewy-soft mouth to brand her as his for all time.

She knew it, too. A crooning whimper rose up out of her throat and she surged closer, as desperate for him as he was for her. But then she seemed to realize what she was doing, or maybe the flaming contact between them was too much. The reason really didn't matter.

All that mattered was that for the second time that night she jerked away from him. Lunging to her feet, she hurried to the armoire just as Keenan rolled back into the room.

The interruption nearly killed Cruz. He cursed and flung himself back against the sofa cushions, his body screaming bloody murder at the loss of her. His skin felt tight, his muscles rigid, his blood boiling hot. He pressed his palms to his temples, praying for control, but God only laughed at him.

Lisa fidgeted with the stack of CDs, looking as agitated as he felt, and that sure didn't help him with his control issue.

Lisa.

He pressed his fingers to his lips to hold her kiss there and imprint it deeper into his flesh. He would make her his or happily die trying.

"What's going on?" said Keenan into the heavy silence.

Judging by the suspicious note in his voice and the hard edge in his expression as he looked to Cruz for an answer, Keenan knew *exactly* what was going on. It could hardly be a surprise; though he'd never openly discussed his feelings for Lisa, Cruz sure hadn't hidden them either.

"We need to talk, man," Cruz told him.

Lisa rushed over, two bright patches of color on her cheeks. "No you don't." Flashing a quelling glare at Cruz, she smiled at Keenan and held out an arm for Atticus, who happily climbed up to her shoulder. "There's nothing to talk about, and Atticus wants to change the music, don't you?"

Atticus chittered with excitement.

"Let's go." Lisa turned back to the stereo, selected a CD

and let Atticus put it in while Keenan studied Cruz with the open distrust he'd probably use on a bridge salesman. The new music started—Santana now, one of Lisa's favorites— and Lisa and Atticus came back.

"Atticus wants to open his present." Resuming her seat on the sofa, she reached out to scratch the thick black thatch of bad-toupee hair atop the monkey's head. "Don't you, buddy?"

Atticus resumed his seat on Keenan's lap and grinned at her, revealing sharp yellow teeth.

"Lisa," Cruz began.

"Not now," she said pleasantly, not looking at him.

Keenan was still staring at Cruz. Actually it was now a full-blown *I'm going to kill you first chance I get* glare, and Cruz waited for him to hurl an accusation or two, but he didn't. Instead, Keenan handed a rainbow-striped gift bag to Atticus.

"Here you go, buddy," he said. "Open. Open."

Manic with excitement, Atticus chattered as he yanked the red tissue paper out, threw it to the floor, and withdrew a box he tried without success to open. He looked to Keenan for help, whining.

"Uh-oh." Keenan's nostrils flared. He fumbled with the box, trying to get his clumsy fingers to slide under the flaps, but no dice.

Cruz shifted uncomfortably, prepared to give Keenan a minute and see how he fared, but Lisa moved to help him. Cruz put a staying hand on her arm just as Keenan shot her an annoyed look.

"I can manage," Keenan snapped, red-faced and deep into one of his flashes of frustrated anger. "I don't need you rescuing me all the time."

Abashed, Lisa held her hands up and backed off. "Okay, okay."

At last Keenan got the box open and Atticus went wild. Screeching and delighted, as though he'd received a lifetime's supply of marshmallows, the monkey went to work extracting his gift. It was a toddler's tool kit, the wooden hammer, wrench, screw driver, and screws painted in bright colors to match the tool box.

Atticus knew exactly what to do with it, too; he stuck one of the screws in its hole in the side of the tool box, turned it a time or two with the screwdriver, and looked around to make sure they'd all observed his brilliant accomplishment.

"Eeeee-eeeee-eeeee!" Atticus screeched. *"Eeeee-eeeee-eeeee!"*

The three humans, having been through this drill before, clapped and cheered. "Good job, Atticus," Lisa said. "Good job."

Atticus rewarded her with another wide grin and then picked up the hammer and started banging it against the box's handle.

"Maybe now you two can tell me," Keenan said, low, his color returning to normal now that his brief bout of frustration was behind him, "what the hell is going on."

"Happy to," Cruz said before Lisa could get a head of steam going. Taking a deep breath, he prayed his oldest friendship could survive the night because he knew Keenan would be furious. "I just told Lisa I'm in love with her."

"Oh, my God," Lisa muttered.

Keenan gaped at Cruz, horror etched on every line of his face. He floundered for several beats, and then the shock turned into outrage. "You're trying to get with *my sister*?" he said, a vein pulsing right down the center of his forehead. "I'm gonna get up outta this chair and knock your teeth down your throat."

Cruz didn't doubt the sentiment or the intent. It was no more than he deserved, he supposed. If he'd been thinking, he would've taken Keenan aside first, told him what he had in mind, and then told Lisa, but his growing impatience hadn't allowed him to do any of that.

"I don't blame you," Cruz said. "Kick my ass if you want. I'll still want to marry her when you're done."

"Marry?" Keenan gasped. *"Marry?"*

"I need your help, though, man." Here Cruz looked to

Lisa. "Because you're the only one who can tell her it's okay for her to rejoin the living—"

"Stop, Cruz," she cried.

"—and she needs you to forgive her."

Lisa gasped and unraveled a little, right before his eyes. She was trembling now, a little pale, and her growing wild-eyed fear scared Cruz as much as it gave him courage. She wouldn't be this upset if he wasn't hitting close to home, would she? Did she need this confrontation as much as he thought she did? Was this the painful conversation that would finally set her free from her self-imposed prison?

Cruz plowed ahead, speaking only to Keenan. "You're better now, man, but what about *Lisa?* Who's going to take care of *Lisa*?"

"You son of a bitch," Keenan snarled.

Atticus froze, hammer cocked, wide-eyed with alarm.

"It's time for you to take a break from *your* physical therapy and *your* struggles and *your* pain and see that your sister is still a young beautiful woman who needs to have her own life now," Cruz said. "And she needs *your* permission to live it."

Lisa got up and made a sickly laughing sound; Cruz knew her pride demanded it. Wrapping her arms around her middle as though she were freezing, she tried to pretend she was fine the way she always pretended.

"I *am* living my life." She raised her stubborn chin. "I don't need—or want—anything other than my work and you, Keenan. Cruz isn't very good at taking no for an answer. That's what's going on here."

But Keenan didn't look like he believed her. He looked like he was coming out of a trance. Blinking slowly, he stared first at his sister, whose lips were now quivering with her effort not to burst into tears, then at Cruz, who met his gaze and let him see his absolute love for Lisa and his determination to make her the happiest woman on the face of the Earth, which was no less than she deserved after the hell she'd been through.

Keenan nodded once at Cruz and seemed to come to an invisible decision. With one hand he absently stroked Atticus's head, and the monkey lowered the hammer and looked up at him.

"*Oooo*," Atticus murmured sympathetically.

"You'll take good care of her?" Keenan asked Cruz.

Cruz shifted his gaze to Lisa because the vow was for her. "Yes."

"Good." Keenan nodded again, more firmly this time, and held his right hand out. "I need a minute with my sister."

"Great." Lisa pivoted, turned her back to both men, and swiped at her eyes. "This is just *great*."

Cruz pressed Keenan's hand and felt the strength that was still there in his best friend's body, curled fingers and wheelchair or no. "Thanks, man."

"I'm going to hold you to that promise," Keenan told him.

"I know." He dropped Keenan's hand and half-turned to go, but Atticus stuck out his right hand, too, wanting to shake. Cruz took the monkey's tiny fingers and had to laugh. Atticus grinned that crooked grin.

Cruz went to Lisa, who again swiped her eyes and resolutely refused to meet his gaze. There was fear in her rigid posture and in the goose bumps running up and down her bare arms. Whether it was the past that scared her the most or the future, he couldn't say.

All he knew was that he loved her.

Peeling one of her cold hands away from where she'd clamped it to her waist, he bowed his head, pressed a lingering kiss to her wrist and took reassurance from her racing pulse.

They were getting closer, he and Lisa. Almost there.

"Come to me, *Lisita*," he told her softly, his need making his voice hoarse and the words shaky. "When you're ready."

Lisa pulled her hand free and turned her stony face away, but the last thing Cruz saw before he left the house was the telltale flicker of emotion in her eyes.

* * *

"Lisa," Keenan said.

She couldn't face her brother. Cruz, damn him, had shaken her so badly she couldn't breathe, much less speak. She felt as though she were on the edge of a bottomless crevasse with her toes hanging over and a stiff wind at her back. Why had Cruz opened all these cans of worms? *Why*?

"I don't blame you for the accident. It was a drunk driver."

"I know that," Lisa snapped.

Wheeling around, she stooped to pick up the wineglasses in her clumsy hands. Of *course* she knew that. This was a stupid, pointless discussion and she was tired and there were dishes to wash. Why did they have to go through this ridiculous and unnecessary forgiveness exercise?

And why was her heart skittering? Why couldn't she breathe? Why was her skin so tight and her flesh so clammy and hot?

"It wasn't your fault you were driving, Lisa."

"I know that," she said again, but there was a new layer of hysteria in her voice, so strong that even she could hear it.

"If you want Cruz—"

"I *don't* want Cruz."

"—then you should go to him because he's a good guy."

"Great. Wonderful." All the wineglasses now collected in her arms, she found the courage to look her brother in the face, to stare him down where he sat in his wheelchair with his ruined legs and his therapy monkey who was supposed to make everything perfect even though Keenan would never walk again. "Glad we got that cleared up. Can I go now?" She took a couple steps toward the kitchen and the only available escape.

"I want you to be happy," Keenan called after her.

"I-I am happy."

The words were faint because no air was getting to her lungs and she just couldn't breathe. There was a noose around her neck . . . a weight . . . a vice . . . and it was slowly choking her to death.

She had to get out of here right now, before she fell apart. The kitchen was her focus. If only she could get to the kitchen. Keenan wouldn't follow her there—he hardly ever went into the kitchen—and once there she'd be able to breathe again. Hurrying to the door, she tried to block out the rush of blood in her ears and the thunder of her erratic pulse—*two steps to the kitchen . . . one step . . . almost there*—but then Keenan said the one thing she absolutely could not deal with: "Be free."

Just like that, she lost it—utterly and completely.

The tears she'd hoarded for two years because she'd wanted to be strong for Keenan erupted from her body on a wailing moan. Desperate for Keenan not to see her fall apart, she dropped all three wineglasses—*shit, shit, SHIT*—and slapped her hands over her face. Weighed down with grief, weak with it, she sagged against the wall, bent at the waist, and gave herself over to ten seconds of unadulterated self-pity. Unable to do anything else, she sobbed and sobbed, aware of Keenan rolling over to rub her back and stroke her hair.

"Shhh," he murmured. "Don't do this to yourself. Come here."

Tugging her arm, he steered her over to the sofa, where she sat, sniffling. Keenan faced her and held both her hands.

"I-It's my fault." With a tremendous effort, Lisa gulped and panted her way to a full breath of air. "I-I should've seen him coming."

"It was a drunk driver."

"I should've swerved."

"You're lucky you weren't killed, Lisa."

"Killed?" Hysteria bubbled up out of her throat and she curled in on herself, nearly choking on her sick laughter. *"You* got paralyzed and *I* didn't even break a nail."

"Stop it." Somehow Keenan got those clumsy fingers tightened around her upper arms and gave her a rough shake, one that made her teeth clack. "Two years is *enough*. Let it go. If you weren't such a control freak, you'd see that none of what happened was your fault."

"I am *not* a control freak." Affronted, she straightened her spine and let him have it with both barrels. "And I don't appreciate you—"

The loud, rattling clang of a cage banging shut jarred her out of her rant and startled her. Swiping at her eyes again, she looked around at the far corner of the room, near the French doors, where Atticus's enormous wire cage stood. The monkey hovered just inside, chattering madly, his soft blue security blanket clutched to his chest. Catching her eye, he held onto the bars and peered through them, scolding her and reminding her of a prisoner contemplating a jailbreak.

Lisa turned back to Keenan and they gaped at each other. "D-did that monkey just lock himself in his cage so he'd be safe from me?" she asked.

"I think so."

Without warning, she and Keenan broke into uproarious laughter. Lisa laughed until her eyes streamed anew. There was a fine line between sanity and madness, and she wasn't sure which side she belonged on. Finally her hoarse throat started hurting and she hiccupped to repress what she hoped was the last sob of the night.

Keenan sobered, too.

"I'm sorry, Keenan," she whispered.

"Don't be."

"I'd take your place in a minute."

"I know you would," Keenan told her. "But has it ever occurred to you that no one but you thinks that way? I'd never change places with you, even if I could."

"Why should I be okay when you're in a wheelchair?"

Keenan shrugged impatiently. "Get that figured out, okay? And then I want you to start working on some of the other mysteries in life. Maybe you can tell the world who killed JFK and how the pyramids were built."

"You're such a jackass sometimes," she said sourly.

"And I think maybe you're a coward."

"What?"

Furious now—how many more times tonight was someone going to call her a coward?—Lisa prepared to blast him, but Keenan studied her with those wise dark eyes and held up a hand to stop her before she got going.

"Don't even try it. I know you better than anyone else, and I've seen the way you and Cruz look at each other." He paused to shudder and crinkle his nose with disgust. "I pretended not to feel the vibes between my best friend and my sister, but I did. I know the deal—"

"Keenan—"

"—and you *do not* have my permission to use me or the accident to hold Cruz off. If you don't want him, fine. Tell him. If you *do* want him, go for it. But don't hide behind me. Are we clear?"

"But—"

"Are we clear?"

Lisa wasn't ready to admit her feelings for Cruz just yet, but there was no denying that she felt better. Better than better—she felt as though she'd shed a layer of heavy armored skin and could now feel the sun's heat on her flesh for the first time in years.

She felt . . . it took her a minute to identify the strange feeling . . . *hope.*

Reaching out, she patted Keenan's stubbly cheek. "You need a shave."

"Yeah, well."

They both grinned and then Keenan opened his arms for her. She scooted into his lap and they held each other as they'd done millions of times before. Some of her tension receded, leaving only the thrum of excitement and the thrill of new possibilities.

"Cruz is a good guy." Keenan smoothed her hair, but she

kept her chin firmly on his shoulder so he wouldn't see the flush in her cheeks.

"I'm scared," she admitted. "I'm not that good at relationships."

"You've never been in one with Cruz."

That made her laugh, but then she thought about what would happen to Keenan if she was involved with someone, wondered who would take care of his many needs.

"What about you?"

Keenan kissed her temple. "Don't worry about me. I've got Atticus. And it's time for me to find my own place. Maybe some sort of assisted living setup, or maybe I'll have a nurse or someone come to me once a day. I'll get it figured out. I'm not going to live with my older sister for the rest of my life. This setup was only temporary. We just let it stretch a little because it's been you and me since Mama and Pops died."

"Keenan," she began.

"Don't argue."

With that, the cage squeaked. Lisa let go of her brother's neck and looked around to see Atticus push open the cage door and peek out. When Lisa didn't shout again, he apparently decided that the coast was clear. Trailing his blue leash, he crept to the wheelchair, his blanket clutched in one tiny hand, and climbed onto Keenan's broad shoulders.

"Hey, Atticus," Lisa said. "It's safe now. I'm done yelling."

"Ooooh," Atticus murmured, and then began one of his favorite activities: grooming Lisa. The three of them sat in companionable silence while Atticus systematically ran his fingers through Lisa's heavy black hair to make sure she didn't have fleas.

CHAPTER THREE

"Jesus," Cruz said a couple hours later, gaping as though he'd discovered Sasquatch making out with a Martian on his porch.

Lisa figured he'd be surprised to see her, but what she hadn't factored into the equation was the shock of seeing him in his negligible pajamas.

Her insistent pounding on his front door had roused him from bed and now he stood illuminated by the porch light in all his glory, which was considerable. His black curls were a wild mess and his eyes were sleepy, but his body was the kind of thing Lisa hadn't thought existed outside of an NBA locker room.

Only a pair of really ugly red plaid bottoms stood between him and the night air, and the bottoms were slung so low over his notched hips that the situation could change with the slightest movement. Perfect tan skin gleamed everywhere she looked: across his sculpted shoulders, down the defined muscles of his long arms, and over the ladder rungs of his tight abdomen. A swathe of sleek black hair ran between his flat brown nipples, over his belly, and disappeared into parts unknown south of his waistband, and Lisa, who'd always admired bare-chested men, found her mouth watering at the sight of it. Big bare feet with strong toes peeked out from under the too-long cuffs at the bottom of his jammies.

It took a lot of effort to shift her focus from that body to the topic at hand, but after a mental head-shake and a deep breath or two, Lisa was ready. "So . . . I had a talk with Atticus."

"Atticus?" Cruz's voice squeaked on all three syllables and he paused to clear his throat. "You did?"

"Yeah."

She edged closer until she could feel the waves of heat flaming off Cruz's big body. With the kind of sexual boldness she'd lacked her entire life until this very second, she circled his belly button with slow fingers—*God, his skin was hot*—and ran her hand up to the middle of his chest. Like magic, his lungs began to heave and his pulse to pound with the force of a marching band.

"I told him there were going to be a few changes."

Flattening her palm, she gave Cruz a gentle push, backed him through the open screen door and into the house, and slammed the door shut behind them. The light was dimmer inside his enormous foyer, with only a small lamp on a table at the base of the staircase to illuminate his gleaming brown eyes. He stared down at her without blinking or moving, but she felt the restless energy vibrating from his body, waiting to spring free and wild at any moment.

Licking his lips, he stared at her mouth. "What . . . kind of changes?"

"Well," she said, reaching behind her back to unzip her dress, "if I'm going to be spending much more time over here—with you—he needs to take good care of Keenan."

"Yeah?" Cruz whispered, eyes bulging as he watched her shimmy out of her dress and kick it to the floor. He stood motionless as she straightened and stood before him in only her black strapless bra and bikini bottom. "What'd . . . what'd Atticus say to that?"

Lisa crept closer and planted her hands on his sides. Shuddering with relief, joy, and the rightness of being with him, she pressed her breasts to his chest, her hips to his. He shifted, letting her feel his size, his want, and his need, and sank his fingers into the hair on either side of her face. Sighing with pleasure, he rested his forehead against hers and held her close.

"What'd he say?" Lisa echoed, trying to remember the topic at hand. "He said, *'Eeee-eeee-eeee,'* but I'm pretty sure he meant, 'No problem, Lisa.'"

That wicked grin, the one that stopped Lisa's heart every time, even after all these years, flitted across his face. "His English is terrible."

"Yeah." Wrapping her arms around his back now, she writhed against his hard length, setting off a wave of contractions that radiated out from her sex. With a gasp—*God, he was going to make her come and he'd barely even touched her*—she turned her face into his neck and absorbed the earthy scent of sandalwood on his skin. "But I think we understood each other."

"Good." He groaned as she scraped his shoulder with her teeth. "He's a—he's a pretty smart monkey."

After that, there wasn't much more talking. Cruz palmed her butt to grind against her aching sex—she was feverish and soaking wet by then—and caught her lips for a nipping kiss that was so sweet and deep she felt it in her throbbing nipples and over every shivering inch of her bare skin.

"I love you," she whispered.

"Yeah?" A faint smile worked the corners of his mouth. "You should. I'm a good guy."

"I know you are. And I've been waiting for this. I've been . . . Ahhh—"

"What? *This?*"

On *this*, he kneaded her butt with a rough, slow caress—down . . . down . . . down. On the up stroke, he thrust his hips and found the exact right spot—*her sweet spot, God, right there, right there*—and she came with a long, keening cry that he caught in his mouth as he kissed her. The pleasure was piercing and bright, strong and deep enough to rearrange her body down to the last atom in the marrow of her bones. Sagging against him, weak now, she was dimly aware of him dragging and half-carrying her to the staircase.

"Bed," he said, his voice hoarse, his eyes glittering and wild. "Now."

They made it in record time and then they were in the darkened bedroom, tumbling onto the massive, rumpled, decadent bed that had luxury sheets, the intoxicating smell of Cruz, and the lingering warmth from his body.

Lying back, she levered up on her elbows, watched as he kicked off those awful pajamas, and caught tantalizing glimpses of his long muscular legs, thick patch of dark hair, and jutting erection.

"Oh, God." She opened her arms and legs to him. *"Oh, God."*

"Shhh, *mi amor."*

He came to her, easing between her thighs, removing her bra and panties, and arranging her limbs the way he wanted them: her legs tight around his waist, her hands in his nape, filtering through his silky curls. Staring down at her, his reverent hands stroking over her breasts, he crooned.

"Mi Lisita," he said, kissing her and swallowing her whimpers. *"Tu eres mi amor. Angelita . . . angelita."*

The kisses became slower . . . deeper . . . and Lisa was beside herself.

"Please." She arched against him, shamelessly rubbing and begging.

"Abra para mí." Pulling back, he palmed himself and

reached for the nightstand drawer. There was the quick flash of a red wrapper as he opened a condom with his teeth and slid it on, and then he was ready. "Open for me, *querida*."

She hardly needed the encouragement. Clutching his shoulder, scratching him in her haste, she angled herself and spread her legs wider, begging him, needing him.

"*Buena.*" A faint smile flickered across his face. "*Tan buena.*"

"So good," she echoed. "*So good.*"

Another heavy-lidded smile answered her. He rubbed against her wet core, lubricating himself, and then inched inside, millimeter by slow millimeter until he was seated to the hilt and she was stretched tight and faint with renewed ecstasy.

And then he began to move in slow, deliberate strokes, each more exquisite than the last, and his eyes rolled closed and his head dropped to the hollow between her neck and shoulder.

"*Te quiero,*" he murmured, his tempo increasing with each pivot of his hips. "*Te quiero . . . te quiero—*"

"I love you, too." Locking her ankles behind his back, she pulled him deeper, held him tighter, and the waves crashed over her again. "Cruz. *Cruz.*"

Her body's powerful contractions sent him over the edge; his body went rigid and his two-hundred-plus pounds of heat and muscle surged one last time, driving her up the mattress as he came with loud, unabashed cries.

"*¡Ay Dios mio! ¡Dios!*"

He shuddered over and over again, whimpered, keened. In that second it felt as though he gave her every ounce of himself, every part of his soul, and wasn't afraid to let her know it. And she loved him all the more.

At last he raised his head to look at her with wonder in his eyes and a smile touching his lips. "We're getting married, okay? Just so you know where this is going."

She'd hoped, but there was nothing like hearing the

words spoken again in that dark velvet voice. "Will you always speak Spanish to me like that?"

His brows quirked. *"Spanish?"*

Reaching up, she smoothed the faint lines across his forehead and then pulled him down for a kiss. "Mmm." Her skin heated all over again. "You told me you loved me in Spanish."

"I love you in Spanish *and* English," he said between nips and nuzzles of her lips. Deep inside her body, she felt him stir again and begin to swell. "And I love that crazy little monkey, too."

"Atticus?"

"Without him, Keenan wouldn't have his job back. He wouldn't be reclaiming his life, and you wouldn't be here with me. Would you?"

"No." She arched, surging her hips up to meet his, and they both moaned. "I think we owe him a big bag of marshmallows, don't you?"

"Absolutely." With complete absorption, he kissed her forehead, both her eyes, and the tiny round mole at the side of her mouth before finally making his way to her lips.

"Here's to Atticus," was the last thing he said for a while.

"To Atticus."

RESCUE ME

Marcia James

*To my husband, James, for his unwavering love
and wicked sense of humor . . .*

*To my friend and critique partner, Patricia Sargeant,
for getting my jokes and going light on the red pen . . .*

*And to Lori Foster and Dianne Castell
for conceiving these wonderful benefit anthologies
and offering me the chance to participate
in* Tails of Love.

CHAPTER ONE

"Rata!"

The shout jerked Adam Baumgardner's attention away from next week's menu, and he scanned his restaurant's dining room. Wasn't *rata* Spanish for "rat"?

"Rata gigante albino!" Rey, his sous chef, stormed from the open kitchen followed by Émile, his maître d'.

Damn. Thanks to Adam's basic knowledge of several languages, he understood his international staff. "There better *not* be a giant albino rat in my kitchen."

"Not the kitchen, the alley," Émile explained.

Rey muttered something about rats and bad omens.

"Actually rats, especially white ones, are considered good luck in India," Émile pointed out in his haughty Gaelic accent.

Before the two could launch into their customary squabbling, Adam stood. "I'll take care of it."

With Rey and Émile trailing behind, Adam headed through the kitchen to the back door. At least this had occurred between the lunch and dinner seatings. The last thing his Nuclear Fusion Restaurant needed was a rumor about rodent infestation.

The alley door was propped open for the warm spring breeze. Sergio, his head waiter, stood in the doorway. "Not *un ratto*," Sergio said in his half-English-half-Italian way. "Dog."

Adam pushed past him into the alley. Sergio was right. The shivering animal huddled against the Dumpster was a small dog. Its pale skin was hairless and mud-splattered. Two sad, black eyes peered anxiously from its dirty face.

Without taking his gaze off the pathetic dog, Adam instructed Émile and Sergio to bring him a bowl of water and some country pâté. They left, both chuckling, obviously anticipating their temperamental chef's reaction to this misuse of his appetizer special. It wasn't long in coming.

"No!" Chien's indignant shout was so loud even the dog cringed. "Pâté for people, not rats!"

Adam sighed. Chien's culinary mastery had earned Nuclear Fusion its four-star reviews, but the Chinese chef's mulish personality was a pain. Before he could remind Chien once again who owned the restaurant, Sergio was back with a slice of pâté on a plate. Émile followed with an empty bowl and bottle of spring water.

Émile shrugged. "You can't serve tap water with that pâté."

Grinning, Adam took the food and water. He didn't approach the dog directly but walked to the left of the door. He crouched, ignoring the pain from the damaged knee that had ended his pro-football career. Then he quietly placed the pâté and bowl on the ground.

April sunlight glinted off the fine china's gold Nuclear Fusion logo as he filled the bowl with water. The trembling animal whined, its nose twitching. Adam retreated to the door and crooned softly, "It's okay. No one's going to hurt you."

Slowly the dog skirted the food, sniffing, then backing away. Finally it nibbled the pâté. Adam released the breath he'd been holding, and Émile and Sergio high-fived. The skinny stray took dainty bites of the food, swallowing without chewing.

Martha, the restaurant bookkeeper, entered the kitchen. "What's up?"

Jared, one of the restaurant's teenaged busboys, made a disgusted noise. "Nuke is feeding some mangy mutt."

Adam grimaced. It'd been two years since he'd retired from the NFL, but people still called him "Nuke." Despite christening his international cuisine restaurant "Nuclear Fusion" as a nod to his football nickname, Adam was getting tired of it.

Martha peered out the door. "Poor thing. It looks starved."

Adam faced her. "What should we do with it?"

Émile sniffed. "Maybe some lemon sorbet to cleanse his palate before the second course?"

Adam laughed with his staff. Even Chien gave a grudging smile before suggesting, "Chocolate soufflé for dessert?"

"Chocolate is dangerous for dogs." Martha glanced away from the stray. "I learned that volunteering at the animal shelter on Caridad Street. That's where you should take it."

"They'd just put it down," Adam protested.

She shook her head. "Rescue Me is a no-kill shelter."

Ten minutes later, Adam was driving the five city blocks to Rescue Me, with a muddy, smelly dog sitting in an empty banana box on his newly detailed BMW's leather seat.

"You reek of Dumpster-diving, little buddy." He kept his voice soft to avoid scaring the nervous dog. Adam lowered his car windows several inches to let in the rich scent of the area's ethnic restaurants—a wonderful mix of exotic spices and fried foods. He inhaled deeply as his passenger's nose twitched.

He maneuvered past double-parked vans, delivering shipments from around the world to this eclectic neighborhood. Adam braked for a man pushing a two-wheeler stacked with Dos Equis beer. Down the street, two Asian women chatted animatedly as they examined produce boxes. The area's amicable quirkiness appealed more to Adam than the ritzier parts of the nation's capital.

Storefronts grew shabbier as he turned right onto Caridad

Street. The short block held two parking lots, an Indian grocery, and Madame Magda's Tarot Card & Palm Reading Parlor. Between the lots was a sooty, two-story brick building with a cheery green sign over the front door. The sign featured a cartoon cat and dog bracketing the words RESCUE ME.

Adam parallel-parked in front of the building. After pumping a few quarters into the parking meter, he retrieved the box from his passenger seat and locked his BMW. Hopefully the car would still be there when he got back.

Inside the carton, the pathetic animal shivered and pawed catlike at the tablecloth he'd used for padding. Thanks to the dog's hairless state, Adam could see its ribs. What if the little thing was too sick to save? He blocked the thought.

"Hang in there," he reassured the animal. "We'll fix you up."

Adam held the box in one hand as he opened the shelter's front door. A bell tinkled when he stepped into an empty waiting room. The furniture was the olive metal and vinyl of government surplus. A hallway led toward the rear of the building.

"C'mon back," a woman called from a room off the corridor.

Adam started down the hall. He peered through the first open door into an examining room. A woman wearing kitten-themed doctor scrubs leaned over a stainless steel table reading a chart. Her chin-length, light brown hair concealed her face.

Then she straightened, turned, and offered her hand. "Welcome to Rescue Me."

Recognition struck Adam with the force of the defensive tackle who'd ended his career. His lungs scrabbled for air, and he resisted rubbing his chest where his heart had taken a direct hit. *Claire.* It was Claire. Her beautiful brown eyes met his, and it seemed like seconds instead of years had passed since he'd made the biggest mistake of his life.

CHAPTER TWO

Dr. Claire Mendelsohn froze, her hand extended toward *Adam*—the man she'd prayed she'd never see again. The icy shock of his appearance stuttered her heart and closed her throat.

What was wrong with her? She'd known this day would come, when she'd heard he'd returned to D.C. and opened a restaurant practically in her backyard. But, God help her, knowing hadn't prepared her for this emotional jolt. Claire dropped her hand and forced the best smile she could muster. "Hello, Adam."

"Um," he began, looking as stunned as she felt. "I didn't know you worked here. I mean, I read in the *University of Virginia Alumni News* you'd gotten your vet degree. . . ."

Her stomach roiled. Was he, too, remembering that awful night after their UVA graduation? It'd been ten years since he'd delivered his ultimatum—go with him to San Francisco or take her scholarship to Cornell veterinary school—but the pain was scalpel sharp. She quashed thoughts of that bitter argument and kept up her end of their oh-so-polite small talk. "Three years ago, I moved back to D.C. to be closer to my parents. I opened this shelter instead of joining an established practice."

Adam nodded, and the tension in the room grew palpable. Claire wanted to weep at how coldly formal they'd become.

She tried not to catalogue the ways he'd changed from the shaggy-haired, twenty-one-year-old she'd loved. But how could she not compare this muscular, well-dressed man to that jeans-clad college kid? Adam's mahogany hair was shorter and expensively cut. Was it still as silky to the touch? And his blue eyes were just as intense today as in her memories. When they'd made love in his fraternity room, he'd stared into her very soul. . . .

Claire cleared her throat. "I read that you'd opened a restaurant. The reviews have been great."

Adam shrugged. "I hired the right chef." He was silent for a moment, then added, "I've never seen you at Nuclear Fusion."

"I haven't been, yet." *Yeah.* Like she'd willingly put her heart through a grinder by visiting his restaurant. She glanced away. "Honestly, I didn't think you'd want to see me."

"Claire—" He stopped as a pitiful whine came from the box in his hands. "Damn, I nearly forgot." He set the box on her examining table. "I found this dog behind my restaurant. Can you help it?"

One look at the shaking animal, and her professional instincts kicked in.

"Oh, poor baby." Claire soothed the animal as it hesitantly wagged its tail. She retrieved several treats for toy-sized canines and offered them to the waif-thin creature. The dog accepted the food after some cautionary sniffing.

Conscious of Adam watching, Claire smoothed her hands over the dog's tiny limbs and torso, then inspected its head, eyes, and mouth. There didn't seem to be any injuries, and the dog tolerated her examination without whimpers of pain.

Her jack-rabbiting pulse calmed as she went through the

familiar routine. Claire started a chart on the dog, recording her observations. After warming her stethoscope on her palm, she checked its heart and lungs. No concerns there, either.

She glanced at Adam, who looked more like a worried pet-owner than a man who'd rescued a stray. "There aren't any obvious problems besides malnutrition. But I'll keep an eye on him for a few days, while I search the missing dog reports."

"Did starving make his fur fall out?" He stroked the matted tuft on the dog's head, his tanned hand as large as the animal's body. "He's only got hair left on his head, ankles, and tail."

Claire smiled. "He's a Chinese crested *hairless* dog."

Adam's jaw dropped, and his fingers stilled on the animal's back. "He's *supposed* to look like this?"

Despite their unhappy history, Adam's incredulity tickled a laugh out of Claire. She rubbed gently at the dirt streaking the dog's sides. "Give the little crestie a break. Once I wash the mud off him, he won't look so bedraggled."

"I'll take your word on that." He met her eyes, and the air thickened again. "Can I come tomorrow and visit, uh, the dog?"

No. She almost said it aloud, but she only had her personal reasons to object. So she nodded. Her assistant, Lucia, could take Adam to see the dog, while Claire did what? Hid in her office? Avoiding him for a decade hadn't killed her feelings.

Absently, she patted the dog, her hand brushing Adam's fingers. Claire registered the warm, familiar feel of his skin before jerking her hand away. The last thing she needed was to remember this man's touch. So she picked up her clipboard and made a note to call the crestie rescue group about missing pets.

"What do I owe you?" Adam asked.

There's a loaded question. Claire bit back a response

about long overdue apologies and explained the shelter's policy instead. "We don't charge people who save lost or abandoned animals. But if you'd like to make a donation, there's a jar on the receptionist's desk."

Adam nodded. Then he smoothed his thumb under the dog's chin and spoke softly to it. "See you tomorrow, bud."

Claire watched the man who'd broken her heart walk down the hall, where he pushed some bills into her donation jar before leaving. Her treacherous mind was bent on torturing her today, noting how fine he looked from the back as well as the front. Why couldn't Adam have turned into an unattractive toad with an obnoxious personality? Instead he was a sexy champion of strays.

After slipping another treat to the crestie, Claire strode to her reception desk and looked into the collection jar. Three hundred-dollar bills lay among the pennies and nickels. She sighed. The man made it hard to hold a grudge.

CHAPTER THREE

Adam drove on autopilot toward his Northeast D.C. home. Despite the work waiting for him at the restaurant, he needed to think. Why had seeing Claire again rattled him so badly?

The cell phone in his pocket played "Neutron Dance," and Adam sighed. He regretted the day he'd let Émile program his phone with the '80s hit. But his maître d' had decided it was an appropriately named ring tone for the owner of Nuclear Fusion.

He slowed for a red light and answered his cell.

"How's the patient?" his bookkeeper asked.

He should've known Martha would be waiting to hear. "Dr. Mendelsohn said he just needs some food and attention. She's going to check for reports of missing cresties."

"That hairless stray was a Chinese crested?" Martha laughed. "You know, they often win the Ugliest Dog Contest."

Adam almost snapped that the poor animal wasn't ugly, just half-starved. Instead, he reined in his unexpected irritation. "Well, Claire will get him fixed up and find his owners."

"*Claire*, is it? You move fast, Nuke," Martha teased him.

Damn. Just because he'd dated a few starlets in his years with the 49ers, he had a rep as a player on and off the football field. And now his friends figured he was always on the make. Before his nosy bookkeeper could pry any further, Adam changed the subject. "Listen, I've got some errands to run, so I won't be in until six. Can you hold down the fort?"

Martha assured him she could, and he ended the call. The last thing he felt like doing was explaining how he knew Claire.

Besides, he didn't really *know* this woman, this competent, compassionate veterinarian. The Claire he'd loved in college had been a shy bookworm, the exact opposite from the blond party-girls his fellow jocks had dated. But Claire had been anything but quiet with him . . . especially when they'd made love.

Regret clenched his gut, and he gripped the steering wheel with whitened knuckles. He'd had his share of bed partners over the years, enough to know *now* how special Claire was and how good they'd been together. If only he'd realized it in college.

The streets became residential and affluent, as he drove in silence with his remorse. By the time he pulled into his drive and punched in the code to open the gate, Adam was cursing the arrogant kid he'd been. How could he have pushed Claire away?

He parked the BMW in his garage and let himself into his McMansion—his parents' nickname for the stone Colonial he'd purchased several years ago. Thanks to a decorator, the main floor was furnished and comfortable, but the only livable room upstairs was his bedroom. The place had great security and was convenient to his restaurant, but it'd never felt like a home.

Adam took the stairs to the second floor two at a time, then strode to the small bedroom at the end of the hall. Inside was a jumble of boxes he hadn't unpacked since leaving San Francisco. He found the carton labeled "UVA" and placed it on the window seat by the room's large, mullioned windows.

He stared at the box, then opened the dusty flap. Why was he doing this? It was hard enough seeing Claire today without this painful trip down Memory Lane. Still, like a glutton for punishment, he shuffled through the carton until he found the picture frame. Picking it up, he peeled off the bubble wrap.

The photo had been taken at their college graduation. Both Claire and he wore caps and gowns, and they were laughing at something he couldn't recall. But it was the way she looked at him with such love in her face that made his chest ache.

He brushed his finger across her image. This young Claire had longer hair than the sophisticated cut sported by Dr. Mendelsohn. In college, she'd tie it back in a ponytail when she had ridden in his old Mustang convertible. Would she be surprised to learn he still had that car—now totally restored?

In the photo, Claire's shapeless graduation gown hid her lean limbs and delicate curves. Today, despite her boxy scrubs, the good doctor was even more attractive, with a woman's fuller body and confidence. How would she feel in his arms now?

Damn, he was a fool for even imagining such things. He'd hurt Claire badly. After signing a football contract that meant more money in a year than he'd thought to earn in his lifetime, Adam had expected Claire to forget her dreams and follow him to California. When she hadn't jumped at his request, he'd issued an ultimatum. And he hadn't even offered marriage in return.

A fresh wave of self-disgust flooded him, and Adam returned the frame to the box. Those days with Claire were the happiest of his life. He'd never been able to recapture the same sense of peace and completion with anyone else.

He'd picked up the phone to call her countless times over the years, then chickened out. What if he'd reached her and she'd refused to forgive him? What if she'd married and built a life with someone else?

Adam looked around the dusty room. All he had from his NFL days was a bum knee and come-ons from women more interested in his money than in him. And too many regrets to count.

Claire wasn't wearing a wedding ring. The thought pushed through his mental pity party and sparked a flame of hope. Was it possible? Could he convince Claire to give their relationship another shot? Adam fisted his hands. Quitting hadn't landed him in two Super Bowls. And he wouldn't throw in the towel on this challenge either.

He just needed a game plan.

Adam grinned, feeling the familiar, powerful resolve that had served him so well with the 49ers. If there was a chance in hell for him and Claire, he was going for it. And with the help of his little crestie buddy, he'd play to win.

CHAPTER FOUR

"It's great to have you back." Claire smiled at her college intern, currently manning the shelter's reception desk. "How was Spring Break? Tell me you didn't end up in a *Gone Wild* video."

Patty laughed. "I spent the week building a Habitat for Humanity house. We kept our shirts on, except the guys. They made it difficult to concentrate." She handed a photo to Claire.

In the shot, eight grinning people stood in front of a partially constructed house. Several were muscular, shirtless young men. Even dirt-streaked, the guys were eye candy. Claire gave an appreciative hum before handing the photo back to Patty.

The shelter's front door opened, and Adam strode in, buff and gorgeous in a body-molding shirt and jeans. Claire forced back the appreciative hum that wanted to resurface. She'd meant to be in her office, in case he stopped by. But when he met her gaze and smiled, her plans to avoid him evaporated like steam.

"Hi." Adam walked up to the desk. "How's the patient?"

"The crestie's doing fine." Claire's voice was steady despite her racing heart. Would she feel this attracted to

Adam if they'd just met, or was this some sort of lost-love lust?

She introduced the intern, who gave Adam the once-over as they shook hands. But his focus stayed on Claire, and she hid her unexpected pleasure at his attention.

"I'll show you to our dog runs." Claire led him past the examination rooms and her office, so aware of the man by her side that her skin actually prickled. What was it about Adam that made her want to forget the past and their bitter words?

Claire concentrated on her tour. "We rent this building and have a year left on the lease before the landlord sells it."

Adam stopped. "Where will you go?"

She sighed, already dreading the move. "We're looking at places in Maryland." Claire continued walking. "We divided this building's storage area into rooms—the largest for the dogs and cats. Feral animals, like raccoons, are isolated in case of rabies. Sometimes we get exotic animals people kept as pets."

She opened the heavy door to the canine section and watched Adam's eyes pop when he heard the cacophony of barks and yips. "They're happy to see you," Claire teased. "Thanks to these thick walls, most of the noise is contained in this room."

She gestured to the runs, several housing a dog. "Each run is built with an inside area, a doggie door in the wall, and a similar outside run, where they can go in good weather. The outside enclosures were built on the old parking lot, which allows us to hose down the runs to clean them."

Adam couldn't seem to tear his eyes away from the assortment of dogs. "What's going to happen to them?"

Claire walked to the first run, slipped her fingers into the mesh surrounding the pen, and petted the terrier inside. "We have volunteers who walk the dogs and play with them. And some foster-parent the dogs or cats," she explained. "They let us know how social and stable the animals are, whether they're good with children, that sort of thing. Then we hold adoption fairs and place as many as we can with good homes."

"You must go through a lot of kibble," he observed.

Claire nodded. That was an understatement. "Food, kitty litter, chew toys . . ." She moved to the next run, where a battle-scarred boxer snuffled her hand before licking it. "We hold fund-raisers, bake sales, etcetera to cover operating expenses."

Adam glanced down the row of runs. "Where's Buddy?"

She grinned. Did he realize he'd named the crestie—often a first step to adopting a pet? "We have him at the end, several pens away from the other dogs, until he gets acclimated." Claire led the way to their newest resident. "He's a little skittish."

The Chinese crested hairless dog was washed, groomed, and fed, appearing strikingly different from the street-worn stray.

Adam gaped. "This *can't* be the same dog. I mean, he looks like my niece's favorite toy, a little fairy pony."

Claire chuckled, his surprised appreciation warming her. "The hairless cresties do look like they have manes and tails."

She knelt down to greet the dog, who cautiously came forward to sniff her fingers. With obvious effort, Adam sat yoga-style beside her. Was his football injury still painful? Claire waited, but he didn't extend his hand toward the crestie.

"Would you like to hold him?" She reached for the spring lock and opened the pen's door without waiting for an answer. "He hasn't bitten anyone since arriving here."

"I wouldn't want to scare him—"

"You'll do fine." She carefully picked up the crestie. "Make a cradle with your palms . . . that's it." She placed the dog in his hands, her heart squeezing at Adam's anxious gentleness.

"Hey, Buddy," he crooned. The dog's ears twitched, and it settled into the nest formed by Adam's hands and chest.

The contrast between the big ex-jock and the tiny dog was amusing, but Claire's thoughts strayed to the time when Adam had held her with the same care. She'd always felt cherished and protected in his arms. That's why it had been so devastating when he'd crushed her heart.

No. She wouldn't dwell on that argument and the awful

months afterward. What mattered now was helping Adam bond with Buddy. Claire cleared her throat. "So far I haven't found any reports of a missing crestie. But I'll keep checking."

"He's about as big as a football and not much heavier." Adam stroked his fingers along the dog's hairless side. "He looks like he has freckles."

"His pink skin has some liver spots." She petted the dog's back, not jerking away today when she brushed against Adam's warm hand. "Cresties can be high maintenance. You need to protect their skin with sunscreen and dress them in sweaters in the winter. They can also develop certain medical problems, but Buddy's as strong as, well, a tiny ox."

Lucia, her assistant, poked her head into the canine area. "Muffin's in second-stage labor. I have her in Room Three."

Claire stood. "I'll be right there." Her assistant left, and she glanced at Adam, amazed at her reluctance to leave him. "Duty calls. But you can visit with Buddy as long as you like."

"Can I come with you?" he asked, his blue eyes searching hers. "Would it bother the dog if I was there for the birth?"

She considered him, the man she'd unconsciously compared to every date she'd had since college. Given their past, she should be avoiding him like rabies. But, God help her, she still wanted to spend time with him. "Sure, but it'll be a little messy."

"After some of the football injuries I've seen *and* experienced, I can handle messy." Adam carefully set Buddy in his pen and promised the dog he'd be back. Then, with a grimace of pain, he stood up and followed her out.

CHAPTER FIVE

As they entered Room Three, the whine of a distressed animal tore at Adam's heart. Could he handle seeing it suffer? On a stainless-steel table against the back wall, a dog shifted restlessly on a padded bed. Its soft brown eyes tracked them.

Claire nodded to her coworker, a Hispanic woman who was petting the dog. "Lucia, meet Adam." Claire walked to the room's sink and turned on the water. She continued as she aggressively scrubbed her hands. "He's the one who rescued the crestie."

Rescued? Adam started to protest. All he'd done was drive Buddy a few blocks to the shelter.

"Hi." Lucia held up her latex-gloved hands. "Sorry, but I can't shake hands right now."

"Lucia's a vet assistant and a godsend here." Claire toweled dry, then powdered her hands before pulling on latex gloves. Each action was confident and economical. Then, she gestured Adam to a nearby chair. "You can sit there, and I'll explain what we're doing . . . that is, if you're interested."

The last was said hesitantly. Adam frowned. Did she

think he'd be bored because he'd been so indifferent toward her career choice during college? "I'm *very* interested," he assured her, as he sat on the uncomfortable chair. "I like watching you work."

Pleasure lit her face, but Claire turned away as if embarrassed by her reaction. Instead of replying, she joined her assistant at the table and stroked the dog's brown-and-white fur. "Hi, Muffin. I hear you're ready to be a momma."

The long-haired dog shuddered, then licked Claire's hand.

"Muffin's a springer spaniel." Claire spoke quietly as she examined the dog. "And the suspected boyfriend is a black lab. Her diplomat-owners were reassigned and had to leave her behind. They trust me to find a good home for her and her pups."

The dog whined louder, and Claire commiserated. "I know, sweetie. Having babies is no fun." She touched her stethoscope to Muffin's abdomen, and Lucia picked up the commentary.

"This padded bed"—the assistant touched its raised sides—"is a disposable whelping box. It gives the dog a soft nest for birthing. We put a heating pad underneath to warm it."

"I think the first mini-Muffin is about to make an appearance," Claire announced in a hushed voice.

Fascinated, Adam watched the dog pant and strain, wishing there was something he could do to help. But this was Claire's domain. She and Lucia stood nearby, ready to step in if Muffin required it. After a *long* ten minutes, the dog expelled a small sack that looked more like a water balloon than a puppy.

"She should help her baby by breaking the membrane and licking the pup clean," Claire explained. "But she's a first-time mom, so we're here in case she needs our help. We don't want the puppy to suffocate."

His stomach clenched, as they waited. Muffin finally nuzzled the puppy and—instinct kicking in—did what was necessary. Claire and Lucia exchanged delighted smiles as the wet puppy wriggled and mewed under its mother's tongue.

Adam grinned, too, as the black puppy suckled its mother's milk. "I didn't know they nursed so soon after birth."

"The *perritos*, uh, puppies," Lucia translated, "need their *madre's* warmth, as much as the milk."

The next hour-and-a-half proved a real eye-opener for Adam as three more puppies were born. Each was a tiny miracle, and he was impressed, then humbled by Claire's skill and knowledge.

He learned about placentas and afterbirth, the messy business she'd warned about. He discovered puppies could enter the world safely head-first or tail-first. And he got an education in genetics, as Lucia explained why three of the four puppies were black and one was brown-and-white like its mom. And through it all, he admired Claire, moved by her compassion.

What would she be doing today if she'd given in to his college ultimatum? Would she have gone to veterinarian school in San Francisco or given up her dream?

His reverie was interrupted when Claire announced, "Here comes the last puppy."

Lucia stroked the dog's heaving side, as the spaniel whimpered. Fifteen minutes passed, then twenty. Muffin shuddered and strained, but nothing happened. The women exchanged worried glances, and Adam could tell something was different this time. Despite the room's comfortable temperature, he broke out in a sweat. At last, another puppy sack appeared, but it didn't slide free of the dog's body as the others had.

"It's lodged in the birth canal." Claire stepped closer, murmuring softly to the spaniel. The concern in her voice as much as her words had Adam anxiously leaning forward.

He clenched his jaw to keep from asking questions, while Claire and her assistant fought to save the puppy's life. Lucia slipped into Spanish, Adam understanding many of her words as she calmed Muffin. Claire, her eyes determined and her movements gentle, finally freed the black puppy. And with Muffin's help, it was soon nursing with its siblings.

Claire met Adam's gaze, and a rush of joy and relief seemed to arc between them. There was triumph in her expression and pride, and he knew he'd never forget this afternoon. How many animals had she helped over the years? How many had she saved, while he'd been throwing a ball around a football field?

"That was amazing," he managed to say, wishing he had the right to hug her close. *You're amazing.*

"Thanks." Claire grinned. "Given the size of those puppies, the black lab daddy must be a bruiser. And he didn't even bother to drop by for their births," she joked.

Adam laughed with the women, and the tension in the room lightened. It'd been an eye-opening and sometimes heart-stopping afternoon. But mother and babies were healthy, thanks to Claire and Lucia. If he'd had a bottle of champagne handy, he'd have toasted Muffin and her human helpers.

Heck, if he thought Claire would agree, he'd treat her to dinner to celebrate. And then he'd do his damnedest to convince her to give him a second chance. He wanted her back in his life.

She gestured to the whelping bed. "We have some cleanup and paperwork to complete before we're really done here. You can head back to the runs, if you want, to visit with Buddy."

"Okay. I'll do that." Adam glanced at his watch so she wouldn't read his thoughts. For all he knew, she was dating someone seriously . . . planning a future with another man. *No.* His gut twisted, and he shoved the disturbing images away.

Adam walked to the door, then faced the woman he knew now he'd never stopped loving. She deserved to hear what had been on his mind all afternoon.

"Claire . . ." Adam willed her to understand how bone-deep sorry he was for everything he'd said and done. "You made the *right* decision ten years ago."

CHAPTER SIX

You made the right decision ten years ago.

It was Friday, a week and a half since Adam had said those words, and the memory of that moment still haunted Claire. The look in his eyes and the regret in his voice had destroyed most of the anger she'd hoarded over his long-ago ultimatum. That simple sentence had been both a vindication of her choice and an apology for the pain he'd caused her.

Claire forced her gaze from the shelter's front door to her clipboard. Adam visited Buddy about this time every afternoon, always stopping by her office to exchange a few words. Like some lovesick girl, she'd let it become the highlight of her day.

Instead of standing in her waiting room watching for Adam, Claire needed to finish her Wish List update for Rescue Me's website. Donations often came from animal-lovers who went online to check the shelter's required items. Her volunteer Webmistress needed the update by this evening.

Of course, with Adam arriving daily with donations, the Wish List was pretty short this month.

As if her intern had read her mind, Patty asked, "What do you think he'll bring you today?"

Claire shrugged. "It'd be hard to top the trunkload of kitty litter he delivered yesterday."

Patty grinned. "You know, he's totally crushing on you."

A blush warmed her cheeks, even as Claire denied the idea. "We're just old friends from college."

"You don't see how he watches you when you're not looking."

Claire fought a swell of hope. She'd be a fool to fall back into a relationship with Adam. Wouldn't she?

The man who'd crowded her thoughts for days walked through the door, carrying two large bags. "Just some chew toys and things," Adam explained. He handed them to Patty, who shot Claire an "I'm right; go for it" look as she left with the bags.

Claire's hands clenched on the clipboard. Was Adam playing Santa because he enjoyed spending time with her? Or was he just here for the crestie? Well, she was about to find out.

"Buddy's strong and healthy," she began, "and since there's no reports of missing cresties, he can be adopted."

Dismay, then determination firmed Adam's expression. "I want Buddy. I can take him, right?"

Claire nodded, her throat closing on a surge of emotions. The dog would live the life of Reilly with Adam, but would she ever see them again? Setting down her clipboard, she managed a few words. "We'll loan you a carrier to get Buddy home."

"Okay." Adam stepped closer, his familiar scent muddling her brain. "But I haven't had a dog since I was a kid. I could probably use some pointers on his care and feeding."

Was he looking for an excuse to get together? She cleared her throat. "We, uh, send printed directions along with pets."

"Oh." He rocked back on his heels, looked at the floor, then met her gaze. "Have dinner with me."

Claire's heart cheered, but her super-developed self-preservation instinct reared its unwelcome head. "Well . . ."

Adam took her hand, his touch tripping her pulse. "You've never been to my restaurant, and I'd like to show it to you. And . . ." He seemed to be mentally searching for a good argument. "And I've been thinking I could hold a fund-raiser at Nuclear Fusion for your shelter." He smiled, but there was a surprising vulnerability in his eyes. "We can plan it over dinner."

Damn his sexy hide for knowing the way to her heart.

Before she could answer, Adam continued, "I'll pick you up at six on Sunday, okay?"

Sunday. Was she crazy? What was she getting into? And what would she wear? Claire nodded, anticipation defeating caution.

* * *

At five till six, Adam parked his vintage Mustang in front of a grand old brick house several residential blocks away from the shelter. The place had been subdivided into condos, Claire had explained, and hers was on the second floor.

He turned off the ignition and pocketed the keys before wiping his damp palms on his black slacks. Geez, he hadn't been this nervous since his last Super Bowl. But tonight could be his only shot at a second chance with Claire.

Adam unfolded himself from the seat, stood next to the Mustang, and spotted Claire on the home's stone porch. In some dim recess of his brain, he registered that she was talking with a woman holding a canine furball. But his focus was on Claire.

The sun glinted off her chestnut hair, softly haloing her face. *Appropriate.* Adam smiled. She *was* an angel to her four-legged patients. His gaze drifted lower, over her coppery, clingy dress, and he forgot to breathe. Two weeks of fantasizing about the body under her boxy scrubs hadn't prepared him for the mouth-watering reality and her long, lean legs. . . .

Claire turned and waved to him, before hurrying down the steps. He circled the car and opened the passenger door for her.

She looked inside. "Adam, is *this* your old Mustang?"

The delight on her face calmed his jitters. "I restored it. There were too many good memories in this car to sell it." *Memories of you.* And he'd love to make new ones, but he kept that thought to himself as she got into the car. He just hoped everything was ready at the restaurant. It had to be *perfect.*

Claire congratulated herself on making small talk the fifteen minutes it took to drive to Nuclear Fusion. Quite an accomplishment when her brain was filled with hot flashbacks of making love with Adam in this car. She clutched her purse in her lap to keep from reaching for his hand like the good old days.

He pulled to the curb in front of the restaurant, tossing his keys to a kid at a valet stand. Then Adam opened the door to Nuclear Fusion, and she entered a world of cool hues and sweeping lines. The walls were curved panels of light, pulsing from blue to turquoise to green. Waves of chrome reflected the living colors and divided the room into cozy booths. Everything, including the sumptuous upholstery and carpet, contributed to the illusion of a futuristic undersea kingdom.

"It's beautiful," she breathed. "A space-age Atlantis."

Adam let out a breath. "I hoped you'd like it." Smiling, he rested a hand on her back—the simple gesture giving Claire gooseflesh—and guided her through the empty dining room. "I reserved my favorite spot for us." He stopped by an oval table backed by a curved, intimate booth for two. Nestled in a private alcove, it was shielded from other tables by a huge aquarium filled with a rainbow of darting fish.

She slid onto the booth's soft cushions. When he joined

her in the snug space, his leg brushed hers and his scent, so tempting and familiar, filled her senses. Claire scrambled for something to say. "Uh, it looks like we're the first customers."

"Actually"—he draped her aqua cloth napkin over her lap—"we're the only customers. Nuclear Fusion is closed on Sundays."

Claire's mouth gaped open like a fish in the nearby tank.

A waiter approached with menus, and Adam introduced him as Sergio. Dazed, Claire studied the list of international dishes, listening to their suggestions before choosing a Thai appetizer and a shrimp pasta entrée. Adam ordered a mix of Chinese dim sum and Spanish tapas, a Kobe beef entrée, and a bottle of California chardonnay before outlining his idea for a shelter fund-raiser.

Throughout the meal, she tried to pay attention, but everything conspired to make her pulse leap and her body ache. He filled the booth, so broad and muscular, practically cuddling against her. If his arm or knee wasn't grazing hers, he was feeding her a bite of his dinner or skimming a crumb off her lower lip. Each touch ratcheted up the sensual tension until she wanted to pull his mouth to hers and kiss him into tomorrow.

When they'd finished and Sergio had cleared the table, Adam shifted to face her, suddenly serious. "There's something I need to know, and it's not about the fund-raiser, which I'm hosting, *no matter what*." He took her hand, his palm warm and slightly callused. "Can you forgive me for what I said after graduation? I was arrogant, stupid, and selfish, a jerk, a fool, an idiot, a real bastard." He grimaced. "You can help me out here any time."

Oh, Adam. Her eyes stung, even as she smiled. "I think you're doing just fine by yourself."

He made a noise between a groan and a chuckle. "God, I've missed you. I want a second chance, Claire. Do you think—"

Yes! The word shouted across her mind, even as she threaded her fingers through his hair and pressed her mouth to his. It was like stirring adrenaline into espresso with a lightning bolt. Claire's lips curved at the thought. No, it was just *Adam*, the man, heaven help her, she'd never stopped loving.

Every persuasion, every apology flew from Adam's brain. For several stunned seconds he just experienced the kiss. Claire's soft, full lips, her sexy perfume, the stimulating slide of her fingers against his scalp . . . Then the weeks of pent-up longing punched through his surprise, and he dragged her hard against him. She gasped, and it was all the invitation he needed to plunder her sweet mouth. How had he lived without her? It was like returning to a treasured past and discovering a blindingly bright future.

Just as Adam was figuring out the logistics for making love in this narrow booth—they'd fit together in the Mustang, hadn't they?—and wondering why some part of his brain was insisting it wasn't a good idea, something barked. *Buddy.*

Adam broke the kiss in time to see a grinning Sergio and Chien disappear behind the aquarium. The crestie barked again, drawing his eyes to the floor by the end of the booth.

God, his special gift. He'd almost forgotten.

Claire blinked up at him, her eyes darkly dreamy and her mouth swollen and so damned tempting. "Did I hear a dog?"

Nodding, Adam picked up the crestie, who was wearing a little yellow vest. Through the leash loop in the back was a rolled document. It had taken Adam half the day to train the dog to walk around with the document, but apparently the tiny mooch would do just about anything for country pâté.

Smiling at the dandied-up crestie, Claire asked, "Is Buddy joining us for dessert?"

"No. He has something to thank you for taking such good care of him." Adam handed the document to her. She unrolled it, and he watched confusion, then astonishment cross her features.

"You can't, this can't—" she began.

Adam rubbed his thumb over her lips to stop her protest. "My accountant was thrilled. I need charitable deductions to balance the profits from this place and my other investments."

"It's too much." She shook her head, stunned. "This says you bought the shelter building and donated it to Rescue Me."

"No strings attached," he said. It was important to make that clear. "Besides, you already agreed to a second chance, if I understood that kiss." She blushed and nodded. "I just found you again, so you can't move the shelter to Maryland. Buddy and I want you near. Being with you these last few weeks has shown me just how empty my life has been."

Claire touched his cheek. "I love you. Even when I should have hated you, I couldn't do it."

A chest-tightening, throat-swelling happiness struck him dumb, so he pulled her close and pressed kisses to her temple. The crestie wriggled between them. "I love *you*, Claire. There's never been anyone else in my heart."

Buddy yipped, making them chuckle. Adam leaned back to give the dog breathing room. "I have to admit, though, this mutt's growing on me. If it weren't for him, I might never have seen you again." He brushed a tear from Claire's face just as Buddy licked the salty moisture from her chin. "That day I brought him to the shelter, you rescued both of us."

Her smile trembled, then firmed. "It was my pleasure."

Adam kissed her again and proved beyond a shadow of a doubt the feeling was mutual.

LORD HAIRY

Donna MacMeans

Yorkshire, 1878

"Dicken saw him on the road last night, blacker than night and bigger than a small man standing," the scullery maid reported, her eyes wide in her pale face.

"The hellhound?" The Waverly's cook sucked in her breath. "Were his eyes gleaming red? Did the dog look straight away at him? It's death certain, if he did."

"Aye. Dicken didn't say, but it's an evil portent just the same."

Hannah Waverly tried to swallow her smile. Though the mouth-watering scent of Patsy's cooking had drawn her to the kitchen, the gossip of the kitchen staff had kept her enthralled. She sampled one of Patsy's dormer pies, tiny scraps of cold meat remnants wrapped in bits of dough, then fried into delicious bundles no bigger than her thumb. She enjoyed them even without the thick gravy Patsy would serve to complete the dish. As it was, she had difficulty restricting herself to just one.

"Mr. Dicken is so old," she said, debating if another dormer would affect her ability to wear her new blue gown to the dance tomorrow night. "He can barely see when the sun is high, much less in the thick of night. One of Mr. Sumner's black sheep must have slipped through the gate again."

Patsy shuddered. "Don't tempt the devil by calling his hound a lamb, young miss. He'll set the black dog on you."

Hannah shrugged and decided that as the dormers were so small, one more surely couldn't hurt. Her fingers reached for another tasty treat.

"And best not tempt your mother by eating those dormers. You know what she'll say."

"Stepmother," Hannah quickly interjected. Surely, her real mother would never be so free with her disapproval. "They're so tiny. I just thought to try another."

"Stepmother," Patsy amended. "I understand, miss, but you know she'll disapprove."

Before Hannah could reply the very woman rounded the corner and scowled.

"Hannah, put that down. Didn't they teach you at that Pettibone School a proper lady does not continually eat?"

Hannah did as she was told, bracing herself for the diatribe that was bound to follow.

Her stepmother curled her lip. "No man wants to marry a woman who eats him out of house and home. What would Lord Ashton say if he saw you right now?"

Hannah thought he might ask for a bite of dormer pie himself, but as she had never met the reclusive viscount, she had no idea of his personal tastes. She wisely kept her counsel while her stepmother continued to lecture.

"You should strive to be more like that Fanny Barnesworth if you want to catch Lord Ashton's favor at the dance tomorrow night. He's the one truly worthy catch in all the district and you shall lose the opportunity to Miss Barnesworth."

"Yes, ma'am," she replied, trying to keep a frown from her face at the mention of Fanny. What man in his right mind would want to harness himself to that wicked piece of muslin? Hannah sniffed, her pride sullied by her stepmother's comparisons. She might be a little plump, but at least she had strength of character. Mrs. Brimley, now the very proper Lady Nicholas Chambers, had told her so.

"Now don't pout, Hannah, it's not endearing," her stepmother chided. She passed Hannah as she crossed the room toward a collection of baskets used for garden produce. She selected one, paused, then turned with a calculating gleam in her eyes and a sly smile on her lips.

"Do you recall Father Medlock's sermon last Sunday on the necessity for charity?" She reached for the bowl of fried dough and dumped the contents into the basket. "I've decided we shall make a charitable gift of these dormers to the poor Mullins family."

Patsy appeared shocked. Hannah's stepmother's uncharacteristic charitable act had just negated her entire morning efforts.

"In fact, I'd like you, Hannah, to take this basket to the Mullins house, but don't go inside. One never knows what sorts of vermin inhabit those hovels. Don't muss your skirts. I understand Lord Ashton has returned from his London trip and is currently in residence. Should he come to call you'll need to be prepared to look your best."

"Yes, ma'am," Hannah repeated. Why Lord Ashton should suddenly call now when he hadn't in the previous five months since he purchased the Beale property was beyond her, but arguing with her stepmother was futile. She imagined Lord Ashton to be as old as Dicken and as demanding as her stepmother. What young woman would wish for that future— even if he was the most eligible bachelor in Yorkshire?

Still, he was to host a dance tomorrow night and many of her friends from the Pettibone School for Young Ladies should be there. She refused to let the thought of her stepmother's ridiculous expectations sully her anticipation of a reunion with her school chums.

She slipped the handle of the offered basket over her arm and retrieved her straw summer hat with two ostrich plumes from the hook by the door. She had paused to tie the ribbons when her stepmother offered her last piece of advice.

"Be mindful of strangers. Gypsies have been spotted in town. Don't dally and don't eat the dormers." This last was said with such an emphasis as to suggest the tidbits had been individually tallied and would be accounted for upon delivery.

As Hannah stepped into the midday sun, she heard her stepmother inquire if Patsy knew how to make pheasant gitana as this was rumored to be Lord Ashton's favorite dish.

"Lord Ashton this, Lord Ashton that," Hannah muttered beneath her breath. If ever she were to meet the mythical Lord Ashton, she was afraid she'd be inclined to tap his leg with a crochet mallet for all the grief his residency had caused. Granted the secluded Beale property had been a grand estate in earlier days. Years of neglect had made it less so. Why would a viscount be interested in property so far removed from fashion?

The trip to the Mullins house would not take overly long. Especially, as she knew a less-traveled path through the woods that wound around a small pond to rejoin the main road before the village church. She remembered walking the path with her mother in happier times. Even though ten years had passed since her mother's untimely death, she still missed her deeply. The path and all the ensuing memories gave her a comfort she could never find at home.

The heavily laden trees shaded the path making the hot summer day more pleasant. She had been fairly well lost in her daydreams when she heard a suspicious rustle behind her. She turned, but saw leaves stirring with the breeze, nothing more.

Her thoughts turned to her stepmother's comments about the Gypsies. They were known to camp in the woods on the Beale property, now Lord Ashton's domain. Of course her stepmother didn't mention that as Lord Ashton was apparently incapable of anything less than perfection. There was no rustling now. It must have been her imagination.

Lord Ashton, Lord Ashton. Hannah smiled to herself. She'd have to remember not to repeat his name in a high, singsong mimic of her stepmother's voice when she was introduced to him tomorrow.

She hadn't traveled far when she heard the rustling again. Closer this time. Even her active imagination could not produce actual sounds. Suddenly, a crashing through the brush sent a surge of panic and alarm through her. Gypsies! She lifted her skirts so as not to hinder her feet and ran from the threat, the basket swinging from her arm.

How foolish to travel the hidden path alone! The sentimentality of a walk once shared with her mother could well cost her life. She glanced over her shoulder to see if anyone followed—anyone of the Gypsy persuasion—and thus failed to see the root that caught her foot and hurled her sprawling onto the path beyond. Her basket freed itself from her arm and took flight, emptying itself of cargo by spewing succulent dormer pies in every direction. The fall to the ground jolted her hat from her head and sent it skittering down the path, ostrich plumes waving farewell.

Lord, she couldn't breathe! The fall had stolen her breath and she couldn't replace it fast enough. Her attacker would be upon her in a second. She gasped for breath, generating a sound not unlike that of a landing goose. If the villain had previously failed to detect her position, he'd have no difficulty now. Footfalls burst through the low-lying shrubs, racing in her direction.

She cringed, squeezing her eyes shut, waiting for the worst to come.

But nothing happened. No one pinned her to the ground. No evil villain pounded the earth in her direction.

Confused, she turned her head toward a gnashing of teeth somewhere on her right.

A huge dog with matted black fur gazed back at her before returning to placidly eating the spilled dormers. Patsy's description of the hellhound sprung into memory. This was certainly no sheep. She wasn't even sure it was a dog. From her current low vantage point, the beast appeared enormous, much larger than any common dog she had ever seen.

"Stop that!" she yelled, thinking at first to save any edible treats. She pushed on her hands and rolled to her side. The black beast paused, then looked in her direction with large baleful brown eyes. A thin strand of white spittle hung from his mouth. He glanced at the doughy treats, then back at her with a sad pleading quality that speared her heart. His long black tail hung low and still. A huge pink tongue slid around the black muzzle, but other than his energetic pant, he didn't stir.

"You're the hellhound, aren't you?" she said, pushing herself to a sitting position.

It's not that she expected the dog to answer. She braced herself in case its response was a menacing growl. Indeed, that would be an evil portent as she was truly defenseless against such a beast, and assistance was unlikely on the secluded path. However, the dog's tail began to slowly sway. The beast continued to pant and again glanced at the food with a clear longing. His black muzzle lifted in the direction of the nearest dormer as if the mere scent was fortifying. If he was the devil's servant, then the help was kept severely undernourished.

"You poor dear, you're hungry." She waved him on. "Go ahead. You might as well finish them. I can't take them to the Mullins all covered in dirt and leaves, can I?"

Immediately, the dog's nose thrust toward the ground and the closest fried tidbit disappeared. His tail waved once back and forth before he advanced on the next morsel and the next, grabbing each off the ground with his massive mouth, and snapping his jowls together repeatedly until all had disappeared.

Hannah watched in amazement. This, no doubt, was Dicken's harbinger of evil: the black dog that stood as tall as a man with fur as black as night. From where had he come? Perhaps the Gypsy camp? She glanced about in sudden alarm, but no man appeared. The black dog, having consumed all the treats bound for the Mullins house, wagged his tail with a force that slashed the foliage from the brush. His mouth hung open in a slobbery mess and he advanced on her as if she were to be his next meal.

Momentarily panicked, Hannah tried to pull her feet beneath her, but her ankle protested. The dog was upon her before she could rise. His massive head pushed at her arm, forcing her hand to rest on his head.

"Look at you. You're nothing but a big baby"—her hand slid down his matted fur—"a big hungry baby."

The dog leaned closer, pressing his body next to hers. She patted his head, then scratched between his ears. His eyes closed as if in enjoyment.

"You like that, don't you?" Hannah said, accepting the dog's reaction as an invitation for more affection. She stroked his long matted fur. "I wonder what your name is." The dog looked at her with soulful eyes, pulling her smile in response.

"I suppose it would be difficult to tell me, wouldn't it? Yet I shall have to call you something." She pulled back to look at the full of him, but the dog crushed close as if afraid she would leave. He fairly knocked her over. "You're as black as soot and covered with"—she brushed her hand across his fur, dislodging a fine dust that floated on air—"ash."

A memory of her stepmother chiding her earlier in the day struck her. "Ash . . . I shall call you Ashton. Lord Hairy Ashton, to distinguish you from the disagreeable viscount at Beale. Do you like that, Lord Hairy?"

The dog responded with a lick on the side of her face.

"Where did you come from, Ashton?"

Lord Hairy responded with a wag of his tail, which of course did not answer her question.

"I can't take you to the Gypsy camp if that's where you're from. I haven't heard of a family in the area having a big, black dog." Given the uproar over the sighting of this hellhound, she was fairly certain that the dog did not belong to anyone local. Whoever had brought him this far had apparently not brought sufficient quantities of food to keep the giant dog fed.

"I can't very well leave you out here to starve, or to scare the villagers." She struggled to her feet, using the dog's back as a crutch to get her from her knees to her feet. Her ankle protested with a jolt of pain that made her grit her teeth, but the pain subsided. She glanced at the dog. "No, Lord Ashton, I will not dance with you no matter how much you beg. It's my ankle, you see."

Lord Hairy tilted his head, his wagging tail stirring up wispy dust clouds. He was certainly a big thing. She chuckled to herself in spite of the painful sprain. "I'd be tempted to ride you, if you were better fed and I less so."

The dog's ears perked and he smiled, or at least it seemed he did.

"I can't very well carry this empty basket to the Mullins now, can I?" She sighed, then glanced down the path for her hat. To her dismay, she saw one of the plumes waving to her from the pond.

"Oh dear!" She hobbled closer to look. "My hat. I'll not hear the end of this for months. My step—"

A black streak bounded past her, followed by a splash. Her new companion nabbed her drowned bonnet, then swam back to the path. He pulled himself from the water and trotted to her with his prize, a soppy, dripping mess of straw and plumage.

"I appreciate the effort but I'm afraid—"

The dog shook the water from his fur, sending droplets over her filthy skirts and disheveled bodice.

"Ashton!" she scolded, but the dog took no notice. His tail continued to wag with pleasure as he placed his trophy at her feet. She set the basket down to retrieve the hat and the dog took the handle of the basket in his mouth. What a sorry pair she suspected they must appear: a disheveled woman who appeared better suited for the gutters of London than a country road, and a massive, matted beast of a dog carrying an empty basket. With few other options available to her, Hannah trudged home with the hellhound following meekly after.

* * *

"Lord God in Heaven, Miss Hannah! What were you thinking to bring that horse in here?"

Hannah wasn't sure if her dirty sodden skirts or the monstrous beast by her side caused Patsy's anxious glance toward the door. Either could have produced the same response.

"Ashton is not a horse, Patsy. He's a dog." Hannah tried to pull the animal away from a fashionably cluttered tabletop, but not before his tail swiped an elaborately framed photograph of her stepmother off the table and onto the floor.

Patsy's face blanched to the color of dormer dough. "The black dog from hell? Don't let him look at me!" She held her hands in front of her face.

"He's not a hellhound, Patsy. Ashton is just rather big"— she glanced down at the dog whose backside was level with her hips—"black and, at the moment, damp. I can imagine the sight of him would scare Dicken. But he's not evil, just friendly."

Patsy lowered her hands just enough to peek over them. "What did you call him?"

"Ashton. Lord Hairy Ashton to be exact." Hannah managed a weak smile. "He's rather fond of your dormers, and the basket they came in." She handed the empty basket to Patsy, noting her raised brow at the gnawed handle. "I've given him a bath, or I should say—"

A crash and a splintering of porcelain interrupted. In directing Ashton away from one potential calamity, she had managed to back him into another. One of her stepmother's decorative plates lay in pieces on the floor.

"He's given me one," she finished sheepishly.

"You can't keep him here, miss." Patsy stooped to retrieve

the broken pieces, placing them in the returned basket. The dog seized the opportunity to thank the woman for his earlier meal with a moist lick, and in the process, knocked her off-balance and into another table. A vase of flowers joined the carnage on the floor.

"I know that, Patsy, and I tried—"

"What's going on in here?" Her stepmother's face drained of color as her gaze took stock of the room's disorder. She gasped. "Merciful heavens, what is that thing and why is it in my house?"

"He followed me home from my call on the Mullins family." It wasn't exactly the truth for indeed she never made such a call. God might consider feeding a starving dog an act of charity, but she doubted her stepmother would feel the same. In an effort to appease the rising storm in her stepmother's face, Hannah repeated, "I've given him a bath."

It didn't help. Even Ashton hid behind Hannah's skirts, knocking a figurine to the floor in the process. Patsy averted her gaze, focusing instead on picking up evidence of Ashton's clumsiness. Her stepmother shook her head with a viciousness that threatened to dislodge her pinned-in curls. "That beast cannot stay in this house. Put him in the stables until your father returns. He can decide what to do with him."

"I tried to leave him in the stables," Hannah pleaded. "But he wouldn't stay. He followed me to the house."

"Tie him up."

"I tried that as well," she said. Her father wasn't expected home from the mill negotiation for another three days. The look on her stepmother's face did not bode well for Lord Hairy Ashton. "His consistent barking whenever I tried to leave scared the horses. Thatcher thought it best if I not keep the animal there."

"There's no answer for it then." Her stepmother fisted her hands on her hips. "You'll have to stay in the stables with the dog."

Hannah gasped. "The stables?"

"Either that or take him back to the woods where you found him and leave him to fend for himself." An accusatory finger pointed at Hannah's skirt, smeared with dirt that had slipped past her apron, a consequence of Hairy's wagging tail. "Look at you. Heaven knows I've tried to turn you into the kind of lady your father could be proud of, but you fight me at every turn." Her eyes narrowed and her face screwed tight. "Perhaps a few days living in the stables will teach you the consequences of conducting yourself like a commoner."

Hurt and shame battled within Hannah, but she ignored the pain for a moment. "But the dance . . . I'll need to prepare and—"

"Dance? Do you think you're still going to the dance?" She laughed, a cruel vindictive sound devoid of mirth. "Everyone of society will be in attendance. Do you think I relish being disgraced by a fat graceless stepdaughter and the unsightly mongrel that won't leave her side? Do you?"

She glared at Hannah, as if she truly expected an answer. Then she shook her head. "I will tell everyone who inquires that you are ill while you mind that beast and await your father's return. Until that time, or until you get rid of that thing"—she shook a hand at the dog cowering behind Hannah's back—"you are not allowed to step foot in this house. Do you understand me?" She waited for Hannah's obligatory nod before she turned on her heel and left without a backward glance.

Tears stung Hannah's eyes but she refused to let them fall. So many poison-tipped arrows had plunged into her heart she couldn't move. Ashton nudged her hand with his head, but even that did not relieve the pain. Her stepmother had said she was fat and graceless, but that did not sting nearly as much as her stepmother had probably hoped. Hannah knew she was never destined to be a thin portrait of elegance. Lady Nicholas Chambers had told her she had womanly curves and a unique grace and Hannah believed that to be true.

No, the deadly dart had been the suggestion that her father

was not proud of her, even though she had tried to be a lady worthy of his affections. She had thought her father could see through her periodic clumsiness, to the innate goodness within, but her stepmother had said no. Her stepmother had suggested she was a common laughingstock, a disgrace.

Her throat constricted so tightly that even breathing was difficult. Her disheveled appearance was not her fault. It could be easily remedied. A wet nose pushed at the back of her fingers, offering solace. She glanced down at Ashton whose ears had set back as if he were the one scolded. He gazed up at her with such mournful brown eyes, a flood of compassion filled her heart.

"What'll you do, miss?" Patsy asked from her position on the floor. "You'll be taking him back to the woods, then?"

The question startled her as she'd forgotten that Patsy had been crouching behind a chair and thus she'd been privy to the whole humiliating conversation.

"I can't do that, Patsy. Look at him. He was so hungry when I found him, I can't take him back." The dog's tongue slipped around her fingers as if to thank her. "He rescued my hat from the pond. He's a talented dog." Ashton's tail began to softly sway. "Now that he's clean, you can see that he's extremely handsome for a hellhound."

"Then you best get him out to the stables before that tail of his destroys more of Mrs. Waverly's things." Patsy's lips curved softly upwards. "I'll send food out for the both of you."

Hannah tickled the hair on the top of Ashton's head then turned to leave the room.

"Miss Hannah?"

Hannah glanced back at Patsy who rose from her position on the floor. "Yes?"

"I think your sainted mum . . . I think she would approve of you taking care of that beast, even if it meant missing a dance. The birds"—she glanced skyward as if she could see them through the ceiling—"they would fly from the Heavens just to sit on her finger. She had a gift with animals, your mum did." Patsy's lips turned in a sad smile. "I think you have it as well."

"Thank you, Patsy," Hannah replied. Tears of a different nature threatened to spill. She remembered her mother's smile and comforting arms that would wrap around her whenever Hannah was moved to tears. The Waverlys' pretty little governess would never offer such comfort, that's why Hannah always ran to her mother. Dear Heaven, she sorely missed her mother.

Her father, worn out by the combined demands of a growing business and a grieving child must have missed her as well. Why else would he have married the socially conscious governess and made her Hannah's stepmother? Of course, there had been rumors at first that Hannah was to have a sister or brother, but nothing ever came to fruition. Only resentment seemed to take root and grow in her stepmother's belly.

Now that she had attended the special classes offered at Pettibone School for Young Ladies, she understood a bit more about her father's needs and actions. But that didn't lessen the tension that built in the household whenever he left on his London trips.

Knowing that her mother would have approved of Lord Hairy Ashton cheered her a bit. Perhaps it wasn't Hannah's lamentable appearance that upset her stepmother so. Perhaps it was the knowledge that in spite of all her stepmother's hostilities, a bit of her mother quietly resided within Hannah. It was a surprising and comforting realization that she needed to dwell upon . . . alone . . . in the stables. She smiled again at Patsy and stood a little straighter. "That means more to me than you know. Thank you."

* * *

After the first night nestled on a prickly mattress of hay with Lord Hairy Ashton, Hannah's back ached but her ankle proved less troublesome. Thanks to Patsy and the other household servants, she and Lord Ashton were both well fed and clean. Thatcher arranged for a clean stall and a rickety table with a lamp so she could read and write in her journal at night. Patsy sent out clean clothes and toiletries. She envied the grooms Thatcher made sleep outside in the clean air. As much as her nose adjusted to the unique scents of the stable, she would have liked to have done the same. However, a lady could not sleep in the open, she reminded herself, just as a lady should not have to sleep in the stable.

Lord Hairy Ashton stayed closer than her own shadow but his company was welcome. She certainly didn't miss the sneering visage of her stepmother, but by afternoon, she did feel sad about missing the dance. She could live without all the fuss and frivolity that surrounded such an event. She found no pleasure in squeezing into a corset and a dress designed to show skin that even the sun had not touched. She'd never mastered the complicated steps of the country dances and wouldn't miss the anxiety that accompanied an invitation to dance, and the anxiety that followed no invitation at all. But it had been several months since she had last seen many of her friends, and she had looked forward to this small reunion.

That is until Thatcher sought her out. He snatched the cap off his head.

"Miss Hannah, Patsy told us what happened with your dog and all, and it just don't seem right. I'll be needing to drive your stepmum to the old Beale place tonight, but if you're amenable, I'll return and take you next."

"That's very considerate, Thatcher. I'd love to go, but I can't arrive looking like this and my stepmother left strict orders—"

"I have an old hip bath in the back and if you don't mind that I've used it a time or two myself, I can have Silas fill it with hot water for you."

"That's kind, but—"

"Patsy moved your fancy dress to the root cellar without your stepmum's knowledge. She asked that I give this to you." He pushed a picnic basket into her hands. Hannah peeked inside to see it stuffed with petticoats, stockings, and gloves.

"Patsy said she has a niece who's wanting to be a lady's maid someday. If the girl can try her hand with your . . ." He pointed in the direction of her head. "She'd be most appreciative."

Hannah flushed, moved by the efforts of the servants. "Of course she can, but this is really too much. What about Lord Hairy—"

"Once the horses are gone, the dog can bark his head off with no nevermind. We can tie him out here so he'll stay out of mischief. Even old Dicken said he'd come by and keep the black beast company."

"Dicken?"

"He says it's clear that the beast was not casting the evil eye on him. He's as hale and hearty as a pig groomed to market. So he thought he might like to sit down and have a talk with the devil himself."

Hannah laughed at the thought of Dicken and Lord Hairy Ashton conferring. "But why are you all doing this? You know my stepmother will not be pleased to see me at the dance."

"It ain't right the way she treats you. Ain't right at all. She wouldn't do it if your father were here but he'll be home soon enough. Besides, she won't know that we helped you."

Hannah smiled. "Won't she suspect I had some assistance if she sees me at the dance?"

Thatcher sniffed. "What if she does? She can't run the place by herself and no one in the region will work for her. It's your father we're beholden to." He smiled, a gleam of mischief twinkling in his eye. "Your father and mother, may she rest in peace."

The possibility took root in Hannah's mind. "It's been so long since I've seen my friends. If I managed to avoid my stepmother, there'd be no possibility of repercussions on your account."

Thatcher shifted his weight and frowned, almost as if he

was disappointed about avoiding repercussions. She smiled. He was a tough old bird and had been in charge of the stables long before the current Mrs. Waverly.

That gesture alone finalized her decision. This was the servants' act of defiance. To refuse their help would seem an insult. She could easily avoid the dance floor. She was seldom asked to dance in the past, and with the numbers attending this, the social event of the season, she could easily get lost in the crowd.

"In that case, I'm honored to use your assistance to attend the dance this evening."

*   *   *

Her stepmother was too busy with her own preparations to inquire as to Hannah's activities. Hannah imagined her stepmother's shock if she had known that as her own maid was artfully styling her hair in her bedroom, out in the stable, another one was decorating Hannah's brown tresses with two rescued and cleaned ostrich plumes.

Patsy had chosen a lovely peach crepe de chine princess gown to smuggle into the root cellar. Hannah recognized it immediately as one of her mother's gowns refashioned to fit more modern times. The excess material that would have laid atop a hoop, had been turned into flounces that would trail behind her with the support of a horsehair bustle. It wasn't the latest Paris creation, nor would the fashion impress the stodgy matrons of the highest strata of society, but wearing the gown made her feel as if her mother surrounded her once again. That gave her the confidence to follow through on this crazy scheme. She'd just have to remember to shake off any bits of hay and straw that might cling to her flounces before she entered the dance.

Guilt nibbled at her when she spied Lord Hairy Ashton with a rope loosely tied around his neck. As she stepped into the empty carriage, Ashton strained against the rope secured to a fence post, all the while barking for her attention. She waved to him from the carriage seat. He wouldn't be able to follow her this time, but she'd be gone for only a few hours and would return to the stable once the dance had concluded.

She arrived at the Beale residence later than the norm causing the doorman to frown even as he granted admittance. The first floor was so full of people she was surprised she had sufficient air to breathe. The voices, the music, the rhythmic pounding of dancing feet on the parquet floor in the ballroom bounced and swirled around her in a cacophony. Now if only she had someone to stand beside her as she entered the crowded ballroom so she wouldn't feel awkward and alone.

She hesitated about entering the throng when her stepmother's voice at the top of the grand stairway spurred her to action. From the sound of the conversation, Hannah hadn't been discovered yet, but that would change if she didn't quickly move. She slipped into the ballroom and navigated her way toward the back wall where open terrace doors could provide a quick exit if needed.

Patsy and Thatcher were confident that their actions would not result in any discipline, but Hannah was less certain. She would take extraordinary measures to avoid being seen by her stepmother. She snapped open her fan and used that as a partial shield to escape discovery.

A cluster of women and girls huddled near the orchestra. Undoubtedly, the viscount stood at the center of all that attention. Although surprised he wasn't leading one of the guests on the dance floor, she was grateful for the distraction the gathering caused. Surely, her stepmother would gravitate toward the sainted viscount and miss Hannah's attendance all together. Still, she'd have to eventually make her presence known to him to thank him for the invitation. It was only proper.

As she slipped near the back wall her school chums spotted her. Charlotte and Alice found her first, but others joined as their animated conversation increased. Hannah was careful to keep her back to the center of the room and her profile hopefully hidden by her artfully employed fan.

"Are you trying to avoid someone? The viscount, perhaps?" Alice observed in a low tone only Hannah could hear. "He's not a bad sort, you know. Nice looking but a little too quiet, if you ask me."

"I'm trying to avoid my stepmother," Hannah confided. "She thought my appearance here would embarrass her and thus decreed I couldn't attend."

Hannah made a quick survey of the room, noting that her stepmother was involved in a conversation on the fringe of the viscount crowd. She shifted a bit so that a giant potted fern would provide partial shielding, then glanced at Alice's frown. Of course, Alice had always been envious of anyone with a mother or stepmother. She didn't understand that sometimes having no mother was preferable to having a spiteful, irritating stepmother.

"I couldn't very well stay away and miss conversing with my Pettibone sisters," Hannah said. "It's been so long since we've all been together."

Alice hugged her before stepping back to further shield Hannah from prying eyes. They both joined in the conversation regarding speculation on who would soon be engaged and who would not. Hannah was so engrossed in catching up that she failed to notice the streak of black that raced through the open terrace doors dragging a length of rope in his wake.

The screams and shouts of others caused her to turn moments before Lord Hairy Ashton discovered her location and eagerly bounded across the ballroom floor directly toward her.

"Ashton!" she shouted, waggling a finger to encourage him to sit.

It was no use. The dog enthusiastically stood on his hind legs and deposited his heavy forepaws on her shoulders. She crumbled beneath the dog's benevolent assault and found herself on the floor with her skirts trussed around her. This new position apparently pleased the animal as he could now lick her face to his massive heart's content.

"Ashton! Get back!" she cried, trying to push his enormous head away from her face. Someone attempted to pull the dog away by the loose rope, but only managed to force Ashton's head up so that she was no longer at the mercy of his tongue. A long thread of spittle, however, dangled from his mouth, threatening to fall on Hannah's face. She frantically searched the floor for her fallen fan. Once her fingers found the handle, she spread the painted paper in front of her face for protection.

"*Achtung!*" an authoritative voice shouted across the ballroom.

Lord Hairy Ashton immediately planted his black rump near her chest, though his head still bobbed over her bodice.

The vibrations of feet dashing across the floor played along her back. The music had stopped. The dog had become the focus of the entire assembly, and by unfortunate proximity, so had she.

Mortification paralyzed her. *Perhaps Lord Hairy Ashton truly is a hellhound.* She certainly could not hide her humiliating predicament with this massive dog guarding her. However, one glance at his joyful face, ears perked forward in excitement, tongue slipped over his jaw, dismissed any thought that the dog was evil. Embarrassed as she was, Hannah was at odds at how to remedy the situation.

The bowed heads of her school chums all gazed at her with concern, except for Fanny Barnesworth whose fluttering fan barely hid a smile.

Suddenly, the circle parted, admitting a tall man, at least from her unique perspective, with intensely compassionate brown eyes. Rich black hair, not unlike that of Lord Hairy, slipped across his brow as he bent down on one knee beside her.

"Have you been injured? Can you stand?" He extended an

arm to help her, but when she didn't readily take it, he quickly glanced toward the dog. "I promise, he won't bite you."

"His tongue worries me more than his teeth," Hannah replied, still hiding behind her fan. Dear heavens, the one time she draws a man's attention and she has to be lying on the floor in disarray with a massive beast guarding her. Her cheeks began to warm. What must he think of her?

"Ashton, shoo!" She tried to encourage the dog's exit with her free hand. "Go away."

"You wish me to go away?" A crease appeared in the brow of the stranger. "I'm offering assistance."

"I wasn't referring to you, sir. I was referring to—"

Did he say 'I'? Alarm robbed her of speech. This well-formed stranger? Could this be the Viscount Ashton that she imagined to rival old Dicken in age? Dear Heavens, not only was she about to insult the host of the dance, but also the very man —the only man—who had come to her aid. She closed her eyes. There was no hope for it. She must have slipped into an outer ring of Dante's hell. Her cheeks certainly burned as if touched by the flames.

"Has she fainted?"

Hannah recognized Alice's voice and the implied hint.

"The girl needs smelling salts!" That would be Mrs. Taylor. Hannah groaned. If Mrs. Taylor was near, her stepmother couldn't be far behind.

There was no hope for it. She couldn't pretend to have fainted away, although that held a certain appeal. She had no skill at dramatic arts and would most likely become an even greater laughingstock if she tried. She opened her eyes and turned her head toward the canine Ashton, afraid to see the reaction in the other. "I was referring to him."

"The dog?"

Lord Hairy continued his toothy smile and turned his head toward each new voice as if he were watching lawn tennis, another game at which she did not excel. The ball, it seemed, remained in the stranger's court.

"You named my dog after me?"

"Hannah Waverly!" Her stepmother pushed through the gathering crowd bristling with familiar disdain. "Why are you lying on that floor? I distinctly instructed you not to come to this dance."

She pointed her finger at Lord Hairy. "And what is that vile mongrel creature doing here?"

Her host's brow creased. He glanced over his shoulder at her stepmother. Charlotte gasped and clenched a fist to her mouth. Alice fluttered her fan in Hannah's direction. But the resulting air current did little to alleviate the situation. What she really needed was for the floor to open beneath her and remove her from sight. She peered over the top of her fan up at her stepmother, who suddenly recognized her error in the hardened glances turned toward her. Her eyes widened.

"Because you're so ill," she protested, modifying her tone. "I thought we agreed, Hannah dear, that you were to stay home in bed." Her stepmother had obviously mastered the acting skills that Hannah herself lacked.

"Is it fever?" a voice in the crowd asked. "If she's flushed with the fever she should be in bed. Someone needs to take her to bed."

Hannah glanced up into the handsome viscount's eyes attempting to suppress the fleeting scandalous image that flitted through her thoughts. Sometimes a little education in the special class at Pettibone could indeed be a dangerous thing. She must end this awkward situation before it regressed further.

"Please, can you help me to my feet?" she asked the man on one knee beside her. "I assure you I can explain."

"Are you sure you don't wish me to carry you to a private room? If you are ill . . ."

"I'm not ill," she replied, trying to decide if that was a wicked glint in his eye or just sympathy for her predicament. Deciding it must be the latter, she tried to sit on her own, though her stays objected to the abrupt change in position.

"My pride has been laid low, but that won't be aided by a scandalous removal."

He helped to pull her upright, though she had the impression that he was sorry to see her so. Once she gained her feet, he squeezed her gloved hand briefly before releasing it to wave a signal to the orchestra. Music filled the room once more and the edges of the crowd began to drift off. He turned, exchanging a few words with those nearby. Her friends discreetly batted out her skirts and misaligned bustle.

He was indeed tall—at least taller than herself by a head—she hadn't been mistaken about that. Nor was she mistaken about his eyes that repeatedly glanced her way with a strange sort of intensity that raised gooseflesh on her arms. If he was indeed the viscount, she'd been mistaken about his age. He looked to be perhaps five years her senior, but with more reserve than those years allowed. Already she wished his hands were still gripping hers and that she remained the focus of his attention.

"I demand an explanation," her stepmother hissed in a low tone as the crowd began to dissipate. Lord Hairy Ashton rose to his feet, his tail wagging furiously, and in the process, banging into her stepmother's gown.

"Yes." The viscount turned, his gaze searching her face. "I believe an explanation is definitely in order."

Though his lips were straight and his brows raised in innocent query, she thought she could discern a flash of humor about his eyes. Her pulse raced in response. His gaze swept the length of her before resting on her lips.

"Perhaps you should begin by explaining why you've stolen my dog."

Her eyes widened. "Your dog?"

He glanced down at Lord Hairy Ashton, then retrieved the length of rope that had failed to keep him in place at the Waverly stable. He pulled the rope through his fingers, stopping at the intact loop that she'd seen secured around a fence post. She bit her lower lip. Either Dicken decided to set the devil free, or the fence post was currently in need of replacement.

"Thor has been missing for several weeks. I had feared someone had stolen him." His gaze searched hers. "Someone apparently did."

"Not so, my lord," her stepmother interceded. "My daughter rescued the beast on the road." She glanced at Hannah as if in warning. "We've taken good care of him. Why, Hannah even stayed with him through the night so he wouldn't be alone."

"She . . . stayed with him?"

There! She saw it again. A wicked glint that teased the corners of his eyes for a moment then disappeared. Heat flashed beneath her stays. She should have paid a bit more attention when the other girls discussed signs of a man's interest in Mrs. Brimley's special classes. But then she had never imagined she would have need of such information herself.

An insistent wet nose pushed the back of her hand. Without thought, she slipped her hand on top of Lord Hai . . . Thor's head and scratched.

"Have no fear, madam," he said. "I do not believe your daughter—"

"Stepdaughter," Hannah corrected without shifting her gaze from the dog's adoring eyes. Why hadn't she thought of this possibility earlier? A magnificent animal such as this could only have come from a magnificent household.

"Stepdaughter . . ."

This time she definitely heard the tease of laughter in his tone. She peeked at her stepmother but noted only a fierce determination. Could it be that only she and the viscount saw humor in the situation?

"I do not believe she stole Thor from me. She hardly seems the sort," he said. "I suspect she merely took pity on him when Thor escaped the true criminals. Now if you'll both excuse me, I don't think this is the proper place for Thor just now. I'll take him to the groundskeeper. Please enjoy the entertainment, ladies." He nodded to the both of them, then tugged on the rope for Thor to follow.

Instead, Thor plopped his bottom by Hannah's feet and refused to budge.

"Ashton." Hannah gently nudged him with her foot. "Go with him. This is your home now."

Still the dog refused to follow direction. He glanced up at her, then looked about the room in total disregard for the man at the end of the rope.

Hannah glanced at the viscount, a soft smile on her lips. "He does like to eat. That's how I came to find Ashto . . . Thor in the first place." She glanced at the dog and scratched his head. "You ate all my dormers, didn't you, boy?"

"Dormers?" The viscount's head tilted, reminding her of his dog. "What, on God's green Earth, are dormers?"

Sweet Heavens above! Perhaps it was the way his lips pursed as they fashioned the words, or the adorable inclination of his voice, but something about the man gave life to illicit thoughts again. Her lips parted, while her gaze made a slow study of the distance from his capable lips to his captivating eyes. He must have noticed as the crinkles about his eyes deepened.

"If you had some food," she said, caught in his gaze, "he might follow you."

"Perhaps if I had you, he would follow me wherever I wish."

The suggestive tone in his voice and mischief in his eyes ignited a small fire within her ribcage that rapidly spread to her extremities. She snapped her fan open in response.

"Accompany me to the groundskeeper so I may properly secure Ash . . . Thor." He laughed, coiling the rope tighter in his fingers. "Now you have me confused. Perhaps as we walk, you can explain how you chose that particular name."

His glance slid to her stepmother but lost some of the humor in the transition. "You are welcome to accompany us, madam. We shall only go as far as the kennel."

"No." She offered a slight smile toward Hannah. "I believe I shall remain here, but for propriety's sake, perhaps one of her friends . . . ?"

"I'll go." Alice stepped forward from the group that hovered on the outskirts of the conversation. She glanced at Hannah. "If that's all right?"

The three left through the terrace doors, the dog obediently at the viscount's heel.

"What kind of a dog is he?" Alice asked.

"A Newfoundland," the viscount answered, shrouded in darkness. "My cousin raises them in Germany as hunting dogs and presented me with one on my last visit. Perhaps you heard my failed attempt to call him to attention earlier?"

The combination of darkness and shared amity added a dimension of intimacy that fanned the spark warming her insides. She hadn't paid attention to his words until he leaned close to her ear.

"I fear you may have broken my dog, Miss . . . Miss . . ."

"Waverly," Alice supplied. "Forgive my manners, but I thought Hannah had been introduced on arrival." She proceeded with the honors.

Hannah managed a slight curtsy in the dark. "On the contrary, I believe I saved your dog, Lord Ashton."

The dog stopped his forward progress and sat down. The viscount's laugh warmed the night. "My dog responds more promptly to my name than I do. You have not explained how you came upon that particular name."

"Is it not obvious?" She patted her thigh as a signal and the black dog continued to accompany them. Hoping a confident tone would forestall questions, she explained, "It's his coat you see. It's the color of soot and ash. So the thought came to me that I might name him Ashton."

She decided it best to keep the "Lord Hairy" part of the dog's name out of the conversation. The viscount himself had remarkably thick black hair, and thus might feel she had named the dog as a jest to him, which in a sense, she had.

"He seemed to respond to the name," she added, "so I thought it would suit."

The viscount did not appear convinced but as they had arrived at their destination, the topic was not continued.

The kennel stood adjacent to the groundskeeper's house. The viscount summoned him with a rap on the door. When the groundskeeper responded, he glanced at the party on his doorstep and blanched.

"My prodigal dog has returned, Mr. Fowler. Please make sure he gets a good meal and fresh water before you lock him in the kennel." The viscount extended the rope, but the man seemed loathe to take it.

"He's come back?" The snarl in his voice suggested that this was not a wished-for occurrence.

"Is this a problem?"

"No, sir. I mean I hadn't expected him to return, sir. After he got out and all."

A tenseness simmered in the air. Hannah glanced at Alice to see if she felt it as well.

"I had thought you said the dog was stolen," the viscount said, very slow and very even. "You suggest now that he merely escaped the kennel? Was it not locked?"

The groundskeeper twisted the hem of his shirt in his hands. "I don't want no trouble, sir. It was your mother, sir. She's the one that told me to leave the kennel open. I didn't want to do it. Even if he is big and black and all." He glanced nervously at the dog.

"My mother?" the viscount's voice raised in surprise. "What has my mother to do with this?"

"She said she didn't want the big dog in the house. She said he was too clumsy around her things. His tail knocked something that broke into a number of pieces. She was fit to be tied, sir."

Hannah fought an inner smile. It seemed she and the viscount had more in common than the affection of a big, black dog.

"She told me to leave the gate open and let him loose in the woods where he belonged. I didn't want to do it, sir. But she insisted."

The viscount glanced at the dog and then the grounds-keeper. He placed the rope in his hands. "You take care of Thor. I'll take care of my mother on the morrow."

He turned from the door muttering something beneath his breath.

Hannah glanced back at the dog, her heart pained at the thought of leaving him. She called after the viscount, "Lord Ashton?"

Thor instantly sat on the doorstep. The viscount turned, equally attentive.

"I wonder if I could have your permission to look in upon Thor on occasion." She scratched the fur between his ears. "I'm going to miss him."

A smile eased onto his face. He advanced toward the women, offering his arms to escort them back.

"Miss Waverly, both you and Miss Darlington have my permission to look upon him whenever you desire. In fact, I believe Thor and I would like to become better acquainted with both of you ladies."

A thrill slipped down Hannah's spine. Although the viscount had properly addressed the both of them, as well he should, she had the distinct impression his words were meant particularly for her.

"However, I do foresee one difficulty, Miss Waverly."

"What is that, sir?"

"Given the way my dog responds to Lord Ashton, I believe you shall have to address me in a different manner."

She remembered how the dog sat at her feet whenever she mentioned the viscount's name and imagined the man responding similarly. She suppressed a giggle. "Did you have a suggestion, sir?" she asked.

He stopped and turned expressly toward her. "I thought perhaps you could address me using my Christian name. I know that implies a familiarity that may be premature in nature."

She could feel the warmth of his breath on her face and prayed that his request was not premature at all. On impulse she moistened her lips and tilted her face toward his. "And what, sir, might that be?"

"Harry," he responded. "Lord Harry Ashton."

To read more about the special classes at the Pettibone School for Young Ladies, see *The Education of Mrs. Brimley.*

DANNY'S DOG

Sarah McCarty

CHAPTER ONE

"No one dies today."

Two or three shelter volunteers looked at Kathy askance, before immediately going back to what they were doing, sorting the living from the dead, the healthy animals from the terminal. The stench of urine, feces, and rotting flesh burned through the mask Kathy held over her face as she surveyed the house. So clean on the outside with its blue siding and cream shutters, so much suffering inside.

Footsteps crunched on the dry grass. Jim, the shelter director, came up beside her. "You know we can't guarantee that."

Only a few inches taller than her five-foot-four he was unassuming in appearance, but when it came to the battle to save animals in need, he had what it took. Commitment and the ability to bounce back from one loss to fight another day. In six months, she'd never learned to do that. Kathy pushed her hair out of her face, her fingers catching on a tangle in the blond strands. Turning her hand, she observed the brassy remnants of her once impeccably maintained highlights. She only knew how to fight.

"You heard me."

Jim motioned a volunteer with a crate of skinny, fussing kittens to the van on the right. Placement in the vans was the first step in a sort of rough triage. The two white vans contained the animals most likely to live. The blue van was for animals with a question mark. The yellow van was for the ones who might be too far gone for saving.

"Be practical."

She'd been practical her whole life, planned everything. Followed through. The only thing she had to show for it was . . . nothing. "That's your job."

Hers was to coordinate the medical care and fostering for the animals that needed it.

She watched as a big black dog with more sores than hair struggled to follow a seasoned volunteer's urging to come with her. From his size, square muzzle, and big floppy ears, she determined he was probably a lab or lab mix. Though every step had to be agony with his infected wounds, the dog went with Susan, even sitting quietly when she stopped in front of the vans. Reflex more than anything else had Susan's hand dropping to the dog's broad head. The dog flinched. Though the touch had to hurt, he leaned into Susan's side and kissed her wrist. At some point in the dog's life, he'd known love. And somehow, he'd lost it. Kathy flinched as her eyes met his across the small yard in silent empathy. Nothing hurt like that. Nothing.

Susan looked at Jim. Mouth tight, he motioned her to the yellow van again. Blinking rapidly to dispel tears, giving the dog another pet, Susan nodded.

"No." The denial burst from her. *Oh, God no.* The dog was so close to another chance. Kathy waved Susan back. Jim cut her a hard look. He'd been doing that a lot lately. Could he see how fragile her control was becoming?

"You find the money, the foster home and I'll save him. Hell, I'll save them all."

It was a fact of life in a shelter. Money was tight. Volunteers tighter. When it came to who to save, it always boiled down to potential adoptability, and big black dogs were the last to be seen as wonderful, even if they were. To make matters worse, because of their size, they were expensive to treat and expensive to house. When operating on a shoe-string, expensive mattered. Kathy and Walt had always planned on adopting a lab mix when Danny got old enough to have a dog. Except Danny was never getting any older, and she'd somehow lost Walt.

"You can't save them all," Jim reminded her in that no-nonsense voice he used on everyone who lost perspective.

You couldn't save him. There was nothing you could do.

The aching sense of loss that had been Kathy's constant companion for the last six months almost swallowed her whole. The horrible sense of guilt and failure followed immediately. She pushed them back. She couldn't take her gaze from the dog's, couldn't stop feeling his trust and joy. He thought he was being saved. "Not him."

Jim frowned. "I don't have a choice. Our budget's stretched to capacity after last week's raid. We don't even have space at the shelter to house this lot, forget what it would cost to save him alone."

She knew that. She didn't care. "Then I'll take him."

"It'll cost more than you pay in rent a month just to get him on his feet, forget what it will take to deal with any hidden issues."

"That's my business."

Jim pulled his ball cap down over his hazel eyes as the first van loaded with dogs and cats pulled out of the drive. He shook his head. "Is this going to be your one?"

She knew what he was talking about. Eventually, every volunteer ran into that one impossible fight from which they couldn't walk away. "Maybe."

Not taking her eyes off the big black dog, watching as he stayed calmly beside Susan despite a small dog snapping at his leg as it was led by, she headed across the bone dry yard they were using as a staging area, her boots crunching on the grass. They'd all been "the one" as far as she could tell. Her reason for rolling out of bed, her reason to keep moving, the happy endings she created for them giving her a desperately needed sense of control over something.

She took the leash from Susan's hand and rested her fingertips on the dog's practically bald head, feeling the inflammation in his skin radiating out in a slow burn. It was impossible to tell what he'd look like healthy—beautiful or ugly—but that didn't matter. All she needed to see was the tentative hope in his big brown eyes. She gently rubbed a patch of hair behind his ear and whispered, "Danny would have loved you."

CHAPTER TWO

Pulling the car up in front of the big cape style house, Kathy turned off the engine. The lilies she'd planted last fall had come up, lining the driveway in a beautiful display of white, yellow, and cream. The grass was cut short and neatly edged. Walt, as always, was handling everything with efficient practicality. Sometimes, she wanted to hate him for that.

Her hands shook as she took the key out of the ignition. She could do this. She gripped the wheel. Walt liked animals. He used to like her. All she had to do was introduce Sebastian to Walt and her mission would be accomplished.

Easing her grip, she stared at the house. Everything was just the way she'd left it. The siding was still white, the shutters still black. Even the artificial wreath she'd hung on the bright red door last December was still in place. She didn't know what she'd expected to change. Something should have been different, but nothing was. The place was exactly as she and Walt had planned. Such a beautiful house to hold so many memories she couldn't face, so much pain she couldn't bury.

Don't come back here again, Kathy, unless you're ready to put this marriage back together.

Oh, God. What was she doing? This was a mistake. She wasn't ready to face anything, least of all her soon-to-be ex-husband. She stretched for the ignition, bumped the keys on a lever. They fell to the floor in a discordant jangle. Swearing, she slammed her hand on the wheel. It didn't help. No physical pain could override her emotional suffering. A whine came from the back seat.

She turned and rubbed Sebastian's head. "It's okay, boy."

It had to be okay. *She* had to make it okay. As Jim had predicted, there was more to Sebastian's issues than a flea allergy and a secondary staph infection. Because he hadn't been on a preventative, he now had heartworms. Advanced enough she'd had to have him treated immediately or there would be no possible recovery.

As if sensing the waver in her attention, Sebastian whined again. She glanced over her shoulder. He was staring at the house with what only could be called anticipation.

"You don't know what you're asking."

He nudged her shoulder. Clearly, while he was sympathetic, he wasn't going to back down. He was fighting for his life while she was fighting for . . . She ran her fingers through her hair. She didn't know what she was fighting for anymore. Everything in the last six months had become a blur. And she was so tired.

The garage door jerked and started to open. Her heart leapt into her throat. Even as she dove for the keys, her eyes stayed glued to the slow revelation. First to come into view as the white door lifted were well-scuffed, brown cowboy boots, then muscular legs encased in faded denims. The tear in the right knee made her want to cry. She knew the exact minute and hour Walt had gotten the tear. He'd been teaching her to play football. She'd been going for a touchdown. He'd tackled her, turning so he took the worst of the tumble. She remembered the laughter in his gray eyes when he'd gotten up, the lovemaking that had begun when the laughter had stopped. The sheer joy being with him had always given her.

The door rose higher, revealing rock-hard thighs, a loose shirt tail framing lean hips, and a slabbed abdomen. She tore her gaze away before the door rose higher. Kathy didn't want to see Walt's bare chest. She pressed her palm over her own chest and felt the small gold disk above her breasts. She hadn't taken it off in thirteen years. She didn't want to know if he'd taken off his.

Her heart beat against her knuckles. Terror or desire? It was so hard to tell anymore. She hadn't taken a thing from Walt after she'd left, refusing his requests to talk, his offers of money. She'd taken enough when she'd taken his son. But now she was back, proverbial hat in hand. Because she didn't have any choice. There was nowhere else to turn.

"This isn't going to be easy, Sebastian. So when we walk up, look sweet."

Sebastian didn't make a sound. His attention was on Walt, who stood in the doorway. She shoved the door open on her beat-up Cavalier. It stuck halfway like it always did. She gave it a kick. It creaked the rest of the way open. A quick glance as she opened the back door showed Walt was standing, legs apart, arms folded across his chest, watching her in that assessing way he had that always made her think of a warrior. He was a cop. It was probably close enough.

Emotions tumbled over her, joy, fear, pain—too many too fast. Pretending to fumble with the leash, she bought herself a little time, but not nearly as much as she needed. Finally, there was no hope for it. She straightened and gently urged Sebastian out of the car. It was only a small step down for him, but he gave a little yelp as his feet hit the pavement.

"I'm sorry."

He had very little skin on his pads. She wished she could afford boots for him to wear until it grew back, but she couldn't afford anything. Donations had covered half his heartworm treatment, but only half. The other half was going to have to come out of her grocery bill, her gas money, and likely her rent. She blew her bangs off her forehead. Mr. Bentley was not going to be pleased.

She rubbed the top of Sebastian's nose. Since this wasn't the first time rent was going to be late, she likely wasn't going to have a roof over her head come August. But Sebastian had a chance. And she needed that more than she needed a roof over her head. Sebastian gave a soft *woof.* "Don't worry, he's not as gruff as he looks."

Not that a body could tell from Walt's expression. That ability to conceal his softer side had been a self-defense mechanism for Walt growing up in a house where his parents waged constant war, and scary as heck to her the day he'd asked her to the sophomore dance. She'd been shy and insecure and head-over-heels in love with him from afar. He'd been so calm, so self-assured, so devastatingly in control, she'd been sure it was a joke, but he'd shown up on her doorstep at the time he'd stated, smiled softly at her stammer, and then swept her away. She'd been his ever since, secure in the belief that nothing could come between them. She sighed and tightened her grip on the leash. She'd been very naive.

Walt didn't say a word or raise his hand as she walked up the driveway, but at least he'd buttoned his shirt. The glance he cut Sebastian wasn't encouraging. When Kathy looked down, she found the dog watching Walt with the same steady assessment.

"Another one of your lost causes?" Walt asked as she got close.

"He's not lost, he's with me."

Her smile felt stiff on her lips, so she wasn't too surprised when Walt didn't smile back. Still, she'd hoped for anything other than the cold implacability with which he leaned against the garage doorjamb and observed her.

"It wouldn't kill you to say hi."

"No, it probably wouldn't."

She sighed. Sebastian leaned against her leg and gave her hand a lick. "But you're not going to?"

"No."

Just that one word—one syllable—that left her nowhere to go, had never left her anywhere to go. Walt had always been so strong, so complete unto himself, she'd never known how to tell him she was falling apart. Until one day, she'd woken up to discover the chasm between them had grown so big that now she was living in a run-down apartment and he was going on about his life as if she'd never been part of it. And the hole she'd tumbled into after Danny's death had just seemed to get deeper and deeper and she'd kept falling and falling with nothing to stop the downward spiral.

Until the day she'd found a kitten behind her house. Too little to survive on its own, she decided to take it to the local animal shelter only to discover they had more than they could cope with already. Standing and watching the goings-on, she'd realized here was a place that needed her. The more she'd helped out, the more she'd gotten involved, the more she'd found a purpose, saving one life at a time until now she'd come full circle, standing in front of the one man whose life she'd destroyed. And she'd come asking favors.

"This was a very bad idea."

Good grief. Had she said that out loud?

The only break in Walt's posture was the cock of his head to the side. Still no smile or even that crinkle at the corner of his eyes that passed as one. "Probably, but let's hear it anyway."

She held up the end of the leash. "I need a home."

His arms folded across his chest. "*You* have one."

"For him." She licked her suddenly dry lips. "Just for two months."

His eyebrow cocked up. "No."

Oh, damn. "I don't have anywhere else to turn."

With every passing moment, Sebastian's weight grew heavier against her thigh. She could feel his heartbeat, or maybe it was her own. She couldn't think when she was around Walt. Just looking at his face, so like her son's, brought back the pain, awakened the guilt until it felt like there was a monster inside her, clawing to get out.

"Whose fault is that?"

"Mine." It was all hers.

With an expression she couldn't interpret, Walt knelt down in front of the dog. She hoped he didn't look closely enough to see what she had when she'd looked into Sebastian's face. Walt didn't need any more pain.

Walt offered Sebastian his hand. The dog wuffled back and then ducked his head slightly in invitation.

Walt hesitated. It was easy to understand why. She'd had the same concern herself. "He'd rather take the pain than go without the pet."

That brought his gaze back to hers. "You know that about him, but you never saw it in me?"

She blinked. The monster inside howled, and raged, tearing strips from her soul. She clenched the leash in her hand. Why did he have to do this? "I knew you hurt."

"But you didn't know I needed you."

Was he asking or telling? "No. You didn't."

He swore. She flinched. Same conversation. Same pattern. Same well of pointless tears choking off her voice. Same pointless effort. "I just need a place for him to stay for two months. That's all."

Sebastian lapped Walt's cheek. Walt rubbed his knuckle under the flap of the dog's big ears. His gaze met hers. "Well, I need a hell of a lot more than that."

She knew that. Had always known it, but she couldn't bring Danny back and didn't have anything of equal value to give. Walt stood. She took a step back. He caught her hand.

Memories flashed through her mind's eye in a raw bleed. Walt holding her hand at their first high school dance. Walt holding her hand when she'd been rejected from her first choice of college. Walt holding her hand as the doctor walked away that fateful night. He'd been her first love, her first lover, first husband, and first failure. She looked down to where his big capable hand swallowed hers. And now another first. The first man she'd used.

His fingers squeezed. "You know my price."

She shook her head, denial, protest, fear. "I just had nowhere else to go."

His mouth set in a straight line. "This should have been your first stop."

"No, it shouldn't."

There was so little holding her together. Just being here was fraying the invisible knots she'd used to bind the pain into a manageable ache, keeping it contained while she ran from fight to fight creating endings she could live with.

"But you're here now." His thumb stroked over the back of hers in a hauntingly familiar comfort. His grip didn't loosen. "I've been waiting six months for this moment, and I've got to tell you, sweet, I'm damn tired of waiting."

The statement lashed over the open wound of her guilt. Tears seared her eyes as the agony rose in a whirling twist, hoarsening her voice. "I'm giving you a divorce. What more do you want from me?"

He took the leash from her hand. His pale gray eyes met hers. "What I've always wanted. My wife."

CHAPTER THREE

She followed as far as the steps. Walt led the dog into the house. Sebastian balked just inside the door, looked back over his shoulder, and whined. She shook her head. She couldn't go back in there, couldn't bear to see the bright interior with all its sunny colors, all its hopes and expectations. They'd scrimped and saved to buy this house, waiting longer for a place of their own because they'd planned on a family and they'd wanted just the right house in just the right neighborhood. They'd wanted everything perfect. And it had been. Perfect house, perfect pregnancy, perfect baby. The only thing they'd forgotten to ask for was the perfect ending. But who could have thought it would end like this? With their baby dead, their dreams in ashes around their feet, and the only thing linking them together anymore a sick dog and loss?

Walt motioned with his hand. "You're letting the air-conditioning out."

"Sorry."

Her feet wouldn't move forward or backward. Even when

Walt dropped the leash and turned, she could only stare at him helplessly, hope rising, panic building. He reached out. She flinched. His hand dropped. Inside the hope that he could forgive her died all over again. And then he did the most extraordinary thing. He cupped her cheek in his hand. The way he'd used to. The way she'd thought he'd forgotten.

"This never stopped being your home, Kathy."

She hugged her arms across her chest. "It seemed like it."

"It took me a while to understand that."

How could he understand what she didn't? "You can't—"

"Accept it?" he interrupted as his fingers curled behind her neck. The calluses dragged across her skin. With steady pressure, he drew her forward. "Accepting how you're seeing things is where I'm struggling."

He was standing on the threshold. One more step and she'd be there, too.

"Don't do this, Walt."

"Don't do what?" he asked in that low baritone that always slipped below her defenses. "Don't touch my wife? Don't hold her? Don't kiss her?"

"Don't try and make it stop hurting," she whispered as she took that last step.

It would never stop hurting and trying just gave her new failures and new guilt.

With a slow, careful move he pulled her into his embrace. "Then how about I just share the hurt with you?"

She blinked, staring at the base of his throat. His pulse was beating faster than normal. She was upsetting him. "You can't."

"He was my son, too."

The black cloud of grief gathering on the periphery of her awareness, rushed forward. Clenching her hands into fists, she pressed them against his chest. If he didn't let her go, she was going to break. "I know. I'm so sorry."

He didn't let go. Why didn't he let go? "It was nobody's fault. It just happened."

That was a lie. She could barely get the words out. "Everything happens for a reason."

And that reason was her.

"Not that, sweetheart."

It was wrong to stand there and let him stroke her hair, rest his cheek on her head, comfort her. She didn't deserve comfort.

"I should have checked on Danny earlier." Why hadn't she checked him earlier?

"You were tired."

She shoved away, stumbling back two steps when he let go. "What kind of mother sleeps while her son is dying?"

He opened his mouth to answer. Shaking her head, she spun around. She didn't want to hear it. She'd been running for months so she wouldn't have to hear him say what she saw in his eyes every time he looked at her. Tears blinded her. Sobs stole her breath. She took a step, misjudged the depth of the stair and fell. Cement rushed to meet her in a wash of gray. Her head hit the garage floor with a thunk that made everything in sight jar out of focus.

"Kathy!"

For a moment, she lay stunned, unable to move while everything around her progressed in slow motion. She saw Walt lean over her, saw the anguish in his eyes. Saw him reach for her head, saw his fingers come back red. She was bleeding. Behind him Sebastian jumped down the stairs, taking them both in one leap. Oh, no. He couldn't jump.

She looked back. Walt was on his cell phone, giving their address.

She tried to talk, nothing came out. Sebastian leaned down, whined and placed a sloppy kiss on her cheek. Walt shoved him back. She struggled harder. He couldn't do that.

"Don't."

His hand pressed on her chest. "Lie still."

She had to make him understand before the darkness rolling toward her took over. "Sebastian. Heartworms. Shot."

If Sebastian got too active, the worms in his heart could break off and just like a blood clot, lodge in his lungs and kill him.

"I'll take care of him later." Her chest was shaking. Or was it Walt? Was Walt shaking?

"Just lie still. The ambulance is coming."

There wasn't time. "Now," she gasped.

She couldn't bear another death on her conscience.

In the distance a loud wailing sounded. Beside her, Sebastian joined in, his howl echoing ghoulishly in the garage.

"Damn it, Kathy! You stay with me."

She tried, she really did, but the darkness was too pervasive, too thick. And just like before, when it rolled over her, she couldn't find him.

CHAPTER FOUR

Walt sat beside Kathy's hospital bed, holding her hand as she lay unconscious. Concussion. They said she had a concussion. He'd known a lot of officers with concussions. They'd always bounced back, but this was Kathy and she was so thin now, so pale from living on nothing but nerves. He didn't see how she could survive anything, let alone a knock on the head. Daniel's death had almost destroyed her. Them.

At the time, he'd been too wrapped up in his own grief to see what was happening to Kathy. He'd overestimated her coping skills, thinking because she went through the motions of their daily life that she was handling her grief better than he. As a result, he'd hidden his own misery, not wanting to burden her. And while he'd been doing that, she'd been building that wall he hadn't known how to get past. That impenetrable wall that had her always apologizing, always running.

It'd taken a counselor to identify it for him. Guilt. He should have seen it for himself. His Kathy had always had an overdeveloped sense of responsibility, but he'd been too busy at the time blaming himself to see anyone else's guilt. In his selfishness, he'd thought he had a monopoly on the emotion. "Ah, Kathy, sweet, how did we manage to screw this up?"

She didn't move. He smoothed his thumb over her short pink nails. He remembered how happy she'd been when Danny had been born. How she'd cherished every day, her endless patience with him when he'd started teething, the way she'd greeted him each day at the door with something new Danny had done. Mostly he remembered how happy he'd been to come home to her.

How, when they'd needed each other the most, had they managed to lose the magic of a couple that had made them invincible? "I'm not giving up on us, sweet."

She still didn't move. She looked so lost in the bed, her blond hair in a neat braid over her shoulder. She'd have something to say about that when she woke up. Kathy hated braids. She also hated hospitals, hated to sleep alone. The doctor didn't like that she was sleeping, but nothing they did could wake her up for more than a few moments in which she snapped at them to leave her be.

Kathy frowned, shifted, murmured. If they were home, he'd snuggle close, kiss her brow, and watch her drift back off to sleep. She'd always slept well in his arms. She rolled to the other side, her frown growing.

What the hell. He stood, shucking his shoes. Very gently, he eased her over before lowering the bar and sliding in beside her. Nothing had ever felt so right as when he eased his arm under her head and tucked her against him. She moaned his name, all the longing he felt inside in that one syllable. It gave him hope.

He cupped his hand behind her head and kissed her brow. "Do you think I don't know why Sebastian means so much to you? He's the spitting image of the dog we dreamed some-day would be Danny's best friend."

A little piece of the future they'd imagined come to life. Not the biggest part, but a part. "I won't let him die, sweetheart. He brought you back to me."

A miracle in itself.

Slipping his hand under the end of her braid, he rubbed the ends between his fingers. They were dry. He frowned at the change. Kathy had always taken care of her hair. "Do you know how long I've been waiting for that? How often I drove by that hellhole you moved into and just sat outside watching over you? I almost broke that door down and dragged you home more times than I can count, but the counselor said you had to make the first move."

He brushed his lips over her lashes, smiling when her lids fluttered. "You're so damn stubborn. I was beginning to think you never would."

But she finally had, and he was never letting her go again. He settled his head beside hers on the pillow. He could just make out the sweet melon scent of her shampoo. Such a small thing, but the memory of how she smelled had haunted his lonely nights, made his arms ache.

She stirred again. "Walt?"

"Right here."

She yawned and winced. Her hand came up. He caught it before it could reach her head, just holding it in his as her eyes opened, revealing the sky blue irises and the confusion.

"What happened?"

"You fell and hit your head."

"How cliché."

Another thing he'd missed. Her sense of humor. His smile was genuine. "Yeah, it was."

He knew the instant she realized where she was. Her eyes widened. "I'm in the hospital?"

"Just for observation."

The tug on her hand let him know other memories had resurfaced also. For a moment, he had the selfish wish she'd lost her memory. He hated the pain that filled her eyes, the immediate emotional withdrawal that put miles between them though their bodies still touched.

"Sebastian?"

"Is fine. Jim took the crate out of your car and has him all set up in the living room."

Keeping her hand in his, he nudged her bangs off her face with his finger. She let him. When he was done, she said, "You can let go of my hand."

"No." He needed that connection. *They* needed it. Immediately, her face closed up. He remembered what the counselor had said about that one-syllable answer and the way he used it could shut down communication. He hadn't believed her. At least when it came to Kathy. Kathy knew him. They'd been together since they were seventeen and sixteen respectively, but seeing its effect on Kathy now, maybe there'd been some truth in the statement. There had to be a reason she'd never come to him.

"It's been too long since I've held you."

Pain flashed over her face, old, pointless, debilitating.

"Talk to me, Kathy girl."

"Don't you think we've said enough?"

They'd said plenty. None of it relevant. "I don't think we've ever talked about a damn thing that mattered."

She jerked back as if he'd struck her. He only let her go so far. "Hell, I'm no good at this Kathy, but I'm willing to try."

"Try what?"

"Talking about what matters. About Danny. About what losing him did to us."

She stared at him, her blue eyes defensive under the bandage covering her brow.

"There's nothing to say."

His first instinct was to argue. His second to withdraw. The third was a small voice in his head courtesy of his counselor. It didn't always need to be a battle. Words had power. Sometimes they just needed to be said to release it.

"Maybe not for you but I'm choking on a hell of a lot of things I want to say."

This time when she tugged on her hand he let go.

"I don't want to hear it."

Before he'd thought when that particular mask fell over her face that she was shutting him out, blaming him for not being there, but now he could see another possibility.

"I know, but I've been waiting six months to say this to you, and I can't go another six with it eating at me."

"So you're going to tell me now when I'm stuck in a hospital bed?"

"Pretty much."

Yet the words wouldn't immediately come. Looking down the barrel of a gun had never left him feeling so exposed. Vulnerable wasn't a comfortable sensation. He could feel the anger build in reaction, the urge to close up increase. If he hadn't had the counselor's warning, hadn't had so much on the table, he would just have responded instinctively, hiding the weakness and letting the consequences fall where they may. Like he had when he'd gotten the call about Danny. He'd rushed to the hospital, taken one look at the devastation on Kathy's face, recognized the pain coming, and simply shut down.

"I loved him, too, you know."

She stared at him like he was about to rip out her heart. Like she deserved it.

"Losing him about killed me. He was our son, part of us, our biggest dream come to life and when he needed me, when *you* needed me, I wasn't there."

She blinked.

"I'm sorry for that, Kathy." He slid out of bed, unable to bear the weight of her silence. "I shouldn't have taken the overtime, should have been there to help you more. And afterward . . ." He shook his head, ran his finger down her arm. Some failures there was no getting around. "Ah, hell, afterward I should have let you scream at me. Whether I thought I could take it or not."

Two blinks this time and a tear he couldn't bear to watch fell. Shit.

"Scream at me, Kathy."

She shook her head. The tear started its downward slide. His determination was nothing against that tear. He'd let too much time pass, too much pain build. Failed her that one critical time. He caught the tear on the edge of his finger before it could blend into her hair and get lost in the bigger distraction. The way they'd lost each other. He touched his thumb to the corner of her mouth the way he had since the day he'd met her, brushed his fingers over the bandage on her forehead, traced the lines of her frown. So much hurt, old and new. But they'd had love, too. More than enough, and if she needed him to carry her for a bit, he could do that. He could be whatever she needed.

"You need to find a way, sweetheart. Kick, scream, shout, bring the house down, but find a way to talk to me."

"Why?"

It was a near soundless question. He stopped it with the pad of his thumb. "Because I love you, and I'm not letting us go."

CHAPTER FIVE

Find a way.

Kathy lay in the hospital bed after Walt left, staring at the door, her mind whirling. Walt wasn't a begging man. He was too take-charge for that, but he'd been begging her there in those last minutes. Or as close as he'd ever come. Begging her to yell at him.

She shook her head. He couldn't possibly think any of what happened was his fault. He'd been the perfect father, the perfect husband. She'd been the one home. The one he'd trusted. The one who hadn't noticed her son slipping away in his sleep.

I'm sorry, Kathy.

Walt didn't have anything to apologize for. He hadn't done anything wrong. But he'd apologized. She couldn't get past that. People only apologized when they felt guilty. She knew all about that. She'd been apologizing in a hundred different ways every day for the last one hundred and eighty days. Not that it seemed to do any good. Not that she ever felt better.

She put her hand to her head, pressing against the throb, wincing when the stitches pulled. A nurse came in the room. Her name tag identified her as Patty.

"You've got quite the lump there."

"I fell down the stairs."

"So that sexy man said when you came in. Raised a few eyebrows for sure."

"They thought . . . ?"

"That he beat you?" Patty checked her IV. "It was a possibility."

"No, it wasn't."

Patty smiled over her shoulder. "So we all decided after looking at the wound and the way he hovered. He loves you very much."

He couldn't. Not anymore. She plucked at a fold in the sheet. "We've had problems."

"What couple doesn't?"

"Not like this." She plucked harder. "Our son died. It was my fault."

The statement hung there in the silence. The nurse paused in checking her IV. "I'm sorry. Car accident?"

She shook her head. "He passed in his sleep."

"Sudden infant death syndrome?"

"Yes."

"That's no one's fault."

"I should have woken up for his three A.M. feeding but I was so tired when he didn't cry, I slept right through." She looked up. "That's when he died."

"How do you know?"

"I read the coroner's report."

"For heaven's sake, why?"

The sheet crushed unresistingly between her fingers. "Because I had to know everything about his death."

Just in case there was something she'd missed.

"Time of death isn't that accurate."

It didn't have to be. Just knowing Danny could have died

waiting for her to come savaged her inside. "But if I'd woken up, checked on him . . . I might have been able to do CPR, bring him back—"

Patty took the sheet from her hand. "I'm a nurse. I know all about the futility of coulda-woulda-shoulda."

Kathy couldn't look up. "He depended on me."

Patty squeezed her hand. "Wait here."

She was back in a minute. In her hand she held a booklet. She laid it on the sheet in Kathy's line of sight. The words "SIDS: Understanding and accepting the sudden loss of a child" jumped out at her.

She pushed it away. She'd read all there was to read on SIDS. Patty pushed it right back. "You've already lost your son. Do you really want to lose your husband, too?"

"No." *Oh, God. No.*

"Then you might want to keep that. You also might want to attend a meeting. This is a support group for people who've been where you are. They're meeting in a half hour downstairs. You should attend."

"Why?"

"You said you wanted to know everything about your son's death? Well"—she tapped the page—"this is part of it, too."

Kathy crumpled the pamphlet in her hand.

CHAPTER SIX

Kathy hesitated at the front door of the house, unsure whether to knock. She knew Walt was home. She'd called the station to check on his shift and his car was in the drive. Still, maybe he wouldn't want to see her. It'd been two weeks since she'd left the hospital. Two weeks in which she'd refused to see him. Two weeks in which she'd fought with herself. Two weeks in which she'd attended support groups, met with a grief counselor, started working through the pain.

This never stopped being your home, Kathy.

The statement wrapped around her with the comfort of a hug. And Walt had never stopped being her husband, yet she'd come so close to pushing him away. Maybe she finally had. The last two weeks had been the hardest of her life, and while she'd ached for him, she hadn't dared see him until she was sure she had herself under control.

She entered the house. He wasn't in the living room or the kitchen. Looking through the patio doors, she didn't see him in the backyard.

From down the hall, she heard a male voice. Walt, and

he obviously wasn't alone. What if he had a woman with him? Her heart sank to her toes, but she held her ground. If Walt was trying to move on, she'd deal with that, too, but she was done running.

Her sneakers made no sound on the thick carpet. The words got more distinct as she reached the end of the hall. He was in Danny's bedroom.

"This was his favorite ball. He had a thing for balls. A lot like you."

She peeked around the corner. Walt was sitting on the floor, beside the crib. Sebastian lay beside him. Walt was showing the dog the soft rubber ball that had been Danny's favorite toy. Sebastian, who was looking much better with the infection gone and his hair growing back, gave it a sniff, tucked it in his mouth, and then put his head back on Walt's leg.

"We used to talk about getting him a dog just like you in a couple years. Someone he could grow up with, play ball with, talk to."

Walt rubbed that special spot behind Sebastian's ear. The dog tilted his head and moaned, but he never let go of the ball. Walt gave it a little tug. Sebastian tugged back. A sad, somehow tender smile played about Walt's lips. She knew what he was remembering. Danny didn't like to give the ball back either.

He ruffled the dog's head. "You would have liked Danny. He had a way of laughing that made everyone around him happy." He stopped rubbing and took a breath. "Just like his mother."

Kathy hadn't laughed in what felt like forever. Hadn't cried, hadn't lived, hadn't done anything worthwhile in more than six months. She'd just shut down, leaving her husband to fend for himself while she punished herself.

"Today's his birthday." He reached beside the dog and picked up a book of matches. "He would have been one."

Tears poured down her cheeks. So Walt was here, in their son's room with a dog they'd talked about getting, celebrating alone. That was so wrong. The match flared. He leaned forward.

She couldn't bear it. "Don't."

He stopped. Sebastian woofed. Very carefully, Walt stood and turned. In front of him she could see a corner of the brightly decorated racing car birthday cake he'd bought.

"It's his birthday, Kathy. I can't pretend he didn't exist, that this day isn't special."

Neither could she. She took a step into the room. Then another, feeling the pain rise up, keeping her gaze locked on Walt's so it wouldn't overwhelm her. She stopped right in front of him, unable to read his expression. She didn't know what to say, except, "I loved him, too."

It was as if she'd given him the world. He shook out the match. His arms came around her, strong and secure the way they always had. "I know."

And standing in them, she let herself feel the love he always had for her, clinging to it as tightly as she clung to his arms while she confessed, "I didn't mean to sleep through his feeding time. I swear I didn't."

His grip tightened. "Kathy, you can't think like that. It wasn't your fault."

"But if I'd woken up I might have—"

His finger caught under her chin, lifting. "If you hear nothing else, hear this. The only person I've ever blamed for Danny's death was myself."

"How could you possibly blame yourself? You weren't even there."

"Exactly. I wasn't there. Not before, during, or after." His thumb tucked into the corner of her mouth with the haunting softness of a kiss. "But you were, and you were hurting and there wasn't a damn thing I could do to make it better. No matter what I tried I only made it worse, until finally, you left."

"I didn't leave."

"What the hell would you call it?"

It sounded so stupid. "Sparing myself the humiliation of you kicking me out."

His grip on her chin tightened to the point of pain, and then he let go, but only to wrap his arms around her and hold her so tightly her ribs hurt. Beneath her ear was the beat of his heart, around her the strength of his arms. And somehow her arms were around his waist, too, holding him just as tightly. It wasn't close enough.

His cheek settled on her head. "I told you the day you gave yourself to me, there was no going back."

He'd been nineteen to her eighteen. So young. "But you couldn't know this would happen."

He couldn't know they'd lose their baby.

His gaze didn't flinch from hers, just held steady with that conviction that was so much a part of him. Once Walt set his path he never varied from it. He was always that sure. "I've always known we were forever, sweetheart, and no matter what life threw at us, I always knew I wanted to go through it all with you."

"Even after . . ."

His thumb pressed, parting her lips. "Especially after." Grief darkened the gray of his eyes. "He was *our* son. It was *our* loss. No one else understood how that hurt, how it still hurts."

Oh God, it did hurt. "But—"

His mouth found hers, cutting off the protest, softly, at first as if he, too, had forgotten the path home, but then his head tilted, his mouth opened and the emotion flowed. Love, passion, grief, joy—it came at her in a dazzling array. All she'd ever wanted. All she'd needed, just waiting for this moment, for her. Just waiting to guide her out of the abyss, back to solid ground.

She locked her arms behind his neck. Oh, God, she'd missed this so much, missed him so much.

I love you. I love you. I love you. The words kept pounding in her head, picking up the pace of her pulse, filling her lungs, her mind, her heart.

"I love you, too."

She breathed in the vow, holding him tighter.

"Don't ever let me go again. Please."

Butterfly kisses brushed over her cheek, nose, and lashes. So many, so soft compared to the steel in his voice. "Never. From now on, Kathy girl, if things get rough, we turn in, not away."

Into each other's arms. Into their love. She relaxed into his embrace. "Yes."

Together they were strong enough to survive anything.

A cold nose shoved between them, brushing the exposed flesh of her stomach. She jumped.

Walt chuckled. How she'd missed that sound most of all.

"I think someone's jealous."

"Yes."

He stepped back, letting the dog between them. Kathy didn't mind. Sebastion needed love, too.

"You might as well know, while you were gallivanting about—"

She pretended to slap his arm. "I was getting help."

He caught her hand, but didn't let go, as if having her near was too new for him, also.

"Uh-huh, well, while you were working things out, Sebastian and I had a talk."

"And?" She knew what was coming. Walt wouldn't invite just anyone to his son's birthday party.

"He's decided he'd like to stay."

It was a statement and a question in one. She looked down at the red, white, and orange cake with the spot on the corner that looked suspiciously like it'd been doggie nibbled. In the middle sat a single red candle shaped in the form of a number one. Danny's favorite color.

She took a breath against the wash of pain, holding Walt's

hand, knowing he was going to be there at the end, making it bearable.

"Kathy . . ."

She squeezed Walt's hand as she imagined Danny there beside the cake, his sturdy body dressed in denim shorts and a shirt, his smile lighting up the room when he saw Sebastian. Tears spilled over her cheeks. Bold and fearless but so sweet. Danny had been such a good boy. The best of Walt and her.

I love you, baby.

The image faded.

"Kathy?" Walt asked again, turning her to face him. "We don't have to keep him."

Her first instinct was to hide what she'd been thinking, but she looked at the cake again. The cake wasn't store-bought. Walt had had it made up specifically for the occasion in Danny's favorite colors with Danny's favorite toys decorating the border. It was exactly what she would have done if she could have. Moving back into Walt's embrace, she put her hand against his chest, feeling the medallion beneath his white T-shirt. He hadn't taken it off.

"I was just imagining Danny here, picturing his face when he saw what you've done." She looked up, catching the same torment in his eyes that lived inside her. "He would have loved that cake, Walt."

For a second, his expression broke. It was such a shame men weren't allowed to cry. The tears he didn't shed roughened his voice.

"I hoped so. Every time I looked back, all I could see was that damned funeral with everyone dressed in black and not a color to be found. It never struck me as right. He was a happy kid. I just wanted . . ." He choked off, his hand clenching in a fist.

She eased her fingers between his, giving him something else to hold onto other than the pain.

"A happy memory?"

"Yeah." He nodded. "A happy memory."

Bringing his hand to her mouth, she pressed a kiss to the center of his palm before wrapping his arm back around her waist, binding them together.

"It's all right, Walt."

And it really was. The cake wasn't perfect. Neither was the dog. Nor was Walt, or herself for that matter, but together they could get a start on something perfect for all of them. A new beginning.

She wiped at her tears before holding out her hand. "Give me the matches."

"Why?"

She leaned back so he could see her face and she could see his. So much love shone down at her it was hard to believe she'd ever thought it gone.

"It's our son's birthday. I want to celebrate his life. With you."

He handed her the matches.

SCAREDY CAT

Patricia Sargeant

To my dream team:

My sister, Bernadette, for giving me the dream
My husband, Michael, for supporting the dream
My brother Richard for believing in the dream
My brother Gideon for encouraging the dream
My friend and critique partner, Marcia James,
for sharing the dream

And to Mom and Dad always with love

Thanks to Lori Foster and Dianne Castell
for including me in this project.

CHAPTER ONE

"Come on, Tom. Stop playing hard to get and come to me."

Kendra Willis balanced on the aluminum extension ladder propped against the single-car garage attached to her town house. She'd reached her right hand toward her suddenly deaf, short-haired tabby American bobtail. Her left hand formed a white-knuckled grip around the edge of the roof. She hated heights.

She masked her fear with a soothing croon. "Come on, Tom. Come here, baby."

Thomas blinked his wide, grass-green eyes and crouched his silver-and-black striped body even closer to the red-tiled roof. He lowered his head to his paws.

Kendra gaped. "You're . . . you're not going to sleep up here, are you?"

"Forget that damn cat."

She glanced down—way down—in response to the grouchy voice. *Crap.* She hated heights.

Her boyfriend, Harvey Sievers, stood on her black-topped driveway. June's early evening sunlight glinted off his silver

BMW. A ruby-red polo knit jersey clothed his lean torso. His tight buns, clad in tan khaki pants, rested against his driver's side door. Annoyance tightened his perfect mocha features.

"I've told you before. Tom has a name."

Harvey crossed his long legs at his ankles. "Leave it."

She narrowed her eyes at his deliberate challenge. "I can't go to the movies with you if Tom's stuck on the roof. We'll be gone for hours."

Harvey checked his silver-and-pearl Rolex, then refolded his arms across his chest. "If we don't go right *now*, we'll be late for the movie."

"Then help me get Tom down." Her voice wobbled with nerves and frustration. "At least hold the ladder steady so I can climb up to the roof."

"If you're so afraid of heights, get off the damn ladder and get in the car."

"I can't leave Tom outside. If something happens to him, I won't be home."

Harvey uncrossed his arms and came off his beemer. "I'm getting tired of this, Kendra. You act as though that cat is your child. It's not."

"I know that." She was precariously balanced on an extension ladder. Did Harvey really need to have this argument now? *Unbelievable.*

Obviously, Harvey wasn't going to steady the ladder so she could climb up, and Kendra was too afraid to come down. Besides, Thomas was still on the roof. She looked up at the brawny bobtail. He returned her gaze with wide, innocent eyes. *Unbelievable.*

She scanned the town house complex, wondering if her neighbors were watching this spectacle. Identical brick-and-concrete homes grew in neat grids framed by narrow, paved roads. Well-tended lawns and young trees decorated each two-story unit.

A couple of houses down, a man stood, hands on hips,

inspecting his yard. He reminded Kendra of an NFL tight end at training camp. Long, sculpted legs extended from black running shorts and a charcoal-gray T-shirt strained across a wide chest. Funny, she didn't recognize him.

Harvey continued his lecture. "It's a stray you took in two months ago. So you saved its life. That doesn't mean you have to turn yours upside down for it."

That made her mad. "Tom isn't a stray. He's my cat. And I'm not turning my life upside down for him. I'm taking care of him. Now, *please* hold the ladder so I can climb onto the roof."

"If I come anywhere near that ladder, it will be to get you down."

Kendra gripped the edge of the garage roof with both hands. Sweat collected on her palms, making her hold slippery. *Oh, man.* If she fell, she'd make her bobtail and her boyfriend really, really sorry.

She looked over her shoulder at her very annoyed date. Well, she was annoyed, too. "What about Tom?"

"Make your choice, Kendra. Me or the cat?"

Had he lost his mind? "You can't seriously be jealous of Tom."

"Ever since you took in that cat, you don't have time for me. I'm sick of it."

Kendra gasped. "That's not true."

Harvey spread his arms. "Tonight is a perfect example. We've been talking about seeing this movie for months. What are you doing? Chasing after your cat. That's not how I want to spend a Friday night."

"I haven't been ignoring you, Harvey. We just spent Memorial Weekend together. Three. Whole. Days."

"That was last week. And it was at your place with your cat."

Harvey would have a problem with parenting. If he couldn't handle one self-sufficient cat, he'd freak with a baby.

He raised his voice. "Are you coming or not?"

Kendra's neck was getting stiff. Her fingers were growing numb. "I won't choose between you and Tom."

Harvey dug his keys from the front pocket of his pants. "You just did."

She watched in disbelief as he climbed into his car and reversed out of her driveway. Without giving her another look—another thought?—he drove away. Leaving her stuck on the ladder. Leaving her. Over her cat? *Unbelievable.*

Kendra met Thomas's wide-eyed gaze. His ears twitched. With one fluid motion, he rose and prowled to the end of the roof. He looked over the front of the garage down to the driveway, glanced back at Kendra, then dove gracefully over the edge.

"Tom!"

She watched, incredulous as he landed on his feet. Without missing a beat, he walked into her open garage, settled into a shaded corner and groomed himself.

"You've got to be kidding. And you couldn't have come down twenty minutes ago because . . . ?"

"Because it's his world and things only happen on his time."

Kendra squeaked, startled into almost losing her balance on the perilous ladder.

"Sorry."

A smooth, smoky voice rose to her from her driveway. The tall, dark-skinned stranger from a few town houses over stood bracing the ladder. Thank goodness she was wearing black linen capris instead of a skirt.

Hallelujah. She was saved.

But Kendra still couldn't move. She was pinned to the ladder, not by fear this time, but by the stranger's liquid brown gaze. His almond-shaped eyes were kind and amused as he stared up at her. High cheekbones and a strong, square jaw completed a very attractive face.

Competent hands held either side of the ladder. His muscular shoulders looked like they could bear her weight if she lost her balance.

"Climb down. I won't let you fall."

Just those words, so casually offered, relaxed her. Kendra believed him.

He never let go of the ladder, not even when she stepped onto the driveway. His long, muscled arms caged her in. He smelled warm and sweaty from his early-evening run. His T-shirt was damp, molding the cotton to his pectorals. Kendra fisted her hands to keep her palms from doing the same.

She ducked under his right arm to put distance between them. Just because Harvey was being a butthead didn't mean she could fall into the sweaty embrace of the first bronze Adonis who held a ladder for her.

"Sorry." Her rescuer dropped his arms. He stepped back, running a hand over his close-cropped hair.

"Thank you for your help." Her voice was husky, making her self-conscious.

"You're very welcome." He offered his hand. "I'm Paul Strahan."

"Kendra Willis. I'm lucky you happened by, otherwise I would've spent the night on that ladder."

He had long, sexy dimples that bracketed full, kissable lips. "I doubt that. You weren't that far off the ground."

"Maybe not from your perspective." The man must be six-foot-two to her five-foot-three. Heights were relative.

"If you're that afraid of heights, why did you climb the ladder?"

"To get Tom."

Kendra looked at Thomas. Her silver-and-black bobtail watched them with a deceptively casual manner, which meant he was paying closer attention than he wanted them to realize. What was he thinking?

"You should have asked your friend to climb the ladder for you."

She had. Kendra returned her attention to Paul. He'd noticed her arguing with Harvey. Had he heard them? She hoped not.

"My boyfriend doesn't care for Tom. I think the feeling's mutual."

"They say animals are good judges of human character."

Kendra eyed him suspiciously. What was he implying?

She saw the interest in his brown eyes. As flattered as she felt, she wanted him to know she was otherwise committed. "I don't know that I agree with that."

Paul glanced at Thomas, then held Kendra's gaze. "Frankly, my money's on Tom."

Kendra had no response to that. She stared at him, speechless and confused.

Paul smiled, his killer dimples coming back. "Enjoy the rest of your evening."

Kendra watched Paul continue his jog down the road, then turned to Thomas.

"Come on, Tom. You've tortured me enough today. Time to come in."

The bobtail dragged his attention from Paul to Kendra. He stood, stretched, then started in the direction Paul had taken.

"No, Tom. This way. You know where we live."

Thomas stopped and looked over his shoulder at her.

Kendra bent forward and held out her hand, rubbing her fingers together as though she had a treat. "Come on, Tom. Let's go home now."

He didn't move.

Kendra straightened and sighed. "OK. But keep yourself safe walking the streets. And, when you're done, remember you have someplace to come home to."

* * *

Thomas watched Kendra reenter her garage. Part of him wanted to join her, to curl up in the warmth of her lap. But he was a cat with a mission. He could be self-indulgent later. For now, he needed to know where the male who'd helped Kendra off the ladder lived.

There was something about the male that made him think he could be the one to make his mistress happy. Thomas turned to chase after him.

He didn't entirely regret the trick he'd played on Kendra. Climbing onto the roof had been an act of desperation. He could smell her fear as she stood on the ladder reaching for him and was sorry for it, but he couldn't let her leave with her mate.

Harvey wasn't the one for her. He was mean and selfish. Kendra was kind and giving. She needed someone who would love her the same way. Unselfishly. Generously. The way she deserved to be loved. Perhaps the male he tracked was that someone. Thomas was going to find out. He had to find a way to repay Kendra's kindness.

Two months ago, Thomas had been beaten almost to death by a gang of strays that protected their territory with vicious zeal. He'd lain bleeding to death on the sidewalk. That's when Kendra had arrived in her vehicle and rescued him.

She'd taken him somewhere to heal. At first he'd hated it. They'd poked, pinched, and pricked him from head to tail. But he'd admit to feeling much better afterward. Well fed and strong. As he'd regained his strength, he realized he didn't mind it there. But then he'd gone home with Kendra, and he liked that even more.

They hadn't understood each other in the beginning. Having lived his entire life on the streets, humans were a mystery to him. He'd had the sense she hadn't been used to cats, either. She'd tried to keep him indoors. The mean streets of Westerville, Ohio, weren't always kind to cats, but he couldn't imagine living behind locked doors.

Thomas watched the male cross the street and turn toward a house on the corner. He froze. That corner belonged to the gang that had almost killed him.

As soon as the thought came to him, a black Bombay emerged from the bushes, followed by an orange Somali and a gray-and-white ragamuffin. Shadow and his crew.

CHAPTER TWO

Thomas had been hungry, weak, and lost when he'd first clashed with the other cats. He'd wandered into this no-cat's land hoping to find food and shelter, just until he could regain his strength.

No sooner had he crossed the street than Shadow and his cats—Red and Decoy—had jumped him. They'd given him the worst beating of his life. He had the scars to prove it, including a deep one bisecting his forehead to the bridge of his nose. And half of one ear was gone.

Flanked by Red and Decoy, Shadow stalked to the curb and hissed, baring his teeth and glaring his hatred. Red and Decoy weaved around their leader, seeming to dare Thomas to cross the street.

He knew the odds didn't favor him. His last encounter with Shadow and his gang had proven that. He'd been lucky to escape with his life. He'd been lucky to meet Kendra.

But Thomas didn't want fear to rule him. He had to make a stand. He arched his back and hissed his response.

Shadow pawed the air, hissing and spitting. Thomas

could feel the other cats' aggression build. He hesitated. Was he doing the right thing? He was all alone. There were three of them. He'd failed before. Would he survive this time if they beat him again?

Thomas scraped together his courage and placed one shaking paw into the street.

Shadow erupted in fury, bunching his muscles and screeching his outrage. His back arched, making him look double his normal size. Red and Decoy joined, hissing and calling, wailing their rage. Together, the gang formed a seemingly impenetrable wall.

Thomas froze. Fear filled him. His whole body shook with it. His muscles went lax from it. He managed to pull back his paw and stumble onto the sidewalk. In shame, he turned and raced back to Kendra.

*   *   *

Kendra half-sat, half-reclined on her fluffy red sofa, feeling Thomas's soft gray fur beneath her palm. The bobtail pressed against her chest. His body heat warmed her. His hind paws braced on her lap. His front paws kneaded her stomach. She gazed into his slumberous green eyes and stroked his wide forehead back to the crown of his head. He leaned in closer, then closer still, then . . . head-butted her. Laughter rushed from Kendra, loosening the melancholy that had gripped her before Thomas had demanded attention.

Still grinning, she nuzzled his forehead. "You're right. I shouldn't waste a perfectly good Saturday morning feeling sorry for myself."

Her doorbell rang. Kendra stroked Thomas's forehead another time or two, then lifted him from her lap and set him on the brown carpet.

He trailed her around the mahogany coffee table to the door. Through the sheer cream curtains covering her side window, she recognized Harvey standing on her walkway.

Might as well get this drama over with. She was happy

to see Harvey, but this make-up talk would come with a price. She straightened her clothes—orange tank top and blue denim shorts—and finger combed her shoulder-length dark brown hair.

Kendra unlocked her door and stepped aside as she pulled it open. He looked good, as usual. Like a male model stepping onto the runway. His cream polo shirt bared sinewy arms while his blue linen pants emphasized his long legs.

"Hi, Harvey."

He kissed her hard and quick on the lips as he crossed her threshold. His spicy cologne teased her. "We need to talk."

"About what?" She locked her door, then led him to the center of her living room. Thomas kept vigil beside her.

"You know about what. That cat."

It really bothered her that Harvey wouldn't use Thomas's name. It was as though he didn't want to place that much value on her pet. But Paul, her rescuer from the prior evening, had used Thomas's name during their first meeting.

"What about Tom? I told you yesterday I wouldn't choose between the two of you."

He patted his soft black curls. "I was talking to Myrna last night."

"Myrna?" Kendra's brows rose at the mention of Harvey's gorgeous and voluptuous coworker. A Vivica Fox look-alike.

"You didn't expect me to waste your movie ticket, did you? It's bad enough we had to make a later show."

"You went to the movie with Myrna?"

"She happened to be available."

In more ways than he claimed to realize. Was he really blind to how much the other woman wanted him? *Unbelievable.*

"And what did Myrna have to say?"

Harvey relaxed. "She told me about a local animal shelter. They take care of strays until they find homes for them."

"Why would Myrna tell you about an animal shelter?"

"You can take that cat there, and they'll care for it until it finds a home."

Kendra had been sucker-punched. Her lips parted but she couldn't breathe. Her eyes widened but her vision blurred. He wanted to take Thomas from her. *Not now. Not ever.*

"Tom has a home—with me."

As though sensing he was the subject of discussion, Thomas began to meow. Kendra glanced down at him seated beside her, but he seemed fine.

Harvey spread his arms. "It's obviously too much for you."

She stiffened defensively. Her voice was tight. "What makes you think that?"

In her peripheral vision, she saw Thomas stand and close the distance to Harvey. He stroked himself against Harvey's leg. Either her boyfriend didn't notice or didn't care. It was probably the former.

"You're always shopping for it and playing with it. You even talk to it. You know, it doesn't understand you."

Kendra begged to differ. "I'm not going to apologize for caring for Tom. I'm sorry you're feeling neglected, but you're not being fair."

Finally becoming aware of Thomas's actions, Harvey glanced down to where the cat was tracing figure eights around his legs. "What in the hell is it doing?"

"*He's* showing you affection. You could learn something from him."

"It's also getting fur on my pants." Harvey lifted his right leg and shook it. "Call it off."

Kendra briefly closed her eyes, then leaned forward, extending her right arm toward her cat. "Come here, baby."

Thomas continued to pace around Harvey's legs.

"It's a cat. Not a baby." His tone was just short of snappish.

Kendra tipped her face up to meet his eyes. "That's a term of endearment. Or should I be offended every time you call me baby?"

Harvey looked away. "You're obsessed with it."

"You're just upset because you no longer feel like the center of my world. I'm sorry for that, but it can't be helped."

"Will you get your cat away from me?" Harvey growled and lifted his right leg again. But this time he used it to kick Thomas away.

Thomas cried out as Harvey's foot connected with his side, bouncing him across the carpet.

"Have you lost your mind?" Kendra screamed as she kneeled to check on Thomas.

Her shaking hands slowly moved over the brawny little body checking for bumps, bruises or—Heaven forbid—broken bones. Thomas stared up at her, stunned. She didn't feel any damage, and Thomas never cried out. Maybe he was OK. But Kendra was fit to be tied.

She wanted to rip Harvey apart. She wanted to kick him even harder than he'd kicked her cat. Instead, she made Thomas her priority, lifting him into her arms and cuddling him close to her body.

She straightened and turned to face Harvey. Her voice was low and shook with fury. "Don't you *ever* touch him again." Kendra shifted her arms to keep hold of Thomas's wiggling body.

Harvey's eyes widened. "He was leaving fur all over my pants."

"So?"

Kendra gasped as Thomas launched himself from her embrace onto Harvey's chest. Harvey shouted and stumbled back. Thomas clung to him, hissing and spitting fury. Harvey tried to grab Thomas's paws while avoiding the cat's unsheathed claws.

Kendra followed them across the living room, managing to wrap her hands around her cat's struggling body. She tugged him back toward her, but Thomas's claws hooked into Harvey's polo shirt.

"Stop. He's shredding my clothes." Harvey scowled and tried to untangle Thomas's claws from his shirt. Once free, Harvey stepped back. "You see? That cat's dangerous."

Kendra was just as furious as Harvey sounded. "You

attacked him. What did you expect him to do? Pack up and leave?" She kept a firm hold on the still hissing-and-spitting Thomas.

"Why didn't you have him declawed?"

"Because he has to be able to protect himself from bullies who'd attack him." She gave Harvey a pointed look.

"That cat is crazy and so are you."

"That should make it easier for you to stay the hell away from both of us."

Harvey's eyes grew so wide, Kendra thought they'd pop from his head. "You're choosing that cat over me?"

"If someone had told me you were capable of hurting a defenseless animal—one that was showing you affection, one that belonged to your girlfriend—I would have told them they were crazy. Little did I know I was a horrible judge of character."

Paul had told her animals were good judges of character. Considering Thomas had never cared for Harvey, she now was inclined to believe him.

Kendra and Harvey locked gazes. Hostility arced between them, and Kendra lost track of time. Thomas continued to screech and struggle in her arms.

Finally, Harvey stepped back. "You deserve each other." He turned, unlocked the door, and let himself out.

"Thank you."

Kendra knew he couldn't hear her, but that wasn't the point. This marked the end of their four-month relationship. But she was too angry to care.

She marched to her front door, intending to close and lock it. As she reached for the doorknob, Thomas leaped from her arms and sped down her walkway.

"Tom." Kendra hurried after him.

Harvey's car was gone. That was quick. She watched as Thomas raced away. Where was he going now? Kendra turned back to her house. Thomas knew his way home. She just hoped he'd be OK.

* * *

He'd taken a risk by weaving around Harvey's legs. Thomas had known the male would get angry. But he hadn't antici-pated that kick. *Meow,* that had hurt. He needed to work on his reflexes.

Kendra had been furious. Her expression and her tone had told him that, as had the fear and concern he'd sensed from her. This was the perfect time for the other male to move in. Thomas would have to play it by ear to persuade the male to take him home to Kendra. That would give them time together while Kendra was still mad at Harvey.

But one thing Thomas couldn't play by ear was entering Shadow's territory. He'd have to get to the male's home by coming from the southeast street corner. It would make for a longer trip, but it should be safer—if Shadow had only marked the southwest corner and not the entire block.

Thomas quickly traveled the detour. It had rained over-night. The ground beneath his paws was damp but warm. Birds sang in the trees overhead, making him hungry. A cool June breeze threaded his fur and tickled his whiskers. It carried with it the scent of warm earth, cut grass, and new roses. Heady fragrances that made him feel alive.

Thomas slowed as he approached the southeast corner of the male's street. He sniffed the air. Something was wrong. He tentatively approached the territory, one paw in the street, the other three still on the sidewalk. The wind rested and the birds quieted. Danger, but from where?

Another step and now three paws were in the road and the fourth remained on the sidewalk. He cautiously brought his fourth paw off the curb and crouched low in the middle of the street. Watching. Waiting.

A rustling from the hedges straight ahead on the opposite sidewalk claimed his attention. Shadow appeared, followed by Red and Decoy. The black Bombay had marked the entire block. That's what Thomas had been afraid of.

CHAPTER THREE

Shadow sauntered to the edge of the curb, his expression vicious, his manner threatening. The black cat hissed a warning and bared his teeth. Thomas's heart drummed painfully in his chest.

What had he ever done to anger the Bombay? Crossed into his territory when he'd been tired and hungry? And for that he deserved to be bullied for the rest of his life?

No. Shadow and his crew stood between him and his goal, finding a suitable mate for Kendra. This mission was too important for Thomas to back down.

Gathering his courage, Thomas raced across the road and sprang into battle. As he leaped toward Shadow, the Bombay raised one paw. The slash cut four deep grooves into Thomas's left cheek, drawing blood and sending him sprawling onto the sidewalk.

Mindful of the other two cats, Thomas ignored his pain. He rolled to his feet, keeping his back clear. Red and Decoy flanked Shadow. The three cats stalked Thomas. He arched his back and hissed his challenge. He wouldn't back down.

He wouldn't show fear. His body was stronger now, thanks to Kendra. He wasn't the same hunger-weakened cat they'd preyed on months ago. And he was ready to prove it.

Shadow charged him, coming in low, then leaping high. Thomas reared up onto his hind legs and swatted his attacker midleap. This time, Shadow landed hard on the curb. But Thomas didn't take his attention off the Bombay's friends.

Red rushed him. There was a tangle of paws and teeth. Red screeched loudly and long as Thomas wrenched free with a portion of the other cat's ear. Payback was sweet.

But he couldn't celebrate now. Decoy had jumped him, clawing his back. Thomas arched in pain. He twisted left, then right, trying to dislodge the ragamuffin. With one last desperate heave, he shook off his assailant—and felt his flesh torn for his efforts.

Dizzy from blood loss, Thomas turned to face the strays. Decoy rose shakily to his feet. He hissed and Thomas screeched back. The other cat's eyes widened before he turned and scampered away.

Red was already gone. That left Thomas to face Shadow. The two locked gazes. Anger and hatred glowed in Shadow's pale gray eyes. And something else. Fear? Respect? Before Thomas could decide, Shadow turned and sauntered away.

Thomas waited until Shadow was out of view before letting down his guard. He sank onto the sidewalk. He was weak, shaky, and bleeding from a multitude of wounds. He needed help. Kendra was too far away, but he could see the male's house. Thomas pushed himself to his feet and limped toward his destination.

It seemed to take a long time to arrive in front of the male's town house. Thomas was winded and weaker. It took everything he had to bat against the screened door once, twice, three times.

The door opened and the male stepped forward. "Tom."

Thomas noted the male's shocked expression. He thought,

You should have seen the other cats, just before he crumbled to the walkway.

Through half-closed eyes, he watched as the male disappeared briefly, then returned with a blanket. Thomas felt himself being lifted with care from the walkway and wrapped in soft yarn. He closed his eyes, feeling as safe as he'd only ever felt with Kendra.

*   *   *

Who in the world was leaning on her doorbell? It had better not be Harvey.

Kendra flung open her front door. Her temper drained and her mind blanked at the sight of Paul Strahan holding a bloody and unconscious Thomas.

"Tom! Tom! Oh, no! What happened?"

"We have to get him to a vet."

Her breath was coming too fast. "Oh, no, oh . . ."

"Kendra." Paul's voice was firm, his gaze direct, pulling her back from hysteria.

"Yes, yes. Of course." She snatched her purse, car keys, and cell phone from a corner cabinet in her living room, then jogged back to her front door on rubbery legs. It took her shaking hands two attempts to lock up.

Paul led her to his car parked in her driveway. "Let's take my car. The engine's still running."

And his doors were still open. "Yes. OK. I'll direct you to the clinic." Kendra climbed into the passenger seat, then reached for Thomas.

"Buckle your seat belt."

Impatient, she strapped herself in, then held out her arms again. Paul helped her settle Thomas on her lap. Kendra swallowed a sob as she studied his wounds. Too many scratches to count. Blood had turned his fur black. Seeing him like this again hurt even more than the first time. Probably because he'd come to mean so much to her. Would he recover this time? *He had to.*

"Oh, Tom. Hold on, baby. Hold on."

Paul reversed out of her driveway and broke the speed limit to the clinic. When Kendra wasn't giving him directions, she was crooning to Thomas.

Paul pulled up to the clinic's entrance. He jumped out of the car and hurried to help Kendra from the passenger seat with the fragile bundle in her arms.

Kendra walked quickly but carefully to the receptionist's desk. "Please. My cat's been badly hurt in a fight."

One look at her bruised and bloodied companion, and the medical staff rushed into action. They took Thomas from her but wouldn't let her follow them to surgery. Instead, Kendra remained behind to give the receptionist her information so they could pull Thomas's chart.

"What's going on?"

Kendra turned at the low, smoky voice. She hadn't expected Paul to join her. Then she saw her purse in his fist.

"Oh, thank you." She shrugged it onto her shoulder. Her mind wandered as she waited for his good-bye.

What cat had attacked her poor Thomas? Was he the same cat from two months ago? Why was he after Thomas?

"What's going on?" As he repeated himself, Paul guided her toward the waiting room chairs. His touch was warm on her cold skin.

Kendra was confused by his behavior until she saw the concern in his eyes. Concern for her cat. He touched a piece of her heart with that look.

"Tom's in surgery." Her voice broke on the final word.

"For how long?" He helped her into one of the cushioned seats.

"I don't know." She was grateful that Paul settled into the chair beside her. She didn't want to be alone.

"He'll be OK."

He seemed to be reassuring both of them. Kendra lowered her head to blink away tears and noticed his afghan in her arms. She shuddered at the sight of Thomas's blood and fur on the yarn.

"Thank you for helping Tom. I'll wash your afghan before I give it back to you."

"Don't worry about it." Paul took the blanket back, folding it so neither of them could see the evidence of Thomas's wounds.

"It's beautiful."

"Thanks. My mother made it."

And he'd wrapped her bleeding cat in it. "How did you find Tom?"

"He came to me. He knocked on my door. I don't know how he knew where I lived."

It took mere moments for Kendra to figure it out. "Tom took a walk right after you left yesterday. He must have followed you home."

"Why?"

She gazed into his brown eyes. He had such kind eyes. "He must have sensed something in you that he liked."

A corner of his full lips curved upward. "Unlike the way he feels about your boyfriend?"

Kendra nodded. "And he's right. Harvey wouldn't have wrapped Tom in paper towels much less an afghan his mother had made for him. And he wouldn't be sitting here beside me waiting for news on Tom's recovery."

"I'm sorry to hear that."

"So am I. That's why we're not together anymore."

Paul arched a brow. "Really?"

"Really. I owe that to Tom as well."

"Smart cat."

Kendra smiled. "That he is. Have you ever had a pet?"

"My family had cats and dogs. And goldfish."

Kendra's smile grew. "A menagerie. We didn't have pets. Tom is my first."

"Where did you get him?"

"I found him in our complex a couple of blocks from my town house. He'd been pretty badly beaten. I wonder if it was the same cat he fought with today?"

"What made you keep him?"

Kendra shrugged. "I don't know. I guess it's because he had nowhere else to go." She huffed a breath and crossed her arms. "Why does he have to roam the streets and get into fights? Why can't he just sit in the window and look cute?"

Paul gave a surprised bark of laughter. "Then he wouldn't be a cat. He'd be an ornament."

Kendra blinked at him, then she laughed, too. "I guess you're right."

They talked about nothing. The act of making conversation kept her nerves at bay. More than an hour passed. Paul offered to get some lunch, but neither of them was hungry.

Finally, Thomas's doctor entered the waiting room. The petite, curvy redhead approached them. The paper booties covering her shoes crunched against the tiled floor.

Paul offered Kendra his hand to help her stand.

The veterinarian smiled her greeting. "Kendra Willis. I remember you from Tom's first fight. Or the first one we know of."

Kendra clasped the other woman's hand. "Dr. Maxwell. I'm glad you were on duty. How's Tom?"

The doctor sobered. "He's lost a lot of blood, and needed a lot of stitches. Well over a hundred. But he should be fine. We'll have to watch for infection."

Relieved, Kendra leaned into Paul. "But he'll be OK?"

"Yes."

"Can we see him?"

The other woman's gaze moved to Paul, then back to Kendra. "Sure, but he's probably still asleep."

"That's OK. We just need to see him."

Dr. Maxwell turned to lead them back through the doors she'd used to enter the waiting area. Her crunching steps led them down a hallway to a small, sterile recovery room.

Thomas lay on his side on an olive green examining bed topped by a paper sheet. He was covered in stitches and bandages from head almost to tail. They'd washed most of the blood from his fur. His stomach rose and fell in a slow, steady breathing pattern.

Kendra quietly approached her dozing cat. With the tip of her index finger, she brushed back the fur from the bridge of his nose over his forehead. His favorite spot.

"Oh, my poor Tom. My poor baby." She crooned in a whisper, not wanting to disturb him.

Paul put a hand on her shoulder, sharing comfort and support. He spoke over his shoulder to the doctor. "When can we take him home?"

Kendra looked at his profile in surprise. Harvey wouldn't have cared about reuniting her with her cat. He probably would have asked Dr. Maxwell if she knew of any animal shelters. Paul had just claimed another piece of her heart.

Dr. Maxwell glanced at Thomas before responding to Paul. "We'll keep him overnight to make sure he doesn't develop an infection. If everything goes well, you should be able to take him home tomorrow after lunch."

Kendra sighed with satisfaction. "Thank you for taking care of him."

The veterinarian nodded with a smile. "I'll give you a few moments alone. Don't tire him." She left, closing the door softly.

Kendra turned back to Thomas. He was watching her through sleepy green eyes. She stroked his favorite spot again and spoke gently. "Hey. You scared me."

Paul squeezed her shoulder. "You scared both of us."

Kendra looked up at her neighbor. This was what she wanted. Someone she could share the important things with. Someone she could share her life with. Was Paul that someone?

She could tell he was attracted to her. Her gaze slipped over his tall, tight form. She was definitely attracted to him. But she wouldn't rush into another relationship. She'd just broken up with Harvey that morning. It had taken her four months to realize how selfish, self-centered, and mean Harvey was. That must be some kind of world record for poor perception.

But Thomas likes Paul. He'd followed him home.

As much as she loved Thomas, she wasn't going to trust her love life to a cat.

Besides, did Paul really care about her cat or was he trying to impress her?

Don't even go there. Paul's concern for Thomas was real. After all, he'd carried Thomas to her wrapped in the afghan his mother had made for him, then raced through Westerville to the clinic with her.

He really cared, and it showed.

Paul gave her a quizzical smile. "What are you thinking about?"

"How glad I am that you're here with me."

His smile softened and the expression in his eyes warmed. "So am I."

Thomas could barely keep his eyes open. He wanted to see what was going on. He wanted to know who was with him, not because he was worried. He was just curious.

Kendra leaned over him, rubbing his nose. He sighed. As always, her touch soothed him, easing his fear of this strange place and his remaining tension from the fight. Shadow and his cats had done a number on him, but this time he'd been the one to chase them off. In the future, they wouldn't challenge him.

He'd also brought the male to his mistress. He was glad. Thomas strained against his drooping eyelids and watched the male smiling down at Kendra. He had a good, kind face. And, despite the concern in her eyes, Kendra looked happy. Content.

His mission accomplished, Thomas closed his eyes to nap.

A MAN, A WOMAN, AND HAGGIS

Sue-Ellen Welfonder

CHAPTER ONE

Loch Lomond, Scotland

'Tis the haggis you'll be wanting, lass.

A sharp, high-pitched bark gave prompt agreement.

Jilly Pepper, American tourist on a mission, dropped her menu and whipped around, ready to tell the aged Scotsman that it wasn't necessary to whisper his recommendation so close to her.

Nor did she need his canine companion splitting her eardrums.

She looked about, frowning.

Not that a scan of the inn's plaid-decorated dining room helped matters. The yappy little dog had high-tailed it. And the owner of the voice wasn't anywhere to be seen.

The cozy pub-restaurant loomed as empty as when she'd claimed a quiet corner behind the bar.

Jilly shivered.

Maybe the Colquhoun Arms was haunted? Yet she'd been

traveling around Scotland for two weeks and hadn't seen a single ghost.

She had heard stories though.

Scotland was full of such tales.

Her heart began to pound and she lifted a hand to her neck, fingering the antique silver locket that rested against her throat. If a Scottish ghost wanted a piece of her, Luss on Loch Lomond would be the place any such spook would come after her.

Or so she was willing to consider until she caught a movement near the door. A crusty-looking Scotsman in a kilt stood there, a walking stick in his hand. He was looking right at her, his blue eyes twinkling.

The dog was there, too.

Little, as she'd guessed. The cheeky creature appeared to be a brown and white Jack Russell terrier. He struck a jaunty pose beside the Scotsman, the same mischievous air about him as his master.

The haggis, lass.

You'll no' regret it.

The words came as before, this time without an accompanying bark. Yap or not, the dog did wag his tail. He also appeared to smile, displaying crooked teeth.

But what really caught her eye was that, for a moment, she would've sworn she could see through the dog's wig-wagging tail.

Jilly blinked. The old man grinned and winked at her. Then he turned on his heel to stride out the door, his little dog trotting after him.

Until both seemed to vanish into thin air.

"Huh?" Jilly's eyes widened. She leaned forward, trying to see out the windows if they'd nipped around the corner to the inn's car-park. But the parking lot looked as empty as the restaurant and nothing moved across the way except a flock of wooly sheep ambling about a large, tree-edged field.

The road down to the loch—Luss's only real *thoroughfare*—

proved equally deserted. Quaint stone cottages hugged the road all the way to the shore, but an air of stillness prevailed there, too.

Jilly swallowed. A chill swept over her. An old man with a walking stick couldn't move that fast. His dog hadn't looked sprightly either. She hadn't missed the telltale white on the Jack's muzzle and brows.

"Have you decided?" The soft voice startled her.

Jilly glanced up at the inn's proprietress. She hadn't even noticed the woman approach her table.

"Do you need more time?" The innkeeper's gaze flicked to the menu.

"No, I know what I want. I'll have haggis." Jilly blurted her choice before she realized what she'd said.

"Haggis?" The woman's brows arched. "Are you sure?"

Jilly nodded, certain her face had run beet red.

Of course, she wasn't sure. Everyone knew haggis tasted like moist, ground shoe leather and made hair grow in places it shouldn't.

But the order had slipped off her tongue and she wasn't taking it back. If only to prove that she was one American who *did* eat haggis.

So she bit back a shudder and flashed her best haggis-loving smile. "I eat haggis all the time," she lied. "I heard yours is really good."

That, at least, was true.

Not that she was about to admit who'd said so.

"Well, then." The innkeeper's eyes narrowed ever so slightly. "Deep-fried haggis with whisky sauce or traditional?"

"Traditional?"

"Haggis served with neeps and tatties." The woman's tone said she knew Jilly had never tasted haggis in her life. "Neeps are mashed rutabagas and tatties are mashed potatoes."

"Oh." Jilly didn't bother to try a bluff. "I'll have traditional haggis."

If only because she was certain most American tourists ordered the deep-fried variety.

But as soon as a server set down her steaming, traditional-looking haggis, Jilly decided it didn't matter if she appeared ignorant.

She'd never seen such an unappetizing pile of goo.

But she'd be damned before she wouldn't scarf down every bite.

She was spared the misery when a fast-moving blur of black and white fur made a flying leap for her table, the dog's loud-slurping tongue lapping the haggis from her plate.

"Gah!" She leaned back against the booth.

The dog—a border collie—was all over her.

Her eyes rounded as one of the beast's muddy paws slid across her thigh, his busy tongue making short work of the neeps and tatties.

The deed done, he kept his paw hard against her leg and simply stared at her.

He also looked incredibly pleased.

"Haggis!" A deep voice, richly-burred and suitably horrified, filled the restaurant. "Have done, laddie. Leave be!"

An enthusiastic tail swish showed the dog had no intention of obeying.

He kept his canine stare pinned on Jilly, totally ignoring the man who drew to a halt beside him.

Jilly looked at him and forgot to breathe.

"Holy heather, lass, I'm sorry!" The man—probably the most gorgeous she'd ever seen—curled firm fingers beneath the dog's collar and pulled him away from her. "He meant no harm, I swear. It was the haggis, no' you."

"The haggis?" Jilly glanced at the clean-licked plate.

Cutie nodded. "He has an insatiable hunger for haggis. That's the reason I have him."

"Oh?" Jilly stared at him, thunderstruck by his dimples and buttery-rich burr.

The dimples deepened, his clear blue gaze not wavering from hers. "Haggis can't resist haggis. He—"

"His name is Haggis?" Jilly glanced at the dog, his wagging tail answer enough.

"Och, aye, he's Haggis right enough." The man smiled. "He belonged to the owners of another inn, but when they couldn't put a stop to his haggis-napping, they meant to put him away. I couldn't bear to think of him in a kennel and so"—he shoved a hand through his dark hair—"he's been mine ever since."

A thump of Haggis's tail against a chair said how much he approved of the relationship.

Jilly understood. With his bold good looks—there was definitely a flair of the Celt about him—she was sure the Scot charmed everyone, including capricious canines.

But it was hard to fully appreciate him with his furry-faced friend still eyeing her as if she might be as edible as her haggis.

Even so, she did note his remarkable blue eyes and the sensual curve of his lips. He had the kind of mouth that would have set her heart to galloping if they'd met under different circumstances.

Such as not in Luss of all places and certainly not with her last clean pair of travel pants stained by mud smears and dog slobber.

She started to tell him to just take his haggis-addicted dog and leave, but before she could the proprietress returned with a glass of water and a small, linen towel.

"Ach, Kieran, whatever are you going to do with that beast?" She flashed him a look as she plunked down the water and the cloth.

To Jilly, she added, "I'll have a fresh plate of haggis for you shortly. If"—she glanced at the dog before hurrying away—"Kieran can shepherd his dog outside where he belongs!"

"He was in my boat where he always is." Kieran snatched up the cloth and dipped it into the water. "He would've stayed there if he hadn't caught sight of some fool Jack Russell running circles on the beach."

"A Jack Russell?" The pretty American's brow knit. "A small brown and white one?"

Kieran wrung out the cloth. "I was too busy trying to call back Haggis to pay much attention to the little bugger. I only knew he bolted away from the strand and made a beeline for the Colquhoun Inn."

He offered the girl an apologetic smile. "With Haggis on his tail that meant trouble."

"Indeed." She glanced at her mud-stained thighs.

She had sweet, shapely thighs. And he was dabbing at them with the dampened cloth.

"Och, sorry!" He jerked back as if he'd scorched himself. "I didn't mean—"

"I'm sure." She snatched the towel and rubbed vigorously against her knee, the color in her cheeks revealing she really had thought the worst of him. "I can get the stains out myself, thank you."

"No, please . . ." Kieran felt his own face flaming. "I'd like to make it up to you. I'm Kieran MacColl, a local . . ."

He broke off, horrified to realize he'd been about to assure her he wasn't some reprobate. Blast, he'd wanted to make amends, not put his foot in his mouth.

Not that she appeared to be listening.

In fact, he was sure she'd dismissed him.

Kieran frowned.

"Look," he began, "I have a boat—the *Salty Seal*—and I'll take you on a tour of the loch. You can meet me at the pier, at four o'clock if you're interested."

"The *Salty Seal?*" She looked up, her hand stilling on her knee.

He nodded. "The name is a story in itself. I'll tell you on the boat."

Her eyes narrowed with a bit too much apprehension for his liking.

Kieran gave her his best I-am-not-an-axe-murderer smile. "You won't be sorry, I swear it."

"I have things to do." She went back to scrubbing her thigh. "I doubt I'll have time."

Haggis chose that moment to lunge forward and lick her hand. Unfortunately, it was one of his full-out slurpy-wet kisses.

She jerked back, dropping the cloth.

Then, to his surprise, her lips twitched. "I'll think about it," she said, looking on as he bent to scoop up the towel. "But I can't make any promises. I really do have a full sched-ule."

"Four o'clock at the pier." Kieran gave Haggis a look that said it was time to go and started for the door, some half-crazed instinct telling him not to give her a chance to say a definite no.

There was something about her that made him deter-mined to see her again. Something indefinable that went beyond her obvious charms.

Something oddly familiar.

He just needed to figure out what it was.

CHAPTER TWO

At approximately two minutes before four o'clock that same afternoon, Jilly caught herself just before she stepped onto the Luss pier. Stopping in her tracks, she gave herself a shake, grateful that Kieran Whatever-His-Name-Was had his back to her. He stood beside his boat, a sturdy-looking craft all gleaming white and with the name *Salty Seal* in bright blue letters on its side.

His haggis-eating dog was nowhere in sight.

Nor were the twenty or so tourists she'd been told to expect onboard for the boat tour. The innkeeper had sworn he never went out empty. She wouldn't have to worry about being alone with him. There'd be no need to make small talk or avoid personal questions with a group of eager-to-see-the-scenery people keeping him busy.

She frowned.

Seeing him alone changed everything.

A soft rain had fallen earlier and low clouds still clung to the hills across the loch while the water gleamed like smooth, polished silver. Standing against such a backdrop gave any man an advantage. When that man happened to be a tall, broad-shouldered, and very good-looking Scot, the results were nearly fatal.

And more than enough reason for her to turn around and leave. She'd been out of her mind to consider joining his boat tour in the first place. After all, she did have other things to do.

Well, one thing.

But it was extremely important.

She lifted a hand to the locket that now seemed to pulse hotly against her skin. Her cheeks felt heated, too, and her heart thundered. She tried to tell herself that she was jittery because of her *mission* and not because the Scotsman on the pier looked so ruggedly handsome. As if he could stride across Loch Lomond's mist-shrouded hills, each blade of grass, stone, and clump of heather acknowledging his birth-right to being there.

Jilly cast another glance at him and was relieved to see he still stood with his back to her. With luck, he wouldn't see her slipping down the lochside path as she made her way to the Luss Church and its graveyard.

A destination she wasn't going to reach because even if Kieran hadn't noticed her arrival and quick turnabout at the pier, someone else was staring right at her.

The kilted man and his dog.

His ghost dog.

Something she was quite sure of because although the old man sat calmly on a bench, smiling at her, his Jack Russell dashed about on stubby little legs, sniffing the damp cobbles and—Heaven help her—she could see the nearby stone wall right through him!

In fact, when the man raised his walking stick in cheerful greeting, she couldn't help but notice that he, too, appeared rather transparent. She could see the loch-front cottages behind him, including the detail of the roof thatch and the colors of the doors, the deep reds and blues standing out against thick whitewashed walls.

Jilly stared at man and dog.

They *were* ghosts!

And *she* was going the other way.

Spinning around, she sprinted for the road. But the instant she nipped into it, she saw the man again. He stood about halfway between her and the inn, admiring the flowers crowding the steps of one of the houses.

The Jack Russell danced at his heels.

See-through as before.

"O-o-oh, no!" Jilly ran in the only direction left to her, dashing onto the narrow stretch of shore beside the pier.

But that escape, too, proved futile.

Haggis sat smack in the middle of the strand, clearly waiting for her. He had a red ribbon-tied scroll attached to his collar and Jilly knew without looking that the message was for her.

A swish of Haggis's tail confirmed it.

Jilly stared at him. She was sure she didn't want to know what the note said. What she wanted was to be back in her bed at the inn with the door locked and the covers pulled up over her head.

Haggis seized the moment, using her hesitation to leap to his feet and bound over to her. He nudged her leg with a cold, wet nose, peering at her expectantly.

His solidity alone kept her in place.

As did her certainty that if she went anywhere else, the old man and his terrier would reappear.

Jilly shuddered.

Then she caved and reached to retrieve her note.

Luss Pier, aboard the Salty Seal

To a certain blond, blue-eyed American . . .
(I've yet to learn your name)

Dare I, Haggis, ask a special favour? The human who

*belongs to me, one most likeable chap named Kieran,
is refusing to give me the haggis that is tucked into a
picnic hamper on his boat unless you join him in
partaking of the other treats he's prepared. Since I
am known to become very unhappy when deprived of
haggis, I hereby beg you to agree.*

*In high hopes of your cooperation,
Haggis*

Jilly couldn't help but smile. She looked down at the dog
and for reasons she was sure had only to do with him, her
heart started thudding. Of course, she wasn't flustered
because of the man she knew had penned the note. And it
certainly wasn't because of that particular man's soft lilting
voice. Nor was it the way his eyes twinkled when he smiled.
From what she knew of Scots, they all had such burrs and
it wouldn't surprise her if eye twinkles didn't rank a close
second on their list of dangerous attributes.

Dimples and dogs were on the list, too.

Haggis leaned in to her then, proving the canine bit of
her theory. She was smiling, after all, and she'd even stopped
worrying about the ghosts. Who could fret about phantoms
when a tail-wagging border collie seemed determined to
lavish his affection on you?

"He likes you."

Jilly screeched as she jumped and spun around, almost
colliding with Haggis's owner.

True to his race, he grinned, eye twinkles and dimples
very apparent.

She frowned. "Do you always sneak up on people?"

"Only those who appear lost." His gaze flicked to the
note. "Has Haggis persuaded you to join us?"

Her fingers tightened on the scroll. "I wasn't lost and—"

Haggis's bark made a liar of her.

His master's eye twinkle said he knew it.

She tucked the note into her jacket pocket. "I knew exactly where I was going."

"Then why did I see you heading down the promenade only to swing back and run for the road?" Kieran lifted a brow. "You then turned again and sprinted onto the beach."

"So?" Jilly tried to look as if she did such things every day. "I wanted some exercise. I've gained weight on this trip."

The Scot's lips twitched.

She flushed. Actually she'd lost a few pounds. Traipsing up and down the super-steep Royal Mile in Edinburgh had surely zapped at least two and all the castles and cliff-top ruins she'd explored had taken care of the rest. She'd never been in better shape.

Something about the way Kieran was looking at her told her that he thought so, too. In fact, if he wasn't the world's greatest actor, his expression indicated he found her attractive, maybe even beautiful.

Jilly glanced at the loch, needing to break eye contact with him.

Add knowing how to look at a woman and make her feel special to a Scot's arsenal of tricks.

She took a deep breath and determined to remain unaffected.

"I think you saw me on the pier and got cold feet." He reached down to stroke Haggis's ears. "You were running back to the inn and—"

"Are you always so concerned with what strangers do?" She swiped at her hair. "And I wasn't—"

"I find myself concerned when that stranger is you." His voice went a shade deeper. "I'd like to know your name."

"It's Jilly." She glared at him, ignoring the way he made her pulse leap. "Jilly Pepper. And I wasn't running from you. I-I saw a ghost—two ghosts, an old man and a dog. I was trying to get away from them."

If she'd hoped to shock him, she'd failed.

Far from backing away and leaving her alone, he stepped

closer. "Ah, well, Jilly lass, then I really would urge you to join Haggis and I. Last time I checked, there weren't any ghosts on the *Salty Seal*."

"You don't think I'm crazy?" She looked at him as if she wished he thought just that.

Kieran bit back a chuckle. "It'd be a rare Scotsman who'd doubt you saw something odd. We're born knowing there's more in this world than can be readily explained. Now"—he decided to take a chance and grip her elbow, gently—"if you're still hedging about letting me show you the loch, then, aye, I might think that's crazy."

"I was expecting a boat *tour*." Her gaze went past the pier and boathouse to where the *Salty Seal* bobbed in the water, bright, innocent, and notably empty. "A crowd of sightseers, not just you, me, and Haggis."

Kieran felt a twinge of guilt.

It passed with lightning speed.

Across the loch, late afternoon sun edged the clouds and a few slanting rays shone on the mica sand that fringed one of the small wooded isles where he hoped to take her for a picnic. He smiled, the Gael in him seeing the turn in the weather as a good portent for him and the American tourist who, for reasons he couldn't explain, struck him as so much more.

The way Haggis had taken to her spoke volumes. He ran circles around them as they approached the pier. Looking and acting younger than his nine years, he held his tail high and his eyes sparkled with excitement.

But if Kieran wished to read anything deeper in his dog's attachment to the girl or even in her apparent agreement to go out on the loch with them, his hopes plummeted when they passed the boathouse and neared the *Salty Seal*'s mooring.

She stopped short, pulling her arm from his grasp. "I saw a poster on the boathouse. It had your tour times and four o'clock was one of them. So"—she eyed the boat suspiciously—"where is everybody?"

Haggis sat down and watched him.

Jilly folded her arms, the look on her face proving her to be more persistent than he would have believed.

"I cancelled the afternoon tour," Kieran admitted, opting for honesty. "Remember I told you there was a story behind my boat's name?" He smiled, hoping to catch her interest. "The boat is named after Salty the seal. He swam into the loch after losing his way in River Leven. He's been here ever since and is quite a character."

"A seal in Loch Lomond?" She blinked.

Kieran nodded. "He's a fine gray seal with an appetite for fish as great as Haggis's for haggis. The local fishermen tried to catch him and return him to the sea, but Salty eluded them. Finally some of us pitched in and bought Salty a fishing license. Just"—he winked—"to make certain that no one got any funny ideas."

She smiled then, the sight warming Kieran to his toes.

He grinned back at her, feeling ridiculously elated. What *was* it about her that made him so determined to win her heart? And, he realized with a shock, that's exactly what he was hoping to do.

"That still doesn't tell me why you cancelled your afternoon tour."

The statement proved he wasn't succeeding.

Kieran did his best not to frown. "Salty was spotted on my earlier tour, the one that went out right after Haggis ate your lunch," he said, going for a half-truth this time.

He had seen the seal, but he'd cancelled the later tour because he wanted to be alone with her.

"I thought," he began, starting to untie the *Salty Seal's* lines, "our chances of seeing him would be greater without a crowd."

"I see."

Kieran risked a glance at her as Haggis leapt into the boat. She'd lifted a hand to her brow and was scanning the loch, clearly keen to catch a glimpse of Salty.

Knowing it was now or never, Kieran jumped into the

boat and turned to reach for her, hoping she'd accept his outstretched hands.

When she did, his heart soared. "If we leave now, we might find him on the far side of the loch." He lifted her on board, scarce believing his luck. "He was basking on a rock near the island I'd like to show you."

He indicated a wicker hamper under one of the thwarts. "We can have a picnic there. It's my way of making up for Haggis ruining your lunch."

"And Haggis?" She pulled the crumpled note from her pocket and waved it. "Will he finally get to eat his haggis?"

"Och! I'm thinking he'll be too full." Kieran laughed and nudged an empty dish with his foot. "He got into the haggis supply before I even—"

He broke off, remembering what he'd written. Equally damning, the picnic hamper was tightly secured with leather straps. Haggis's haggis dish sat in plain sight, the smeared remains of his favorite treat irrefutable evidence that he hadn't been denied a thing.

Haggis barked, sounding amused.

Heat shot up Kieran's neck. "Er . . ." He tripped over his tongue. "I can explain—"

"Please don't." Jilly settled herself on a bench and started smiling again. "It's been a long time since a man went to such trouble to get my attention."

She reached to pet Haggis when he thumped down beside her. "I'm quite flattered and"—she looked out over the loch as the boat started away from the pier—"a seal sighting and a picnic sound wonderful."

Kieran grinned and swung the *Salty Seal* toward their destination. If the loch gods were kind and with a little help from his four-legged friend, this afternoon's outing would be the first of many.

Jilly Pepper was a keeper.

He had no intention of letting her go.

CHAPTER THREE

Hours later, Jilly sat on her bed at the Colquhoun Arms and kept telling herself there was no such thing as love at first sight. Even so, she couldn't resist slipping to her feet and going to the dresser where her digital camera and a handful of smooth, round pebbles proved her wrong.

Photos didn't lie.

And the way her breath caught when she touched the stones only confirmed her suspicion. Gathered on the shore of the islet where Kieran had taken her for a picnic, the pebbles were more than mementoes.

They transported her back to the moment she'd collected them and heard Kieran's shout that he'd spotted Salty. She'd thrust the pebbles into her pocket and grabbed her camera, aiming it to where the seal frolicked in the water. Enchanted, she'd watched as he rolled belly up and peered at them with his round, inquisitive eyes.

"O-o-oh!" she'd cried, snapping pictures as she ran to Kieran at the water's edge.

Losing her footing on the wet shingle, she'd plowed right into him. He'd whipped around, catching her by the shoulders and then held her just a breath longer than was necessary for her to regain her balance.

In that instant, her world tilted. She'd also seen a flash of heightened awareness in his eyes. The air shifted, crackling as if charged with electricity. He'd lowered his head to kiss her, but she'd jerked free, breaking the magic.

And there *had* been magic.

Remembering sent shivers through her and made her heart thunder.

If he'd kissed her, she'd have been lost.

Jilly flattened her hand across the pebbles, pressing down on them until they stopped feeling like living, breathing memories and were once again nothing more than stones from the shore.

A pity she couldn't do the same with the photos.

Frowning, she studied the camera lying so innocently on the dresser. Maybe if she stared at it long enough the incriminating pictures would disappear. Or at least morph into something less damning.

Unfortunately that wasn't going to happen.

And she knew she wouldn't be deleting the shots.

But she *could* remind herself why the photos shouldn't matter.

So she reached for her grandmother's locket, its age-smoothed silver warm beneath her fingers. Heart-shaped and engraved with two thistles, the stems entwined in intimate embrace, the locket held a twist of auburn hair and a tiny cutting of plaid.

Treasures Margo Clare had cherished all her days.

Remnants of the tragic love affair that had stolen the light from her life and left her soul bereft. Jilly tightened her fingers around the locket, more aware than ever of its sobering message.

Long distance romances didn't work.

And it was always the woman whose heart would be broken.

Of course, according to Jilly's grandmother, Alastair MacColl had been worth the risk. Big, brawny, and with a shock of red hair, he'd had flashing blue eyes and more charm than was good for him. As a gifted artist and passionate kilt-wearer, he'd needed less than a glance to bring world-traveler, Margo Clare, to her knees.

Her plans to hop trains and see Europe in a summer vanished as Jilly's grandmother spent her holiday in the Scotsman's arms, only returning home to announce her pending marriage and move to Scotland.

Alastair's letter ending their relationship reached the States before Margo. The missive's cold tone proved what a fool she'd been.

Now the letter rested inside Jilly's purse, yellowed, brittle, and ink-faded. Waiting, as did the locket, for her to perform a *closure ceremony* at Alastair MacColl's grave. A ritual she'd agreed to do because it'd been her grandmother's dying wish.

Only if she burned the letter and tucked the locket into the cold, waiting earth would Margo Clare find peace in Heaven.

Or so the old woman believed.

Jilly's heart began to hammer and she could almost feel the locket pulsing against her skin again, each silvery vibration admonishing her with five echoing words. *Don't make the same mistake. Don't make the same mistake. Don't . . .*

Frustrated, she spun away from the dresser and started toward her bed.

She took exactly three steps before she huffed out a breath and wheeled around to snatch her camera and retrieve her photos of Salty.

But it wasn't the seal's black domed head that caught her eye.

It was the back view of Kieran as he stood on the shore looking out at the loch. The width of his shoulders and how the evening light glinted on his dark hair, revealing a touch of chestnut she'd only noticed on studying the photos.

She also couldn't miss how companionably Haggis sat beside him and that in one of the photos Kieran was scratching the dog behind his ears.

A man who loved dogs couldn't be bad.

How people felt about dogs had always been her measure of a person.

She clicked through the photos, the memory of their almost-kiss burning inside her until she shut down the viewing screen and tossed the camera onto the bed.

She couldn't—*wouldn't*—get involved with a Scotsman from Luss.

Or could she?

She honestly didn't know.

But she did recognize the need to get out of her room, pleasant as it was. A glance at her watch told her that the inn's pub would still be open. She could sit at the bar, sip a pint of ale, and soak up the coziness until she was ready for bed.

As it happened, upon slipping downstairs and into the late night quiet of the lounge, a red-cheeked man in a tweedy jacket swung round in his chair and grinned at her the instant she stepped through the door.

"Ho, there's yourself!" He waved his dram glass in greeting. "I saw you went straight to the source today, what? Well-met, lassie, well-met, indeed."

Jilly paused, blinking.

For a moment, she thought he was the ghost. But this man wasn't kilted and was definitely solid. He also didn't have a see-through Jack Russell.

Even so, he seemed familiar and his words caught her off guard.

Then she remembered speaking with him at the Luss Post Office on the day she'd arrived. He'd suggested she stay at the Colquhoun Arms and, much to her relief, he'd also assured her that she'd find Alastair MacColl's grave in the village churchyard.

"The source?" She started forward again, not sure what he meant.

"Why, young MacColl, of course!" He slapped his dram glass on the bar. "He's Alastair's grandson. I saw you with him on the strand, not far from his gallery."

Jilly's heart sank and her legs went rubbery.

Tweedy beamed. He had no idea he'd turned her world upside down.

"His gallery?" She stared at him, not caring if she sounded like a parrot. "The man I talked to runs boat tours."

"Och, don't we all these days!" The man chuckled. "Ferrying visitors around the loch, weaving, or piping at hotel-sponsored ceilidhs, the summer tourist trade gets us through the winter."

Jilly nodded, unable to speak.

Her mouth had gone dry and she was beginning to feel sick.

"As for MacColl . . ." The man leaned forward. "You know what they say"—he winked—"the apple doesn't fall far from the tree. Some hereabouts think he's more talented than his grandfather."

"So he's an artist?" Jilly could hardly get the words out.

"He's a driftwood artist." He spoke as if that made a difference. "He makes animal sculptures out of driftwood. Horses, sheep, dogs, birds, you name it. Says the pieces he collects speak to him, telling him what they're meant to be. Then he sets to work."

Jilly swallowed. "I'm sure his work is . . . beautiful."

"Aye, so it is." The man reached for his dram, emptying the little glass. "You should stop by his studio. It's at the end of the road, across from the pier but a bit hidden behind the trees."

"I will." Jilly forced a smile.

She had no intention of visiting the gallery. And she

already knew where it was. Her grandmother had described its location to her.

No way was she going there.

What she *was* going to do was remember to listen better when people introduced themselves.

Looking back, she was sure Kieran mentioned his last name. But his dog's haggis attack startled her so much the name hadn't registered.

Luckily it did now.

Too bad the revelation made her feel so lousy.

*   *   *

Somewhere in the small hours, just as Jilly finally fell into a deep sleep, Kieran sat bolt upright in his bed. His heart pounded, the sheets were twisted, and cold sweat damped his brow. He shoved a hand through his hair and glanced at the clock on his night table, not at all surprised to see that it was after two A.M.

Not that the time mattered.

What counted was that he'd remembered what was so familiar about Jilly Pepper.

It wasn't the girl at all.

Not really, although now that he'd made the connection, he couldn't deny she had the same deep blue eyes and shining, honey-blond hair. He suspected she'd also inherited the full, round breasts though it was hard to tell beneath the jacket she always wore.

His gut clenched. How ironic that it was something else she wore that revealed her identity. Margo Clare's locket was unmistakable. His grandfather had fashioned it for the woman, giving it to her as a token of his undying love.

She'd sworn to wear it always.

Then she'd left Scotland never to be heard from again.

"Damn." Kieran scowled and leapt to his feet, promptly stubbing his toe on a chair leg. "Owwww!" he roared, resisting the urge to kick the chair.

Limping around the darkened room, he glared at the black-out shades at his windows as he snatched up his clothes and dressed as quickly as his throbbing foot allowed. Then he let himself out into the light summer night and strode straight across the damp grass to the small studio that had once been his grandfather's.

He needed several tries to open the rusty-hinged door, but once inside enough of the night's luminosity spilled through the windows to show him what he'd come to see.

His pulse racing, he went to where some of his grandfather's earliest paintings were propped against a wall. He knew which one he wanted. It was the only painting covered with cloth.

It was hidden from view, though he knew his grandfather had often lifted the cloth to peer at it. Something he'd done with increasing frequency in later years. The long hours he'd spent in the studio, mooning over the portrait, had never failed to break Kieran's heart.

But he'd understood.

Margo Clare had been the only woman Alastair MacColl had ever truly loved.

"Damn!" He cursed again as he found the painting and ripped away the cloth.

He stared down at the beautiful woman, scowling.

Her painted face smiled back at him. Poised, serene, and looking absolutely incapable of wreaking the kind of damage she'd done to his grandfather.

Kieran stepped back and folded his arms, his gaze focused on the painting. A true masterpiece, it showed the woman perched on a rock somewhere near the summit of Ben Lomond. She wore a blue dress and Jilly's locket glinted brightly at her throat.

She appeared about the same age as Jilly.

And she seemed—no, she *felt*—so alive Kieran would have sworn she really was looking at him.

He narrowed his eyes at her, uncomfortable.

"Does Jilly know what you did? Did you ever tell her how you promised to return and then vanished into thin air? Did you laugh each time you received one of my grandfather's letters, begging you to come back to him?" The questions left his lips before he could catch himself.

He frowned.

Only crazies talked to oiled canvases.

He might be halfway to falling in love with an American he hardly knew, but other than that he was quite sane.

Sound-minded enough to regret dashing out without tossing on a jacket. He shivered and rubbed his arms, certain his grandfather's cluttered little studio was colder than an arctic winter.

Ignoring the chill, he pulled the draping back over the painting. He'd seen enough. Jilly's locket was indeed the same one worn by Margo Clare.

But when he turned to leave, he also saw the lady was no longer wearing it.

She hovered in a shaft of soft light near the door, a mere shimmer against the night. Decades older, she was beautiful as before, and still in her blue dress. And rather than glinting at her neck, the locket dangled from her outstretched hand.

Her eyes pleaded.

The shimmering light around her intensified as she drifted nearer.

It wasn't as you think.

The words rippled the air and lifted the fine hairs on Kieran's nape. But before he could blink, she vanished, taking the odd light and the cold with her.

Only clarity remained.

Something between his grandfather and Margo Clare had gone horribly wrong. And now—he was sure of it—he had a chance to make things right.

He just hoped he wasn't too late.

CHAPTER FOUR

"I knew I'd find you here."

The words came soft in the cool damp of the rain-misted churchyard. Rich, deep, and with enough burr to make Jilly's breath catch.

She froze. Kneeling beside Alastair MacColl's grave, with one hand braced on his headstone and the other about to shove her grandmother's locket into the wet mossy earth, left her in a vulnerable position to greet the man's grandson.

She swallowed, not ready to face him.

"Don't do it." He was coming closer. She could hear the crunch of his shoes on the gravel path. The rustle of bracken and heather, sounds that let her know his dog bounded along with him.

"It's over, lass." His hand settled on her shoulder, squeezing. "The locket is yours now."

That did it.

She shot to her feet and swung around. "What do you know of it?"

His gaze pierced her. "Not as much as I'd like, but enough to guess what you were doing."

Jilly glared at him, not liking the look on his face. "I wasn't *doing* anything," she lied, heart racing. "The locket dropped and I found it on the grave."

Haggis pushed between them, whining.

Kieran folded his arms. "See? Even he knows you're telling a tall one."

"My business here is my own." Jilly stood her ground. "I was about to leave anyway."

"I know." He looked equally determined. "I went to the inn. They told me you'd checked out."

"Then you'll understand I'm in a hurry."

Rather than answer her, he glanced at Haggis. The dog sidled over to him, deftly helping him block the path out of the churchyard. Unless she wished to follow Haggis's lead and lope through dripping underbrush.

Jilly frowned. "Just what do you want?"

A chance for us.

Kieran caught himself before he blurted the truth burning so hotly inside him. There were other things they needed to settle first. "Let's say I'd like to avert another tragedy."

She blinked. *"A what?"*

"I know you're Margo Clare's granddaughter." He watched her carefully as he said the words. "At least I think that's the connection."

The high color that flooded her face proved it.

"Then maybe you should just turn around and walk away." She jammed a hand on her hip, the sudden glitter in her eyes making him regret his bluntness. "Leave me alone so I can see to her last wishes."

"I can't do that." Kieran shook his head. "I believe she changed her mind. If you'll give me five minutes"—he steeled himself, expecting a rebuff—"I think you'll agree."

Her eyes flashed. "How could you know what she wanted?"

"Because"—he took a breath—"I saw her ghost last night."

Her jaw slipped but she didn't argue.

Kieran smiled, encouraged. "Five minutes is all I ask."

She glanced through the trees to the loch, then back to him. "Five minutes where?"

Kieran swiped a raindrop off his brow. "I'd like to show you something in my grandfather's studio. You'll understand when you see it."

"I don't know . . ."

The hesitation in her voice made Kieran's heart flip. Hope tightened his chest and he reached out a hand, willing her to take it.

Sharing his excitement, Haggis barked and ran to the churchyard gate, clearly certain they'd follow.

"You'd no' let him down would you?" Kieran seized his chance, not missing how her gaze followed the dog. "Besides"—he glanced at the darkening sky—"this drizzle is about to worsen."

Already rain splattered the path. Whether for that reason or because of the chill wind sweeping off the loch, she took his hand and let him lead her back to the promenade. Haggis shook himself and trotted beside them for the short walk to Kieran's cottage.

But she hung back when they entered his garden and approached the studio. "I'm not sure—"

"It's just a portrait." Kieran opened the door. "My grandfather painted it of Margo Clare on Ben Lomond. She's wearing your locket and when I saw her last night she held it out to me. I'm sure she meant—"

Jilly stopped on the threshold with a gasp.

She wasn't staring at the painting of Margo Clare, but at a self-portrait of his grandfather and his favorite dog, a Jack Russell named Argyll.

"That's the man I saw at the inn!" She stepped into the studio, one hand to her breast. "He was in the road, too, with that same dog. I'd know them anywhere."

"Looks like he knew you, too." Kieran joined her at the portrait. "You know who he is, don't you?"

Jilly nodded, her mouth too dry for words.

"I suspected it was him. And Argyll." He slid an arm around her. "They were inseparable. As I believe he and Margo Clare would have been if she hadn't left him."

"She didn't." Jilly jerked free. He had it wrong. "Your grandfather ended the relationship. He broke my grandmother's heart. See"—she pulled the faded letter from her purse—"it's all here."

She thrust it at him, watching as he read. He blanched and then two bright spots of red colored his cheeks.

"Bloody hell!" He looked up. "My grandmother wrote this. Her handwriting is unmistakable."

"Your grandmother?"

He nodded. "She loved my grandfather since childhood. But he thought of her as a sister. Until—"

"He didn't hear from my grandmother again," Jilly finished. "He never knew she believed he'd written to say it was over."

"It doesn't make sense." Kieran frowned. "Grandfather sent letters begging Margo Clare to return."

"Perhaps your grandmother intercepted them?" It seemed a possibility.

He frowned, ran a hand through his hair. "I sure hate to think so, but we'll never know." He reached for her, drawing her close just as Haggis nosed between them, tail wagging. "Jilly . . ." He looked down at his dog, then at her. "Whatever happened, we do know they brought us together. They want us to have the future they were denied. Maybe—"

"But . . ." Jilly glanced aside, not wanting him to see the brightness in her eyes.

"Lass." His voice said he saw anyway. "Does this mean you feel it, too?"

Jilly swallowed the tightness in her throat. "Feel what?"

He laughed and caught her chin, turning her face back

to him. "That our grandparents are together again? And that they're happy?"

She nodded, believing.

"And do you feel this, too?" He lowered his head and kissed her. "The attraction that's been crackling between us since we first met."

Jilly blinked. She did feel it. But the swirling mist and rain and the studio's thick whitewashed walls reminded her of how far from home she was, how impossible their chances.

Somehow, though, she'd slung her arms around Kieran's neck and despite Haggis still wriggling between them, he'd pulled her even closer.

"I was going to fly back tomorrow . . ." She trailed off when he kissed her again. "I—"

"You can stay here, Jilly." He smiled down at her. "There's a holiday cottage at the rear of the garden. You can have it for starters. After that—"

Haggis thrust his beaming black and white face up at them, his eyes saying what they both knew. They were meant to be together and if this wasn't a classic happy ending, it was a wonderful beginning.

COPYRIGHT NOTICES

ABOUT THE AUTHORS

Lori Foster is a Waldenbooks, Borders, *USA Today*, *Publishers Weekly*, and *New York Times* bestselling author. *Romantic Times* honored her success twice with Career Achievement Awards in 2001 for series romantic fantasy, and in 2004 for contemporary romance. Lori's *Too Much Temptation* became Amazon's #1 selling romance title in 2002, and *Servant: The Acceptance,* written as L. L. Foster, was a #1 Editor's Pick in romance.

Lori is passionate about giving back to the community and has been pivotal in raising money and awareness for causes including battered women, animal adoption, and children with special needs. For more information, visit www.LoriFoster .com.

Stella Cameron is the *New York Times*, *USA Today*, *Booklist*, and *Washington Post* bestselling author of many contemporary and historical novels. She and her husband live in Washington State.

"My first fictional characters were cats, dogs, horses, mice, hedgehogs, frogs—creatures I've always loved. In the beginning, I drew them. In years to follow I still drew them, but they 'spoke' in cartoonlike balloons floating over their heads. At last came people, also in cartoon form, but eventually I put them all together into little stories, then longer stories, short books, and then longer books. I'm still writing about the trials and love people share and in every story there is at least one animal with an important part to play.

"I have shared my whole life with animals, too. I've dedicated the story in this book to a few of them. Doing my best for the ones who have done their best for me is one of my passions and I hope that with *A Knotty Tail*, I showed you a little of how special animals are to me."

Kate Angell resides in Naples, Florida. She's an avid reader, a sports enthusiast, and an animal lover. She has a household full of dogs and cats. Her terrarium holds two green frogs. She believes feeding one pet is as easy as feeding a dozen.

USA Today bestselling author **Dianne Castell** has won *Romantic Times*' Reviewers' Choice Award, been on the cover of *Romantic Times* magazine, and has made the Waldenbooks bestseller list. Dianne lives in Cincinnati, where she cooks chicken biscuits and gravy for her two cats and writes fun, sexy, Southern stories with a touch of mystery and a ton of romance.

Ann Christopher is a full-time chauffeur for her two over-scheduled children. She is also a wife, former lawyer, and decent cook. In between trips to Target and the grocery store, she writes the occasional romance novel featuring a devastating alpha male. She lives in Cincinnati with her family, which includes two spoiled rescue cats, and she loves to hear from readers via her site, www.AnnChristopher.com.

Marcia James writes hot, humorous romances and was a finalist in eleven Romance Writers of America chapter contests before selling her first comic romantic suspense, *At Her Command*, to Cerridwen Press. An advertising copywriter and marketing consultant, Marcia presents author promotion workshops and writes PR articles. In her eclectic career, she has shot submarine training videos, organized celebrity-filled non-profit events, and had her wedding covered by *People* magazine. After years of dealing with such sexy topics as how to safely install traffic lights, Marcia is enjoying "researching" her novels' steamy love scenes with her husband and hero of many years. Please visit her on the web at www.MarciaJames .net.

Donna MacMeans made a wrong turn many years ago when she majored in accounting in college. What was she thinking? Balancing books just can't compete with crafting plots and inventing memorable characters. She finally broke free of her life as a CPA to write witty and seductive historical novels for Berkley Sensation in what can only be described as her dream job.

When not at her keyboard, Donna enjoys painting, traveling, and creating luscious desserts. She lives in central Ohio with her husband of thirty-five years, her two adult children, and her constant canine companion, Oreo—an Australian shepherd–terrier mix. Donna loves to hear from her fans. Please contact her at www.DonnaMacMeans.com.

Sarah McCarty has been active in animal rescue for more than twenty years. She specializes in critical care medical rescue, working with shelters around the country, taking in and rehabbing those dogs, cats, and birds that through neglect and/ or abuse are in too critical condition for the strained resources of a shelter. Sarah's belief that animals enrich our lives is reflected in her stories. Whether she's writing a fast-paced western historical or a pulse-pounding paranormal, Sarah's tales of love always contain a four-legged character who, right along with the hero and heroine, make us laugh, cry, and believe.

Award-winning author **Patricia Sargeant** writes romantic suspense and contemporary romance. In addition to her love of reading and writing, Patricia enjoys jogging, movies, coffee, and cookies. Raised in New York City, Patricia lives in Ohio with her husband. Find out more about Patricia on her website, www.PatriciaSargeant.com.

Former flight attendant **Sue-Ellen Welfonder** has three grand passions: Scotland, the paranormal, and dogs. All can be found in her medieval romances and the paranormals she writes as

Allie Mackay. She is proud of her Scottish descent, spent fifteen years in Europe, and now just tries to live quietly—although she never misses a chance to visit Scotland. She's devoted to her Jack Russell terrier and wishes dogs everywhere were equally loved.

Turn the page for a special preview of
Erin McCarthy's next Fast Track Novel,

JACKED UP

Coming soon from The Berkley Publishing Group!

Nolan Ford wasn't listening to Eve Monroe as she chewed him out. It wasn't that he was trying to be disrespectful but, Lord, the woman could start an argument in an empty house.

Besides, the top button on her blouse was straining, and each time she lifted her arm and waved it around, he held his breath, waiting for the button to pop. He'd had something of a crush on Eve for years, always aware when she was around the track or the garage, stomping around in her heels and severe office clothes. She thought no one noticed that she was a woman, and seemed to work damn hard to make sure it stayed that way, but Nolan had always noticed.

Eve was hot. Full-on smokin', jalapeño-pepper hot. From that lustrous deep brown hair with a hint of red, to her gold-flecked eyes, down past an amazing chest, to slim legs and a perky behind, she was all that and a bag of chips, in his opinion.

"I mean, seriously, I don't care what kind of underwear you wear, just wear some!" she said, making a sound of frustration. "I mean really, let's show a little decorum."

Nolan fought the urge to grin. She looked so serious when talking about his underwear. Or lack thereof. But he knew if he so much as curved the corner of his mouth up, her head would blow off her shoulders. Eve was not happy about the little incident during the race the other day. "Well, ma'am, it's hot in those crew suits. Some particular parts need air circulation."

She drew in a deep breath, obviously struggling for control, but it only made her blouse pull tighter. Nolan stared in fascination as the button slipped halfway through the hole. If that thing gave, he was going to see her bra. He wasn't sure he was capable of not getting a hard-on if that happened.

And since he wasn't wearing any underwear today either, she would probably notice.

"Stick a bag of frozen peas in your drawers. Just wear them." Her hands went up to rake her hair back away from her face. "Don't pretend you don't understand that this is a big deal. You have been in the business for years. Sponsors want a friendly, wholesome image for the sport their name is attached to. As do the team owners, and the powers that be in stock car racing. When a jackman goes over the wall and rips his suit, the whole world doesn't need to see his back end."

Nolan had to agree with that. He certainly hadn't intended to tear the seat of his pants going over the wall into the pit road when Evan's car had stopped for a tire change. Or for his ass to end up on YouTube. But it had. So what could you do about it? That was his philosophy in life: Don't sweat the small stuff. Or bare butts.

"I do understand, Eve. I'm proud to be a member of Evan's crew and I take my job seriously. It was an accident. I believe they even have a term for that—*wardrobe malfunction*."

She started talking. He stopped listening again. As her arms waved, the button gave up its good fight and parted ways with the hole it had been in. Her blouse sprung apart. He was assaulted with the sight of lots of pale creamy flesh bursting out of a hot pink bra, the cleavage high and perky. It was a gorgeous surprise, all that breast she'd been hiding under her crisp tailored shirts.

But then that was what he thought of Eve in general—that she was hiding a whole lot of woman under the attitude. It was a thought that had intrigued him more than once as he'd seen her typing furiously on her smart phone, clipboard in hand. What it would be like to see every inch of her naked body, to get her to totally come undone . . .

"That's just an excuse," she was saying. " 'Wardrobe malfunction.' Give me a break. Are you even listening to me?"

Nolan nodded. "They do happen, you know," he drawled, really savoring the moment of triumph. Forcing his eyes away from her chest, he let his grin win out. "You seem to have one happening right now."

He pointed to her blouse, wide open and catching the breeze.

She glanced down and turned as pink as the lace bra she was wearing.

"I think they call that tit for tat," he told her.

The Promise of Love

SIX ORIGINAL STORIES EDITED BY *NEW YORK TIMES* BESTSELLING AUTHOR

Lori Foster

INCLUDING NOVELLAS FROM

LORI FOSTER   ERIN MCCARTHY   SYLVIA DAY

JAMIE DENTON   KATE DOUGLAS   KATHY LOVE

Six award-winning and bestselling authors present a never-before-published anthology touching upon the obstacles people confront in their lives—and those who help heal their hearts.

These stories feature women who are survivors of stormy pasts, and the good men who have become stronger for understanding them. Together they can overcome anything, with a love born of compassion…

The authors are donating all of their proceeds from *The Promise of Love* to One Way Farm, a charitable organization.

penguin.com

M929T0811

The Gift of Love

EIGHT ORIGINAL STORIES EDITED BY
NEW YORK TIMES **BESTSELLING AUTHOR**

Lori Foster

INCLUDES NOVELLAS FROM

**LORI FOSTER   JULES BENNETT   HEIDI BETTS
ANN CHRISTOPHER   LISA COOKE
PAIGE CUCCARO   GIA DAWN   HELENKAY DIMON**

In this heartwarming anthology of never-before-published stories, eight award-winning and bestselling authors come together to celebrate their love of family and the enduring bonds that enrich all our lives.

The love that connects families is universal. Whether it is the love of parents for their children, the love between a husband and wife, the love between siblings, a love that transcends generations, or even the love for a family member never met, the family ties that bind us to one another are the strongest and deepest emotional connections we experience. In *The Gift of Love*, eight exceptional writers offer a variety of unique perspectives on what family love means and how it impacts our lives in ways profound and often surprising.

**The authors are donating all of their proceeds from
The Gift of Love to The Conductive Learning Center of
Greater Cincinnati, a charitable organization.**

penguin.com